A
SEASON
of
LOVE

Also by Amy Clipston

For Sue Brower

GLOSSARY

ach: oh
aenti: aunt
appeditlich: delicious
Ausbund: Amish hymnal
bedauerlich: sad
beh: leg
boppli: baby
bopplin: babies
brot: bread
bruder: brother
bruderskinner: nieces/nephews
bu: boy
buwe: boys
daadi: granddad
daed: dad
danki: thank you
dat: dad
Dietsch: Pennsylvania Dutch, the Amish language (a German dialect)
dochder: daughter
dochdern: daughters
Dummle!: hurry!
Englisher: a non-Amish person
fraa: wife
Frehlicher Grischtdaag!: Merry Christmas!
freind: friend
freinden: friends
freindschaft: relative
froh: happy
gegisch: silly
gern gschehne: you're welcome
grandkinner: grandchildren
grank: sick
grossdaddi: grandfather
grossdochdern: granddaughters

grossmammi: grandmother

Gude mariye: Good morning

gut: good

Gut nacht: Good night

haus: house

heemet: home

Ich liebe dich: I love you

Kannscht du Pennsilfaanisch Dietsch schwetze: Can you speak Pennsylvania Dutch?

kapp: prayer covering or cap

kichli: cookie

kichlin: cookies

kind: child

kinner: children

kumm: come

liewe: love, a term of endearment

maed: young women, girls

maedel: young woman

mamm: mom

mammi: grandma

mei: my

mutter: mother

naerfich: nervous

narrisch: crazy

onkel: uncle

Ordnung: the oral tradition of practices required and forbidden in the Amish faith

rumspringa: running around; the time before an Amish young person has officially joined the church

schee: pretty

schtupp: family room

schweschder: sister

Was iss letz?: What's wrong?

Wie geht's: How do you do? or Good day!

Willkumm heemet: welcome home

wunderbaar: wonderful

ya: yes

zwillingbopplin: twins

Kauffman Amish Bakery Family Trees

(boldface are parents)

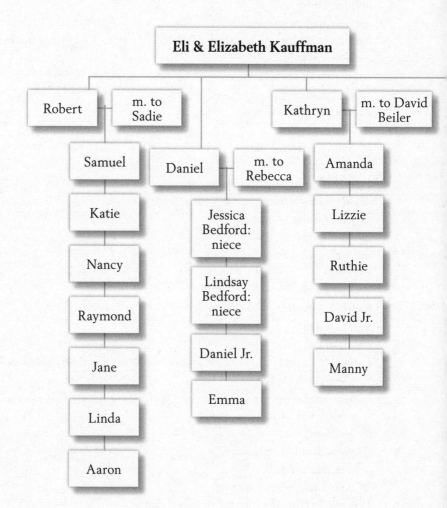

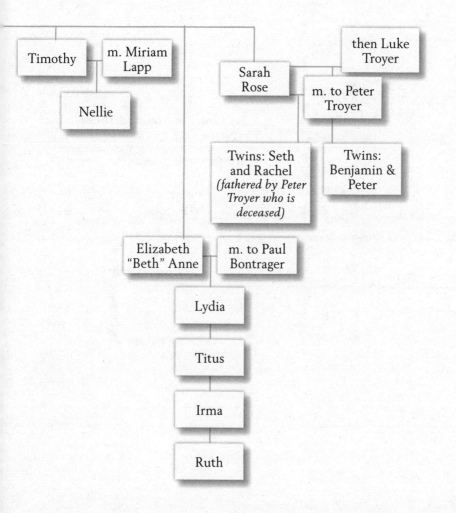

Timothy — m. Miriam Lapp

Nellie

Sarah Rose — then Luke Troyer

m. to Peter Troyer

Twins: Seth and Rachel *(fathered by Peter Troyer who is deceased)*

Twins: Benjamin & Peter

Elizabeth "Beth" Anne — m. to Paul Bontrager

Lydia

Titus

Irma

Ruth

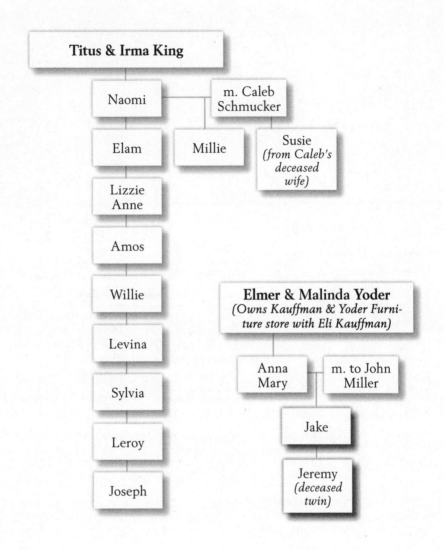

Titus & Irma King

Naomi — m. Caleb Schmucker

Elam

Millie

Susie
(from Caleb's deceased wife)

Lizzie Anne

Amos

Willie

Levina

Sylvia

Leroy

Joseph

Elmer & Malinda Yoder
(Owns Kauffman & Yoder Furniture store with Eli Kauffman)

Anna Mary — m. to John Miller

Jake

Jeremy
(deceased twin)

NOTE TO THE READER

While this novel is set against the real backdrop of Lancaster County, Pennsylvania, the characters are fictional. There is no intended resemblance between the characters in this book and any real members of the Amish and Mennonite communities. As with any work of fiction, I've taken license in some areas of research as a means of creating the necessary circumstances for my characters. My research was thorough; however, it would be impossible to be completely accurate in details and description, since each and every community differs. Therefore, any inaccuracies in the Amish and Mennonite lifestyles portrayed in this book are completely due to fictional license.

1

Katie Kauffman carried a tray filled with breakfast foods down the hallway toward her aunt Rebecca's bedroom. Balancing the tray on her hip, she tapped on the closed door. "Breakfast time, *Aenti* Rebecca!" she called.

"Oh," Rebecca said through the door. "Come in."

Katie pushed the door open and smiled at her aunt, who rested propped up in bed. Katie had spent most of the summer helping her pregnant aunt in place of her best friend Lindsay Bedford, who had come to live with their aunt Rebecca four years earlier after her parents died in a car accident.

Lindsay had left their community of Bird-in-Hand, Pennsylvania, to visit her parents' dear friends Trisha and Frank Mc-Cabe in Virginia Beach, Virginia, and help Trisha heal from an accident in which she had broken her leg. After Lindsay had left, Rebecca's pregnancy complications had worsened, and Katie had moved in to help care for her aunt Rebecca and uncle Daniel's young children.

"How are you feeling today?" Katie asked, as she placed the tray on the nightstand beside her aunt. "You don't look quite as pale as you did yesterday."

"I'm doing better, *danki*." Rebecca smiled. "How are the *kinner?*"

"They're doing well," Katie said, pulling up a chair and

sitting beside the bed. She handed her aunt a glass of orange juice. "They're eating breakfast with *Onkel* Daniel, but I have a few minutes before his ride arrives to take him to work."

Rebecca sipped her juice. "How are you today, Katie?"

"I'm doing well." Katie lifted the plate filled with scrambled eggs, hash browns, and sausage and handed it to her aunt. She then gave her the utensils. "I made your favorites."

"*Danki.*" Rebecca bowed her head in silent prayer and then scooped a pile of eggs into her mouth. "Katie, this is delicious, as usual. Not only are your breakfasts always *wunderbaar*, you're a fantastic baker."

"*Danki.*" Katie smiled. "It's my goal to be the best baker at the Kauffman Amish Bakery. I'm working with *Mammi* to learn all of her recipes and even invent some of my own."

"Maybe someday you'll run the bakery for your *mammi* when she's ready to retire," Rebecca said.

"I would love that," Katie said, smoothing her apron over her lap. "That would be a dream come true for me. Hopefully Amanda and Ruthie will continue to work there with me. I would love to keep working with my family, you know?"

Rebecca nodded. "I bet you can't wait to go back to the bakery, *ya*?"

Katie hesitated, not wanting to hurt her aunt's feelings. "I love being here, but I do miss the bakery."

"You're allowed to miss the bakery." Rebecca smiled. "I bet you miss your friends too."

Katie nodded. "I do. I'm looking forward to when Lindsay gets back, and we can all be together. It's been a long time since Lindsay, Lizzie Anne, and I have all been together. I miss *mei* best *freinden*."

"I'm certain you do." Rebecca swallowed some hash browns and then sipped more juice.

"I really miss Lindsay since it seems like Lizzie Anne is

spending more and more time with *mei bruder,* Samuel," Katie said, hoping she didn't sound selfish.

"Have you heard from Lindsay?" Rebecca asked.

"I need to go check the messages." Katie glanced toward the window and wondered if Lindsay had received the letter she'd written a few days ago. Against her aunt's wishes, she'd written to her friend to tell her Rebecca had taken a turn for the worse and was restricted to full bed rest. Though she knew she was disobeying her elders, she felt Lindsay needed to know the news as soon as possible. "I'll check the messages today and see if Lindsay has called."

"*Danki,*" Rebecca said. "I hope she's doing well." She smiled. "I'm certain you and your friends will be back together soon, and you'll be back at the bakery making your *wunderbaar* desserts."

"*Ya*, you're right, *Aenti* Rebecca," Katie said. "Things will be back to normal soon." Smiling at her aunt, Katie hoped she was right.

⌒⌒

Lindsay Bedford held her breath as the bus pulled into the station in Lancaster, Pennsylvania. She touched her prayer covering and then smoothed the skirt of her black bib apron, which covered her purple frock, making sure both were presentable before grabbing her tote bag from the floor. It seemed as if it took a lifetime for the line of passengers in front of her to file off the bus. When she finally stepped onto the sidewalk, her heart swelled.

"*Heemet,*" she whispered, her lips curling up into a smile.

"Lindsay!" a familiar voice called.

Turning, she spotted Matthew Glick waving from a few yards away. He was dressed in a dark blue shirt, black trousers, and suspenders. His dark brown curls peeked out from under his straw hat, and his golden-brown eyes shone as he made his way through the crowd toward her. A smile split his handsome face, and her heart thudded in her chest.

"Matthew!" she called as he approached. *"Wie geht's?"*

"Doing great now." Matthew reached for her bag. "May I carry that for you?"

"Danki." She smiled, but held the bag closer to her body. "How about you carry my luggage instead? My duffle bag is pretty heavy."

"I'd be happy to," he said, gesturing toward the bus station. "Let's go inside and get it. I'm certain you're in a hurry to get *heemet. Mei schweschder* rode along with me. She'll be happy to see you too."

"Oh, that's nice. I can't wait to see Betsy," Lindsay said. "It's so *gut* to be *heemet.*"

After retrieving her duffle bag, they both climbed into the back seat of the waiting van.

Betsy waved from the front passenger seat, where she sat next to the driver. "Lindsay, *willkumm heemet.*"

"Danki, Betsy. I appreciate your coming to get me," Lindsay said, as she settled into her seat and buckled her belt. "You both kept my arrival a secret, *ya?*"

"I kept my promise." Matthew lifted his hat and smoothed his curls. "Betsy and I haven't told anyone."

"I'm certain Daniel, Rebecca, and the *kinner* will be *froh* to see you again," Betsy said.

"How is *mei aenti* doing?" She held her breath, hoping her aunt Rebecca hadn't taken a turn for the worse.

"I haven't heard that anything has changed," Matthew said. "Don't worry about her right now. We'll get you *heemet* as soon as we can." He smiled. "Tell me about your trip. Did you have a *gut* time?"

"I did." Lindsay angled her body toward him and also glanced at Betsy as she spoke. "My aunt Trisha and uncle Frank live right on the beach, and I walked out there every day. It was so nice to feel the warm sand between my toes. I even swam a bit. I love the ocean. I spent some time with friends from school, and I attended the church where I grew up. I volunteered at a nursing *heemet* too, which was nice. I told you in my letter I helped Mrs. Fisher, the patient who spoke only *Dietsch.*"

"Oh, how nice that you helped out in a nursing *heemet,*" Betsy said. "I'm certain the patients enjoyed seeing you."

"*Ya,*" Matthew said with a nod. "That was really *wunderbaar gut* how you helped Mrs. Fisher communicate with the nurses when she fell and hurt herself."

Lindsay's smiled faded. "She passed away Friday night."

Shaking his head, he frowned. "I'm sorry. I know she was very special to you."

"I'm so sorry too, Lindsay," Betsy said. "How very sad."

Lindsay cleared her throat in the hopes of not getting emotional in front of them. "But I'm glad I was able to help her some. She dictated a letter to me, and I sent it to her estranged *dochder.* It was a way for her to make peace between them before she passed away."

"That's very nice of you," Betsy said. "What else did you do while you were in Virginia Beach?"

"Let's see," Lindsay said, touching her chin. "Aunt Trisha, Uncle Frank, and I went to some of my favorite places to eat, and we ordered pizza from my favorite pizza parlor."

"Oh, I love pizza," Betsy said with a grin. "I bet it was *wunderbaar gut*!"

"*Ya.*" Matthew grinned. "I bet that was a nice treat."

"It was. I would love to take a group of *mei freinden* to visit Virginia Beach sometime. I know it's Katie's dream to see the beach."

"Maybe someday we can take a trip down there," Matthew said.

"*Ya.* Aunt Trisha has a third level in the house with plenty of space for guests."

"You should do that," Betsy said. "You're only young once."

"It sounds like you stayed pretty busy while you were there. Did you have time to do anything else?" Matthew asked.

Glancing out the window at the morning traffic, Lindsay thought of her GED and hesitated, wondering how he'd feel if he knew she'd worked to achieve it. However, she didn't want to keep any secrets from him, since he was her good friend.

After a moment Lindsay faced him and took a deep breath. "I also did something that was more work than fun," she began.

"Oh?" He raised his eyebrows with curiosity. "What was that?"

"I hope you won't be upset with me." Lindsay glanced at Betsy. "And I hope you won't think badly of me."

Betsy smiled. "Lindsay, I'm certain you couldn't do anything to make me think badly of you."

"Why would I be upset?" Matthew's expression became one of concern.

"I wanted to prove to myself that I am smarter than Jessica thinks I am." Lindsay bit her lower lip.

"You don't have to tell me," Matthew said. "I respect your privacy, Lindsay."

"I studied really hard, and I got my GED." Lindsay braced herself, waiting to see if he would be upset.

Matthew paused. "*Ach.*"

Lindsay studied his eyes, finding disappointment mixed with concern there. "You're upset." Out of the corner of her eye, she saw Betsy turn toward the front of the van as if she didn't want to interfere in the conversation.

"No." He shook his head. "I'm just wondering why you wanted a GED if you're planning to stay in the Amish community."

"I just wanted to try," Lindsay said with a shrug. "I had to see if I could do it. I was so tired of Jessica beating me down with snide comments about not finishing high school. I had to do this for myself."

He nodded slowly. "Does that mean you want to use your GED to get a job in the English world or go to college?"

"No," Lindsay said quickly. "I don't want to get a job in the English world, and I also don't want to go back to school. While I was in Virginia Beach, I figured out what I want to do with my life."

"And what do you want to do with your life?" His words were hesitant.

"Join the Amish church." Lindsay sat up straight in the seat as confidence in her decision filled her. "I know for certain this is where I want to be."

His warm smile was back. "*Gut.*"

"Betsy," Lindsay said, "do you think it's okay I got my GED?"

Betsy smiled at Lindsay. "I think it's fine you wanted to get your GED. But I also think it's *wunderbaar* you want to join the church."

"*Danki,*" Lindsay said.

Lindsay asked Matthew about the furniture store, and he talked about his latest projects as the van bumped up the road toward her aunt Rebecca's home in Bird-in-Hand. She also asked Betsy about her family, and Betsy talked about her children and the weather. Although she listened to Matthew and Betsy, Lindsay's thoughts returned to Rebecca. She prayed her aunt was going to be all right and the complications with her pregnancy hadn't worsened in the past few days.

Lindsay's trip to Virginia Beach was cut short when she received the letter from Katie that told her Rebecca was restricted to complete bed rest after her blood pressure spiked. Since Trisha was no longer immobile, Lindsay rushed out on the first bus available in order to return home to help her aunt. Lindsay informed only Matthew she was returning since she planned to surprise the family.

The van turned into her aunt's rock driveway, and Lindsay's

heart fluttered. She couldn't wait to see her family after nearly three months. She'd missed them terribly.

The van came to a stop near the barn, and Lindsay fished her wallet out from her tote bag. "How much was the ride?"

Matthew shook his head. "Don't be *gegisch*. I'll pay the driver after he takes Betsy *heemet* and me to work." He gestured toward the door. "You go inside. I'll get your bag."

"*Danki*." Lindsay said good-bye to Betsy, hopped out of the van, and rushed up the porch steps. She glanced through the glass of the back door and saw Katie washing dishes at the kitchen sink. Lindsay pushed the door open, and Katie looked up, her blue eyes rounding as they met Lindsay's.

"Lindsay!" Katie yelled. "You're *heemet*!"

"Hi," Lindsay said, dropping her tote bag on the floor with a clunk.

Katie rushed over, embracing Lindsay in a tight hug. "I'm so glad you came back."

"I booked my ticket as soon as I got your letter." Lindsay studied her eyes. "How is *Aenti* Rebecca?"

"She's doing okay," Katie said. "She's been very *gut* about staying in bed, which is what the doctor instructed her to do. She goes back to see him next week."

"*Danki* for taking care of her," Lindsay said. "I'll be sure she follows his orders."

A thud sounded behind her, and Lindsay turned to see Matthew standing by the door, her duffle bag beside him on the floor.

"*Danki*," Lindsay said, walking over and lifting the bag. "I appreciate the ride from the bus station."

"*Gern gschehne*," Matthew said. "I'm glad you called me." His eyes were intense. "I hope to see you soon."

"*Ya*," she said. "You will."

"Have a *gut* day. I need to get to work." He nodded toward them both and then slipped out the door to the van.

"Lindsay!" Daniel Junior called, running from the family room to the kitchen. *"Willkumm heemet!"*

Dropping to her knees on the floor, Lindsay pulled her little cousin into a hug. "It's so *gut* to be *heemet.*"

With a squeal, Emma toddled over to join them, and Lindsay tugged her into a group hug with Daniel Junior.

"I have something for you both," Lindsay said with a grin. She pulled her tote bag over and handed Daniel Junior a toy car and Emma a doll. She had picked up the toys for them before leaving Virginia Beach.

The children thanked her for the gifts and then hurried back into the family room to play.

"Is *Aenti* Rebecca awake?" Lindsay asked as she stood. "I'd love to let her know I'm *heemet.*"

"She's resting," Katie said. "But I think she's awake."

"I'm going to go see her," Lindsay said, hoisting her bag up onto her shoulder. She looked at the clock above the sink. "Is it time for the *kinner* to nap?"

"Ya," Katie said. "I can bring your duffel bag for you if you want to carry Emma. We can go up together."

Lindsay smiled. "That sounds like a *gut* plan." She carried Emma up the stairs, kissing and nuzzling her while the little girl giggled. After tucking her into her crib, Lindsay kissed Emma's head and then moved to Daniel Junior's room where she kissed him as well. She found Katie standing in the doorway to Lindsay's room.

"They're very *froh* you're *heemet,*" Katie said, with a smile. "I am too." She gestured toward Rebecca's room at the end of the hallway. "I'll let you go see *Aenti* Rebecca alone. I've been sleeping in your room, so I'll pack up my things. I'll see about getting a ride *heemet* in a little bit."

"No, don't leave. Why don't you stay today so we can spend some time together?" Lindsay dropped her tote bag near the doorway. "I'll be right back. I don't want to take away from her rest time."

Moving down the hallway, Lindsay stood at Rebecca's door and peered in, finding her aunt lying on her side, facing the opposite wall. Her eyes filled with tears as she thought of how much her aunt must have missed her when she began to feel ill. A sob gripped her and she sucked in a breath to prevent it from escaping.

Rebecca rolled over and gasped as she began to sit up. "Lindsay? You're *heemet?*"

"*Ya,*" Lindsay said, wiping her eyes as she moved into the room. "How are you?"

"*Ach,* Lindsay." Rebecca opened her arms. "*Kumm.* It's so *gut* to see you."

Lindsay leaned over into her aunt's arms as hot tears streamed down her cheeks. "I'm so sorry I wasn't here when you got *grank.*"

"Don't be *gegisch,*" Rebecca whispered, her voice sounding thick. "It's not your fault, and Trisha needed you." She looked up at Lindsay. "How is Trisha?"

"She's doing well." Lindsay sat on the edge of the bed. "She's walking around now with a soft cast."

"What brought you back so soon?" Rebecca asked while holding Lindsay's hand. "I wasn't expecting you for a few more weeks."

Lindsay hesitated. She couldn't bear to tell her aunt a fib, but she also didn't want to cause any trouble for Katie who had only done what she believed was right.

"Did Katie call you?" Rebecca asked, raising her eyebrows with suspicion.

"She wrote me," Lindsay said. "But please don't be upset with her. She's very worried about you, and she knew I would want to know what was going on. She felt she had to tell me."

Rebecca smiled and touched Lindsay's cheek. "I'm not angry."

"*Gut,*" Lindsay said, relief flooding her.

"I just didn't want you to feel obligated to come back *heemet* since Trisha and Frank needed you," Rebecca continued. "I wanted Trisha to be well before you came *heemet*. You'd made a promise to her first."

"But I want to help you," Lindsay said. "You're my family too."

"It's so *gut* to see you," Rebecca said while squeezing her hand. "I've missed you so much."

"I've missed you and everyone else too," Lindsay said. "I had a *gut* time, but this is *mei heemet*." She paused and took a deep breath. "I have made a decision. I want to join the church."

Rebecca sucked in a breath and tears filled her eyes. "Are you certain?"

Lindsay nodded. "I'm absolutely certain. I'm ready."

"*Ach*, Lindsay." Rebecca squeezed her hand again. "That's the best news I could ever hear." She wiped her eyes. "I'm so *froh*."

Lindsay told her a little bit about her trip, sharing the same news as she'd told Matthew in the van. When Rebecca yawned, Lindsay stood. "I should let you rest. We can talk later."

"That's a *gut* idea," Rebecca said. "Did Daniel know you were coming *heemet*?"

Lindsay shook her head. "No, he didn't."

Rebecca looked confused. "How did you get *heemet* from the bus station? Did you get a taxi?"

"No, I didn't take a taxi." Lindsay's cheeks heated. "Matthew arranged for a ride *heemet* and met me at the bus station."

"Matthew?" A smile turned up Rebecca's lips. "You called him and asked him to pick you up?"

Lindsay nodded. "I didn't call *Onkel* Daniel because I wanted to surprise you all."

AMY CLIPSTON

"That's sweet," Rebecca said. "I'm glad to hear Matthew picked you up. He's a *gut* young man."

"I know. I'll let you rest for a while," Lindsay said. "I'll bring you your lunch after your nap."

"*Danki, mei liewe*," Rebecca said.

Lindsay gently closed the door behind her and headed back to her room. Stepping through the doorway, she found Katie sitting on her bed and frowning while holding Lindsay's cell phone.

"This fell out of the pocket of your tote bag when I moved it out of the doorway." Katie frowned. "Where did you get it?"

"It was a gift from Aunt Trisha and Uncle Frank," Lindsay said, sitting next to Katie on the bed.

"A gift?"

"*Ya*," Lindsay said, taking the phone from her. "They bought it for me after I got my GED."

Katie looked alarmed. "You got your GED?"

Lindsay nodded.

"Why would you do that?" Katie's expression turned to confusion. "I thought you loved living here. I thought you liked being Amish and couldn't stand when your sister said you were selling yourself short."

"I do love it here," Lindsay said. "And I know for certain I want to be Amish."

Katie shook her head. "You're not making sense. You say you want to be Amish, but you got your GED."

"I know." Lindsay stuck the phone in the front pocket of her tote bag. "But I was so tired of Jessica hassling me that I wanted to prove to myself I could do it. Since I got my GED now, before I'm baptized, it shouldn't be a problem, *ya?*"

"That's true." Katie paused, and a smile grew on her face. "Does that mean you want to be baptized and join the church?"

Lindsay nodded, and Katie grinned.

"I'm so excited to hear the news," Katie said. Her expression became curious. "How did you get Matthew to pick you up at the bus station?"

"I called him," Lindsay said. "We'd written a couple of letters back and forth, and I knew he'd keep a secret if I asked him to. He's a *gut* friend."

"I'm glad you're back." Katie stood and picked up her own bag, which contained all her clothes from her overnight stays. "I guess we should go downstairs, so we don't disturb the *kinner* and *Aenti* Rebecca while they nap."

"I appreciate all you've done." Lindsay stood and hugged her friend. "I'm going to unpack before I come down. I want to get organized."

"That sounds *gut*." Katie hefted her bag onto her shoulder. "I packed everything of mine, so I'll be ready to go when *Onkel* Daniel arrives *heemet* from work. It will be strange to go back *heemet* after being here for a while. I had fun, though." She looked curious. "Are you hungry? Can I make you a snack?"

Lindsay touched her stomach as it rumbled. "*Ya*. That would be *wunderbaar*. I had some crackers on the bus, but I haven't had breakfast yet."

"I'll make you something." Katie started toward the door. "I'll have it ready soon, so hurry down."

"*Danki*," Lindsay said.

While Katie disappeared into the hallway, Lindsay contemplated how much she loved being back in Bird-in-Hand. She'd first moved here four years ago from Virginia Beach. Lindsay and her older sister, Jessica, had come to Bird-in-Hand to live with her mother's sister, Rebecca, after their parents were killed in a car accident.

When Lindsay and Jessica first arrived, they both felt as if they'd entered another world, or perhaps another century, since Rebecca, Daniel, and the rest of the community lived simple, plain lives without modern clothes, television, electricity, or other up-to-date conveniences Lindsay used to take for granted.

Lindsay had embraced life in the Bird-in-Hand community, quickly becoming a member of the Kauffman family. By contrast, Jessica protested and fought against the changes until she was permitted to move back to Virginia and live with their parents' friends Frank and Trisha McCabe.

Lindsay pulled her dresses and aprons from her duffle bag as she thought about her sister. Jessica was Lindsay's polar opposite, beginning with their appearances. Jessica had dark hair and eyes, and Lindsay had deep red hair and bright green eyes. Jessica had finished high school, graduating with honors, and then moved on to college. She was now finishing up a high-profile internship with an accounting firm in New York City.

On the other hand, Lindsay kept with Amish tradition and didn't continue her education beyond eighth grade, other than achieving her GED while staying in Virginia Beach with Frank and Trisha. Instead of going to high school, Lindsay began working in the Kauffman Amish Bakery, owned by Elizabeth Kauffman, with Rebecca and Rebecca's sisters-in-law.

After placing her dirty clothes in the hamper, Lindsay hung her clean dresses and aprons on the hooks on her wall and then put her undergarments in her dresser. Once all of her clothes were properly put away, she stowed the bag under her bed.

Heading to the stairs toward the smell of bacon and eggs, Lindsay smiled. This was truly her home, and it was so very good to be back where she belonged.

2

Later that evening, Katie rode next to Daniel in his buggy and discussed the weather as they drove back to her house. She spotted her father and her older brother, Samuel, as Daniel guided the horse toward the barn near her house.

"*Danki* again for staying with us," Daniel said as he halted the horse. "You were a great help to us."

"*Gern gschehne, Onkel* Daniel," Katie said, while grabbing her bag from the floorboard. "I was *froh* to help."

Katie's father, Robert, and Samuel approached as she and Daniel climbed from the buggy. Katie greeted them and lifted her bag onto her shoulder.

"*Wie geht's,*" Robert said, shaking Daniel's hand. "What brings you and Katie out here tonight? I thought she was working for you all week."

"Lindsay surprised us and arrived *heemet* today," Daniel said. "We appreciate all Katie has done for us. *Danki* for allowing her to work for us, Robert. I know she has obligations at the bakery."

Samuel shot Katie an accusing look, and her shoulders tensed.

Squaring her shoulders in defiance, Katie frowned at her brother and then turned toward Daniel. "I'm going to head inside and see if *mei mamm* needs any help," she said. "*Danki* for bringing me *heemet.*"

"Please tell your *mamm* hello and *danki* again for allowing you to stay with us, Katie," Daniel said. "We couldn't have gotten by without you. You're *wunderbaar gut* with the *kinner*."

"I will tell her," Katie said. "*Gut nacht.*"

Katie heard her father ask about Rebecca as she hurried up the steps and into the house. She dropped her bag at the base of the stairs and found her mother, Sadie, sitting at the kitchen table with her sister Nancy while they created a shopping list.

"Hi," Katie said as she stepped into the kitchen. "*Wie geht's?*" She hugged her mother and then grabbed an apple from the bowl on the counter and bit into it. When the juice trickled down her chin, she snatched a paper towel to wipe it away.

"Katie," her mother said, her eyes round with surprise. "I'm so glad you're *heemet*. Is Rebecca doing better?"

Katie shook her head and dropped into a chair across from her mother while taking another bite of the apple. "No, she's about the same, but Lindsay came heemet today and surprised everyone."

"She did?" Nancy asked. "How was her visit to Virginia? Did she have fun at the beach?"

"She had a *gut* time." Katie shared a few of Lindsay's stories about walking on the beach, working at the nursing home, and frequenting her favorite restaurants. "She's back for good now. She told me she wants to join the church too." She bit into the apple again, enjoying the tart sweetness.

"That's *wunderbaar*," Nancy said with a smile. "When did she get *heemet*?"

"Earlier this morning," Katie said. "Matthew picked her up from the bus station." She took two more bites of the apple and then wrapped the core in the paper towel.

Their mother glanced at Nancy. "Why don't you go see if the *kinner* are ready for bed? I'll be up shortly to tuck them in. I'd like to speak with Katie alone."

"Yes, *Mamm*." Looking disappointed, Nancy stood and started for the stairs. Katie assumed her younger sister wanted to stay and find out more about Lindsay's trip and homecoming.

"Did you eat supper?" Sadie asked, gesturing toward the apple core.

"*Ya*, I did eat supper, but I was still hungry," Katie said, placing her hands on the table. "Lindsay and I made chicken pot pie. *Onkel* Daniel was very glad to see Lindsay was *heemet*. He was really surprised. He told me to say *danki* for allowing me to stay over and help them out."

"It's the proper thing to do when family members need help." Sadie looked curious. "Matthew picked up Lindsay from the bus station? How did he know she was coming *heemet*? She must've called him, *ya*?"

"She did." Katie bit her bottom lip and wondered if her mother was going to grill her about Lindsay and the situation at Rebecca's house. While Katie loved her mother, Sadie was known in the community for having a loose tongue. Katie knew things she shared with her mother might be repeated at an upcoming quilting bee.

"How's Rebecca's spirit?" Sadie asked. "Is she holding up okay despite her complications?"

"I think so." Katie shrugged. "She seems very tired and a little frustrated that she can't get up and do things around the house. She's *froh* Lindsay is *heemet*, and she thanked me for everything I've done just like *Onkel* Daniel thanked me. I'm glad I was able to help them out."

Sadie looked suspicious. "How much fun did Lindsay have in Virginia Beach?"

Katie paused, choosing her words with care. "She spent time with old *freinden* and enjoyed the beach but spent most of her time taking care of her *aenti* Trisha." Although Katie understood why Lindsay had gotten her GED, she knew her mother wouldn't. She figured it was best to keep that information to herself since Lindsay was going to join the church. She glanced at the list in front of her mother in hopes of distracting her. "Are you planning on going shopping tomorrow?"

Her mother sighed. "*Ya*, I think so. I was hoping to wait until Friday, but we're out of quite a few things. Are you going to go back to work at the bakery tomorrow?"

Katie shrugged. "I was planning on it. Do you want me to help you with the shopping instead?"

Her mother waved off the question. "I can handle the shopping, Katie. Your *mammi* will be happy to have you. I'm certain the bakery is still very busy even though there are more bakers working there now. Elizabeth told me she hired three new bakers—Hannah, Fannie, and Vera—when you went to work for Rebecca since tourist season was in full swing."

"I miss baking, and it will be nice to get back to working with *mei aentis* and cousins." Katie stood. "I better go out and ask *Dat* to arrange a ride for me." She stepped onto the porch and found her father and brother climbing the stairs. "*Dat*, I'm going to go back to work in the morning. Would you please arrange a ride to the bakery for me?"

"*Ya*, of course," her father said. "I'll call right now." He headed toward the small shed that housed their family's phone.

Samuel's stare was accusing. "You told Lindsay about *Aenti* Rebecca, didn't you?"

"I did," Katie said, crossing her arms over her apron. "I prayed about it, and I felt it was the right choice. Lindsay has a right to know *Aenti* Rebecca is sick, because *Aenti* Rebecca is like her *mamm*."

Samuel's frown softened. "Are you saying you didn't get in trouble?"

Katie shook her head. "No, I didn't. Even *Onkel* Daniel understood. Both *Onkel* Daniel and *Aenti* Rebecca are glad she's back."

Her brother rubbed his chin. "I guess in this situation you were right to follow your heart." He smiled. "Lizzie Anne will be very excited to see Lindsay again too."

"Oh *ya*! I'm so excited *mei* two best *freinden* and I will be back together again. It's been such a long time since we've been able to talk," Katie said. "I better get upstairs and unpack."

While climbing the stairs with her bag on her shoulder, Katie smiled. She was glad to be home. Life would get back to normal again.

☙

Lindsay brought the platter of eggs, fried potatoes, sausage, and bacon to the table where her uncle and cousins sat. She then grabbed the basket of bread and placed it in the center of the table before sitting next to Emma. After a silent prayer, she retrieved a piece of bread, sliced it, and slathered butter on it before handing it to Emma, who giggled with delight as she bit into it. Lindsay then filled a plate for Daniel Junior before looking at her uncle, who was cutting up his scrambled eggs.

"*Aenti* Rebecca looked *gut* this morning," Lindsay said. "She seemed to have some color back, *ya?*"

Her uncle nodded and lifted his cup of coffee. "*Ya,* she does."

Lindsay scooped a pile of fluffy yellow eggs onto her plate and thought about the question that had haunted her through the night. She wanted to share it with her uncle, but she felt doubt nipping at her.

Lindsay glanced at Daniel Junior, who bit into a hunk of bread and chewed with a grin on his face, his mouth open. "*Appeditlich,* Lindsay."

"*Danki,* but please chew with your mouth closed, Junior." Looking back at her plate, Lindsay again considered talking to her uncle about her burning question: Should she talk to the bishop about joining the church? She met his curious eyes.

"Is something bothering you, Lindsay?" Daniel asked. "You don't seem like yourself this morning."

"I've been thinking about something," Lindsay began as she placed her fork on her plate. "It kept me up most of the night."

Daniel looked sympathetic. "Do you want to talk about it?"

She nodded. "I want to be baptized."

"Ach." He looked surprised. "That's a big decision. Are you certain?"

"Oh yes. I'm positively certain." She gripped her fork again. "I want to be baptized with *mei freinden,* though I know I've missed most of the classes. Do you think there's a chance I could join them somehow?" She absently cut up her egg while she considered her options. "I can always join another district next year, but it would be even more special to be baptized with *mei freinden* this year."

Daniel set his coffee mug on the table and touched his beard. "You remember when your *aenti* Miriam was baptized, *ya?"*

"Ya," Lindsay said. "I do remember that. It was after she moved back here from Indiana. She started dating *Onkel* Timothy not too long after that."

"She received special permission from the bishop," Daniel said. "Timothy told me she had to go talk to the bishop and explain why it meant so much for her to join the church." He speared some potatoes with his fork. "Do you feel comfortable doing that?"

"I don't know." Lindsay lifted her napkin and thought about Bishop Abner Chupp. "Bishop Chupp is a fair man, but he's a little imposing."

"He's really not imposing." Daniel smiled. "He's just a humble man like me. We're all the same in God's eyes."

"But you're *mei onkel.* It's easy to talk to you when I want to tell you something very personal and serious, like my decision to join the church." Lindsay wiped her mouth. *"Aenti* Miriam spoke to the bishop and explained she wanted to be baptized, and he allowed her to come to classes, right?"

"That's what Timothy told me," Daniel said, before wiping his beard with his napkin. "I believe she met with the bishop during the week at different times to make up the discussions she'd missed, and she was baptized in the fall of that year with the rest of the group. Her father wasn't well, and she wanted to be baptized as soon as she could in order to have him there with her."

Lindsay scooped some egg into her mouth and chewed while considering his words. She knew joining the church was what she wanted to do with her life, and she certainly could make time to see the bishop in order to complete the discussions she'd missed while she was in Virginia. "I can do that," she said finally.

"I think you can too," Daniel said.

"*Brot!*" Emma exclaimed, reaching for another piece of bread.

"You want more *brot?*" Lindsay asked, and Emma clapped her hands in response. "I'll get it for you."

While she buttered another piece of bread, Lindsay thought back to her GED. Although she'd doubted herself at first, she'd studied and passed the test on her first try while she was staying with her aunt and uncle in Virginia Beach. She understood the baptism classes were more like lectures where the ministers spoke, and she wouldn't have to study and take a test like she had for the GED. However, she knew the emotional impact of the baptism instruction would be just as taxing as the GED exam had been.

After handing the bread to Emma, Lindsay looked back at her uncle.

He lifted his coffee mug and nodded toward Lindsay. "You can do anything you set your mind to, Lindsay. You're a very smart *maedel.*"

"*Danki,*" Lindsay said.

A horn tooted outside, and Daniel hopped up from the table. "I have to run off to work." After kissing the children's heads, he fetched his lunch pail and hat before rushing toward the door. "See you tonight."

"Have a *gut* day." Lindsay watched him disappear out the door, and she wondered if her uncle was right. Could Lindsay explain to the bishop why she wanted to be baptized with her friends, and would the bishop give her permission to make up the classes she'd missed?

⧗

The following evening, Lindsay wiped down the counter and filled the sink with water after supper while Emma sat in her high chair and munched on a cookie. The clip-clop of hooves drew her eyes to the window above the sink where she spotted a horse drawing a buggy toward the barn.

"I wonder who's here to visit," she said to Emma, who giggled in response. "We weren't expecting anyone."

Lindsay scrubbed the dishes and placed them in the drain board before moving her eyes back to the window, where she spotted her uncle and Daniel Junior standing with Matthew by the buggy. She smiled, and her stomach flip-flopped. Had Matthew come to visit her, or her uncle? Or perhaps he wanted to see them both.

"Matthew is here to see us, Emmy," Lindsay said as she wiped her hands on a dishrag. "Do I look okay?" She touched her prayer covering, and Emma laughed. "I hope that means *ya,*" Lindsay muttered.

She straightened the canisters on the counter and wiped a stray crumb into the sink before opening the refrigerator. She was searching for any leftover whoopie pies that Katie had mentioned bringing from the bakery after her mother stopped by last week. Lindsay knew whoopie pies were Matthew's favorite treat, and she wanted to offer them to him if he came in to visit her.

Finding no whoopie pies, she set the percolator on the stove for coffee and pulled a container full of peanut butter cookies from the cabinet. She was glad she'd decided to bake for the children earlier in the day and glad she had something to offer Matthew, even if it wasn't whoopie pies. After placing mugs and the cookies on the table, she pulled two glasses from the cabinet.

The back door opened, revealing Matthew clad in a brown shirt that seemed to make his brown eyes more golden than usual.

"*Wie geht's,*" he said as he stepped into the kitchen. He removed his straw hat, revealing a messy pile of dark brown curls. When Emma squealed, he laughed. "How are you, Emma?"

"Matthew," Lindsay said, smoothing her hands over her black apron. "What a pleasant surprise. What are you doing out this way?"

"I needed to talk to Daniel about a work project and also needed to borrow some tools," he said.

"Why would you need to talk to him and borrow tools when you'll see him tomorrow at the furniture store?" Lindsay eyed him with suspicion.

Matthew grinned. "That was my excuse to come and see you." He gestured toward the table. "May I visit with you for a few minutes?"

"*Ya.*" Lindsay smiled.

Matthew sat in front of her and talked to her cousin. "Is that a *gut kichli*, Emma?" He touched her arm. "Did you save one for me?" He glanced at the plate of cookies in the center of the table.

"Please help yourself," Lindsay said, gesturing toward the cookies. "They're peanut butter. I made them earlier today."

She lowered herself in the seat across from him and Emma. "I would've made you some whoopie pies if I'd known you were coming."

"Ach." Matthew looked disappointed as he took a cookie. "I should've told Daniel I was coming by. I've been craving whoopie pies." He brightened as he bit into the cookie. "Maybe next time we get together we can have some whoopie pies."

"I'll see if I have the ingredients. If so, I'll make some tomorrow." Once the percolator was finished, Lindsay hopped up and grabbed it from the stove. She poured coffee in each of the two mugs on the table and then placed the percolator back on the stove.

"Danki. How's Rebecca?"

Lindsay nodded. "She looks better today. Her color has come back some. How are you doing?"

"Fine." He glanced at Emma. "These *kichlin* are *gut*. You were right, Emma."

Emma poked Matthew's arm. *"Gut kichli,"* she said.

Lindsay laughed, enjoying the interaction between her cousin and Matthew. "What was the project you asked Daniel about?"

"I'm working on an entertainment center that's giving me trouble. Your *onkel* is very *gut* at building them." He grabbed another cookie off the plate. "But I also came here for the desserts. I told you you're a better baker than *mei schweschder.*"

"Oh?" Lindsay couldn't hide her grin. "What would happen if I told your *schweschder* you despise her cooking?"

"I didn't say I despised it," he said as he bit into his cookie. "I said you're better at it."

"Is that so?" Lindsay shook her head and broke a cookie in half while enjoying the easy banter with Matthew. "You might regret that statement if I repeat it to your *schweschder.* You'll find yourself very hungry."

"I could always come over here and grab a meal," he said with a nonchalant shrug.

Lindsay paused. Was he inviting himself to supper one night?

"I'm only joking," Matthew said. "How was your day?"

"*Gut*," Lindsay said. "I had fun with the *kinner* and also did some cleaning. It's really *gut* to be *heemet*."

"Will you be at the youth gathering Sunday night?"

Lindsay wiped her mouth with a napkin. "I believe so. I haven't discussed it with *Onkel* Daniel, but I'm fairly certain he'll let me go."

"I hope so." Matthew handed Emma a cookie, and she shook it over her head. "Look how she's holding that above her head. I think she may want to join us for volleyball soon."

Lindsay shook her head. "You're *gegisch*." She bit into the cookie. "How's the furniture store?"

"Busy. But busy is *gut*. Some *Englishers* are already ordering furniture for Christmas gifts. It's difficult to believe the summer is almost over. We'll be inundated with orders soon as fall approaches."

"I imagine you will stay busy." While sipping her coffee, Lindsay thought of Jake Miller, the Mennonite grandson of one of the store owners, Elmer Yoder. Jake and Lindsay's sister, Jessica, had been close friends until a disagreement earlier in the summer. "How's Jake doing?"

"He's been really quiet," Matthew said. "He keeps to himself." He looked curious. "Are you wondering if he's mentioned Jessica?"

Lindsay nodded while biting into a cookie. "The last I heard from Jessica she hadn't spoken to him. It's a shame they aren't talking."

Matthew shook his head. "He hasn't mentioned her."

Lindsay felt a twinge of disappointment for her sister and then pushed the thought away. Jessica's relationships were her own business. She remembered her conversation with Daniel at yesterday's breakfast and took a deep breath. "Matthew, do you think it would be possible for me to talk to the bishop and ask to be baptized with Katie and Lizzie Anne?"

Matthew's eyes brightened. "You want to be baptized this fall? I didn't realize you wanted to join the current baptism class."

"*Ya*, I do," she said. "Even though I wasn't born into this community, I feel as if I belong here. My heart is here with my family and my cousins."

"*Gut*," Matthew said. "I'm very glad to hear you say that."

"*Danki*," Lindsay said. "I talked to *Onkel* Daniel about it this morning, and he told me *mei aenti* Miriam was able to join a class that was already in session by making up the lessons. Maybe I could explain I've been away in Virginia caring for my aunt Trisha, and I just got back. Do you think that might work?"

"*Ya*," Matthew said. "I think it's a possibility. When do you want to talk to him?"

Lindsay shrugged. "I don't know. I was hoping maybe *mei onkel* Daniel would take me to see him this weekend."

The back door opened with a bang, revealing Daniel Junior, who was standing in the doorway. He was frowning and covered from head to toe in mud. The mud soaked his clothes, shoes, and hair.

Emma burst into giggles while calling, "*Gegisch bruder!*"

"Junior!" With a gasp, Lindsay stood. "What happened to you?"

"I fell in a horse stall." Daniel Junior grimaced. "*Dat* told me to ask you to please give me a bath right away."

Lindsay swallowed the urge to laugh as she turned to Matthew. "I guess I better say *gut nacht*."

With a grin, Matthew stood, his chair scraping the linoleum floor. "I guess so." He swiped a few cookies from the plate and stuffed them in his pockets. "I'll enjoy these during the ride *heemet*."

"Okay." Lindsay turned to Daniel Junior and pointed toward the mudroom by the door. "Go take off your boots, pants, and shirt, and then go straight on to the bathroom. I'll be right there." She glanced at Matthew. "It was nice seeing you."

"You too. *Danki* for the *appeditlich kichlin*." Matthew started for the back door.

Daniel Junior hurried by Lindsay, stopping in the doorway to the mudroom. "Is Matthew your boyfriend?"

At a loss for words, Lindsay felt her cheeks heat as she stared at her cousin. *Could his timing possibly get any more embarrassing?*

"Not yet, Junior, but I'm working on it," Matthew said with a smile. *"Gut nacht."*

Her cheeks aflame and her mouth gaping, Lindsay turned toward the back door just as Matthew slipped out, closing the door behind him.

Chocolate Oatmeal Cake

Mix and let cool:
　 1 cup oatmeal
　 1½ cups hot water

Blend together:
　 ¼ cup oil
　 1¼ cups sugar
　 2 eggs

Combine both mixtures with the following:
　 1 cup flour
　 1 teaspoon baking soda
　 ½ teaspoon salt
　 1 teaspoon vanilla
　 ½ cup cocoa

Mix together and bake at 350 degrees for 50 minutes.

3

Friday evening, Katie descended the bakery steps toward the parking lot. Her cousins and aunts hurried toward the van waiting in its usual spot by the sidewalk. When she spotted Samuel sitting in a horse-drawn wagon, she eyed him with confusion.

"What are you doing here?" she asked, approaching the wagon. "I thought I was riding with *Aenti* Kathryn like I do every day."

"I have to stop by the furniture store for *Dat*, so he told me to pick you up." He gestured toward the passenger side. "Hop in."

After waving to her cousins and aunts, Katie climbed onto the wagon. "What does *Dat* need from *Daadi*?" she asked as the wagon approached the intersection to Highway 340.

"*Daadi* has some supplies we need to fix the fence," Samuel said. "He offered to help *Dat* out so he can save some money."

"Oh," Katie said.

They drove in silence and soon Katie spotted the familiar business her grandfather, Eli Kauffman, had built with his friend Elmer Yoder before she was born. Samuel guided the horse into the parking lot, and Katie spotted the Kauffman & Yoder Amish Furniture sign displayed at the front of the single-story white building.

She followed Samuel up the stone path that ran to the steps leading up to the store. Samuel wrenched open the front door, causing a bell to ring, announcing their arrival. Large windows lined the front of the shop, and the walls were covered in crisp, fresh, white paint. She silently marveled at how clean her grandfather and the rest of the carpenters kept the store. It almost appeared to be brand new, rather than a couple of years old. The building had been rebuilt after a fire four years ago.

Katie glanced around the open area, taking in the sample pieces, including mirrored dressers, hope chests, entertainment centers, dining room sets, bed frames, end tables, and coffee tables. The familiar aroma of wood and stain permeated her nostrils.

A long counter covered with piles of papers and catalogs sat at the far end of the room, blocking a doorway beyond which hammers, saws, and nail guns blasted while voices boomed in Pennsylvania Dutch.

"I'm going to find *Daadi*," Samuel said as he headed toward the work area.

"I'll be here." Katie ran her fingers over the top of a mirrored dresser, silently marveling at the beautiful craftsmanship. She studied the brass hardware on the drawers and wondered what it would be like to have a bedroom set this pretty in her and Nancy's room. But she knew this furniture was expensive and would be too extravagant for her.

Glancing up at the mirror, she spotted Jake Miller standing behind her. "Jake," she said with surprise. "How long have you been standing there watching me?"

"I just walked out front and spotted you," he said. "I can't ignore a customer."

Katie laughed as she faced him. "I'm a customer?"

"You're looking at our samples, aren't you? Would you like to order a dresser?" Jake asked, grinning. "We're running a special end-of-the-summer sale right now, and I could get you a great deal. It could be yours before Christmas if you order today."

"That sounds like a *gut* deal. I think I'd like to order a whole bedroom set," she said, playing along. "How much would that cost me?"

"Let me think." He touched his clean-shaven chin. "Since you're family, I'll sell it to you for only fifteen hundred."

"Fifteen hundred dollars?" Katie guffawed. "That's the family price?"

"Oh yes," Jake said. "Everyone else pays three thousand."

"Wow." Katie touched the dresser. "Did you make this?"

"This piece?" Jake moved past her and examined the dresser. "I would guess your grandfather made this one." He pointed toward another dresser without a mirror. "I think my grandfather made that one."

"They make beautiful furniture." Katie studied Jake, taking in his dark hair and bright blue eyes. He stood several inches taller than she did, probably close to six feet. "Your *daadi* and *mei daadi* have been friends a long time, *ya*?"

"That's right." He lowered himself onto a hope chest beside the dresser. "I'd say more than fifty years. They went to school together."

Katie nodded. "That's a long time."

"What brings you out here this fine day?" Jake asked, crossing his arms over his chest.

"Samuel said he needed to get some supplies from *mei daadi*." She jammed her thumb in the direction of the workroom. "He picked me up from the bakery before continuing on his way here. I came along for the ride."

"Oh." Jake gestured toward a dining room chair across from him. "Why don't you have a seat while you wait?"

"That sounds nice." Katie sat and smoothed her hands over her apron and dress. "How have you been?"

"Fine," Jake said. "Busy." He pointed toward the desk. "The phone has been ringing nearly nonstop. I'm splitting my time between manning the desk and working on small projects. I'd like to become a full-time carpenter. I've been spending a lot of time at my grandfather's house on Saturdays working in his shop."

"Oh." Katie fiddled with the ties to her prayer covering while she studied him. "You're very close to your *daadi, ya?*"

"Yes, I am." Jake glanced down at his dark T-shirt and jeans. "I guess I don't look like an Amish carpenter, but I'd like to be one."

Katie chuckled. "I think you'd make a *wunderbaar gut* Amish carpenter."

"Danki." He grinned. "I've heard the bakery is very busy too."

"Ya, it usually stays that way until the cold weather comes in," Katie said. "Then the tourist groups disappear until spring."

"Eli told me Elizabeth wants new display cabinets installed at the bakery," Jake said. "She's pushing him to do the renovations this fall and winter when the bakery isn't very busy."

"Really?" Katie asked in surprise. "I had no idea." She considered the shopping area in the front of the bakery. "I guess the bakery still has the original cabinets from when it was built nearly thirty years ago, *ya?*"

He shrugged. "That's what Eli said."

"That will be a nice change," Katie said.

"What's your favorite dessert to bake?" he asked.

Katie considered the question and thought about the many desserts she prepared every day. "I guess it would have to be chocolate chip cookies."

"Really?" Jake raised an eyebrow. "Chocolate chip cookies?"

Katie frowned. "What's wrong with that?"

"That's so ..." He paused. "Ordinary."

Her frown deepened. "You haven't tried my chocolate chip cookies, so how would you know if they're ordinary?"

He held his hands up as if to surrender. "I guess you got me there, Katie. I'll have to try them and see if they are truly extraordinary."

Katie wagged a finger at him. "That's a deal. I'll have to make you some and then you can judge."

"Jake," Samuel called from the doorway leading to the shop. "Can you help us load some wood into the back of the wagon?"

"Of course," Jake said, standing and walking toward the work area. "I was asking about your sister's baking."

Samuel grinned. "You'd be surprised how *gut* she is. I like her cooking and baking more than *mei mamm*'s."

Surprised by her brother's compliment, Katie smiled as she followed Samuel and Jake through the shop. She waved as she passed her uncle Luke and other familiar carpenters on her way out the back door. Katie nodded and greeted her grandfather and her uncles, Timothy and Daniel. Together, the men loaded wooden planks and tools into the back of the wagon.

Once they were done, Samuel shook their hands and climbed into the wagon. Katie said good-bye to her uncles and grandfather and climbed up next to Samuel.

"Hey, Katie," Jake called from the back door of the shop. "Don't forget my chocolate chip cookies."

"I won't, Jake," Katie said. "I promise."

Jake waved before heading back into the shop.

"What was he talking about?" Samuel asked as he guided the horse through the parking lot.

"*Kichlin*," Katie said with a shrug.

⚬⚬⚬

Lindsay stepped into Rebecca's bedroom Saturday night. "They're asleep." She lowered herself onto the hope chest across from where Rebecca sat propped up in bed. "They wore themselves out today running around outside." She studied her aunt's pale complexion. "How are you feeling?"

Rebecca frowned. "I feel the same as I do every day. I'm

frustrated I can't get up and take care of *mei kinner*." She sighed and placed the Christian novel she'd had in her lap on the night stand. "It's funny how I miss the little things. For example, it seems like an eternity since I gave the *kinner* a bath. I would love to hear Emma giggle and splash in the water again."

"This is temporary," Lindsay said. "Remember how you said this time would fly by, and before you knew it, you'd be holding your new *boppli* in your arms?"

Rebecca ran her fingers over her headscarf. "I was wrong."

"You were wrong about what?" Daniel stood in the doorway.

"*Aenti* Rebecca is frustrated about being stuck in bed." Lindsay pushed her prayer covering ribbons behind her shoulders. "She wants to get up and take care of the *kinner*, but I reminded her she said the time will pass by quickly."

"And I was wrong," Rebecca repeated. "Time isn't passing by quickly. A few days feel more like a few weeks."

Daniel looked at Rebecca with a tender expression as he touched her shoulder, and Lindsay wondered if she should leave so her aunt and uncle could speak in private.

"It will pass by quick enough, *mei liewe*," Daniel said. "Before you know it, you'll be complaining the newborn *boppli* isn't allowing us any sleep."

"I hope so." Rebecca touched his hand and then smiled at Lindsay. "*Danki* to both of you for reminding me this time will pass. The Lord has *wunderbaar gut* plans for our family in the future."

"That's very true." Lindsay started toward the door. "I'll go finish cleaning up the kitchen."

"Wait," Rebecca called. "You don't need to leave."

Lindsay stopped in the doorway while Daniel moved to the other side of the room. "I thought you and *Onkel* Daniel might want some time together. I just wanted to check on you. Do you need anything?"

Rebecca shook her head. "No. I'm fine, *danki*."

Lindsay glanced at her uncle, who was sitting on a chair while pulling off his socks. "*Onkel* Daniel, would it be okay if I go to the youth gathering tomorrow night?"

"Of course," Daniel said. "Why wouldn't it?"

Lindsay's expression became serious. "That would mean you'll have to care for the *kinner* and put them in bed."

Daniel grinned. "I believe I can handle *mei kinner*, but I can always ask Rebecca for advice if I get confused."

"I think you can figure it out, Daniel," Rebecca said, readjusting the pillow behind her head. "You're a smart man."

He chuckled. "I'm glad you still believe that, Becky."

Lindsay fiddled with the seam on her bib apron. "Do you think I could visit the bishop tomorrow? Maybe I could go see him before the youth gathering?"

"That would be fine. I'm *froh* you've decided to do it." Daniel smiled at her.

"What are you two talking about?" Rebecca looked confused. "Why do you need to see the bishop?"

"Tell Rebecca what you shared with me at breakfast a couple of days ago, Lindsay," Daniel said.

"I want to ask the bishop if he'll allow me to be baptized with *mei freinden* this fall," Lindsay said, leaning on the doorframe. "I'm going to go meet with him and see if he'll let me make up the lessons I've missed like he did for *Aenti* Miriam when she was baptized."

Rebecca's expression brightened. "That's *wunderbaar.*"

"I think it's a *gut* idea to visit him Sunday afternoon," Daniel said. "I'll take you over to his house on the way to the youth gathering. I can get *mei mamm* to come and watch the *kinner* while I'm gone. I'm certain she'd love to visit with the *kinner* and Rebecca."

"That sounds perfect." Lindsay's stomach fluttered at the thought of speaking to the bishop, but in her heart, she knew she had to do it. It felt right. All of her doubts about joining the church had dissolved after her visit to Virginia Beach. This was the path God was leading her down.

"I'm so very *froh* to hear the news, Lindsay," Rebecca said, reaching for her hand. "Your *freinden* will also be excited."

"*Danki.*" Lindsay held Rebecca's hand for a moment and then gestured toward the doorway. "I'm going to go check the messages. I was thinking of *mei schweschder* today. If she hasn't called me, I'd like to call her and see how she's doing."

"Be certain to tell her hello for us," Rebecca said. "And come back to say *gut nacht* before you head to bed."

"I will." Lindsay padded down the hallway, descended the stairs, and grabbed a flashlight by the back door before heading out across the rock driveway to the small shed. She stepped into the shanty, which contained a phone, stool, and counter. She lifted the receiver and dialed the voice mail. After entering the code, a recorded voice told her she had one message. She punched the button to retrieve her message, and her older sister's voice rang through the receiver.

"Hey, Linds," Jessica said. "I got your voice mail explaining you were back in Pennsylvania. I've been trying to call your cell phone but it goes straight to voice mail. I guess the battery's dead, huh? I just wanted to check and see how Aunt Rebecca's doing. Give me a call. Bye!"

Lindsay deleted the message and then dialed her sister's cell phone.

Jessica answered on the second ring. "Hey, Linds! How are you? How's Aunt Rebecca? I've been waiting to hear from you."

"We're doing okay," Lindsay said, noticing it was quiet on the other end. "You aren't out tonight?"

"No." Jessica sniffed. "I think I'm coming down with a cold. I'm really beat."

"I bet it's those long hours you're working," Lindsay said,

lowering herself onto the stool in front of the counter. "You said this was supposed to be an internship, but you've been working fifty hours a week, right?"

Jessica sighed. "I know. I'm working too hard and now I'm getting sick. You sound like Mom."

Lindsay grinned. "Thank you. I take that as a compliment."

"Fill me in on the news," Jessica said. "You said Aunt Rebecca is okay? You scared me with the message you left when you said you rushed home."

"I'm sorry I scared you. I was scared myself. *Aenti* Rebecca is on strict bed rest, so she's really frustrated about not being able to do things around the house. She looks tired and a little pale, but she's okay. I'm keeping an eye on her."

"Good," Jessica said, sniffling again. "Where's your cell phone? Is the battery dead?"

"It's turned off," Lindsay said. "I put it in my dresser drawer. I decided not to use it."

"I didn't know you turned it off. I assumed the battery had died when I kept getting your voice mail." Jessica sounded surprised. "I've been thinking of you all and praying for you. I talked to Aunt Trisha and Uncle Frank. They're doing well. Aunt Trisha is very happy with her walking cast."

Lindsay smiled while wrapping the phone cord around her finger. "That's good. She was doing the dishes and telling me to get out of the kitchen when I was there."

Jessica laughed. "I can see her saying that. How are you doing?"

"Fine." Lindsay bit her lip and debated telling Jessica her news about meeting with the bishop. In the past, she'd endured Jessica's constant negative comments about Lindsay's desire to be Amish. However, a surge of confidence in her decision flowed through her. She wanted her sister to know about her choice. "I'm going to see the bishop on my way to the youth gathering at Lizzie Anne's tomorrow night."

"Really?" Jessica sounded curious. "Why? Did you get in trouble for something? Is it like being called to the principal's office?"

Lindsay rolled her eyes. When would her sister take the time to learn more about the Amish lifestyle? "No. It's not like that at all. I'm going to ask him if I can be baptized in the fall with my friends. I've missed some discussions, so I want to try to make up the lessons. If I miss this opportunity, I'll have to be baptized next year with another church district. The baptism discussions are only held every other year."

"Oh," Jessica said. "You're serious about this?"

"Yes, I am," Lindsay said. "I'm comfortable with my decision, and I wanted you to know about it."

"Let me know how it goes," Jessica said.

"I will." Lindsay continued to wind the cord around her finger. She couldn't help but smile. She was certain her sister would lecture her on how she shouldn't join the church without going to college. However, to her surprise, Jessica had accepted her choice.

"Other than your cold," Lindsay began, "how are things?"

"They're okay," Jessica said. "I'd love to see you, but I need to pack and get back to Richmond. Classes start soon."

"Are you stopping by here on your way back to school?" Lindsay asked.

"I don't think I'm going to have time," Jessica said. "I need to finish up a few projects at work, but I'll see."

"It would be great to see you, and maybe you could see Jake. You didn't leave things on a good note with him, and I imagine you never called him. Am I right?" Lindsay fiddled with the phone cord while she waited for her sister's response.

Jessica sighed again. "You're right. I haven't called him, and he hasn't called me either."

"Have you thought about calling him?"

"I've thought about it." Jessica sneezed and then coughed.

"Jess," Lindsay said with a frown, "you sound terrible. Have you been to the doctor?"

"No." Jessica moaned. "I need some of Mom's homemade soup."

Lindsay's mouth formed a sad smile. "I wish I could whip some up and bring it to you."

"I do too." Jessica coughed again. "I guess I better go. I feel like crashing on the couch with a good movie."

"I think you need sleep more than you need to watch a movie," Lindsay said.

"Yes, Mom," Jessica responded with a weak laugh. "I'll talk to you soon. Give my love to Rebecca, Daniel, and the kids."

"I will. They send their love to you too. Bye, Jess."

"Bye," Jessica said.

Lindsay hung up the phone, grabbed the flashlight from the counter, and headed back to the house. While stepping into the kitchen, Lindsay smiled. She'd finally gotten Jessica to accept the fact that she was going to be Amish. Bridging that gap of understanding between her and her sister was a weight off her shoulders. Perhaps Jessica would finally respect Lindsay's decisions. *It's about time.*

⁓≈⁓

Katie smiled while walking between Lindsay and Lizzie Anne through the streets of Bird-in-Hand Saturday afternoon. "I'm so glad *Mammi* could come over today and take care of *Aenti* Rebecca so the three of us could go out."

"I agree," Lizzie Anne said. "It's been too long since we've all been."

Lindsay pointed to a bookstore. "Can we stop in here? I wanted to get something for *Aenti* Rebecca since I didn't bring her a gift from Virginia."

"That's a great idea," Katie said. "I know she loves to read to pass the time. I'll get her a book too."

"*Wunderbaar*," Lizzie Anne said. "Let's shop!"

For the next thirty minutes, Katie, Lindsay, and Lizzie Anne browsed the store, holding up Christian novels and comparing the covers.

Katie perused the bookshelves, glancing at the non-fiction books beside the rows of novels. When she found a baby name book, she lifted it and grinned. "Lizzie Anne and Lindsay," she called. "Look at this. Should we get it for *Aenti* Rebecca?"

Lizzie Anne took the book. "Oh *ya*," she said, playing along with Katie's joke. Let's look at the girls' names." She flipped through the pages. "How about Tiffany? What do you think of Tiffany Kauffman? Isn't that Amish?"

"My turn," Lindsay said, grabbing the book. "I found a boy name. How does Colby Cody Kauffman sound?"

Lizzie Anne and Katie laughed so loud that other bookstore customers turned to study them.

"Let me look," Katie said, and Lindsay handed her the book. "I'll see if there's a better girl's name since I have a hunch *Aenti* Rebecca is going to have a girl." She turned back to the section of girls' names. "I got it. Paris Brittany Ashley Kauffman." She and her friends had to wipe tears from their eyes after their laughter ended.

"That is the best Amish name yet," Lindsay said.

"I agree," Lizzie Anne said.

Katie noticed other customers were still watching them while they made their way back to the inspirational novel section. "We better pick out a few books before we're asked to leave for being too rowdy," she whispered.

"*Ya*, but it was fun," Lindsay said. "I haven't laughed that hard in a long time."

Lizzie Anne nodded in agreement. "That's why I love our shopping trips the best."

"I do too," Katie said.

They studied the shelves of Christian novels, comparing covers and titles. When they narrowed their search to three books, they made their way to the cashier. Each of them bought one book as a surprise gift for Rebecca.

"*Aenti* Rebecca is going to be so excited when she sees these books," Lindsay said as they headed down the sidewalk.

Katie pointed toward a restaurant. "Can we grab a quick lunch before heading back to *Aenti* Rebecca's?"

"That would make this day absolutely perfect," Lindsay said.

They sat at a small booth and glanced at the menus. After ordering their food, they each sipped from their cups of ice water.

"I think we should've bought that baby name book as a joke," Lizzie Anne said. "That could've been fun."

"But a waste of money, *ya?*" Katie said. "But fun all the same."

Lindsay shook her head. "I guess I shouldn't be laughing since I have the most un-Amish name here."

"Maybe your name will become Amish because of you," Lizzie Anne said with a shrug. "You'll start a new trend."

"*Ya,*" Katie said. "I'll name my future *dochdern* Mary, Rachel, Anna, Fannie, and Lindsay."

The three girls laughed, and Katie noticed they were yet again drawing attention.

"I fear we may be asked to leave the restaurant now because we're having too much fun," Katie said.

"There's no such thing as having too much fun," Lizzie Anne said. "That's what friendship is all about."

"That's so true," Lindsay said.

Leaning across the table, Katie touched her friends' hands. "It's so *gut* to spend time together like this. We need to do this more often."

"*Ya,*" Lindsay and Lizzie Anne said in unison before laughing some more.

Katie smiled. This was the best afternoon she'd enjoyed in a long time.

STRAWBERRY SHORTCAKE

½ cup butter or margarine
1½ cups flour
1 cup sugar
¼ teaspoon salt
2 eggs
2 ¾ teaspoons baking powder
½ cup milk
1 teaspoon vanilla

Cream butter and sugar, then add one egg at a time. Beat well. Add sifted dry ingredients alternately with milk. Add vanilla. Pour in greased pan. Bake at 350 degrees for 45 minutes.

Let shortcakes cool and then top with strawberries and whipped cream.

4

Sunday afternoon, Katie followed Lizzie Anne and Lindsay out to the pasture at her aunt Kathryn's house after the service and noon meal. The warm sun kissed her cheeks and caused her to squint.

"It's lovely out today," Lindsay said, smiling.

"*Ya*," Katie agreed.

"*Ach!*" Lizzie Anne exclaimed, pointing across the pasture. "They're picking teams for volleyball. Let's go play!"

Katie spotted a group of young men and women gathered around the volleyball net. Her brother Samuel and Matthew stood together while Matthew held the volleyball. Katie loped alongside her friends as they raced toward the net.

"I want to play!" Lizzie Anne announced, approaching the net. "Pick me."

"I do too," Lindsay chimed in.

"We'll take Lizzie Anne," Samuel told Matthew.

Matthew smiled at Lindsay. "I guess we'll take Lindsay then."

"What about me?" Katie said as her friends lined up with their teams.

"I'm sorry, but we're full," Samuel said with a frown. "You'll have to play next time."

"Oh." Katie glanced at Lindsay, who mirrored Samuel's frown in response.

"I'm sorry, Katie," Lindsay said. "You take my place next time around, all right?"

"That's fine." Katie sank onto the warm grass. She hugged her knees to her chest and watched her friends laugh while bumping the ball back and forth. She wished she could be part of the camaraderie, but instead tried to smile and enjoy the game. After all, it was a beautiful day and she was with her church community.

When the game was finally over, Lizzie Anne and Lindsay rushed over, panting and laughing.

"You really missed that shot, Lizzie Anne," Lindsay said with a chuckle. "Did you fall asleep on the court?"

"No!" Lizzie Anne said with feigned annoyance. She pointed to Samuel. "It was his fault. He missed the pass, so I missed the shot."

"No," Samuel responded as he and Matthew walked over. "That was all your fault, Lizzie Anne. You were asleep just like Lindsay said."

"I'm thirsty," Lindsay said. "Let's all get a drink, *ya?*"

Matthew gestured toward the barn. "That's a *gut* idea."

"But I was going to play volleyball," Katie said, falling in step with her friends.

"We'll play again," Lindsay said. "Maybe this time Lizzie Anne won't miss the shot."

"You missed one too, Lindsay!" Lizzie Anne said, tapping Lindsay's arm.

Katie smiled, wishing she could participate in the conversation. Although she'd watched the game, she didn't quite see the humor they did. She assumed she would've been able to feel a part of it if they'd had room for her on one of the teams.

Katie climbed the steps behind her friends and trailed them to the kitchen where they filled plastic cups with cold water from a pitcher. They moved to the family room, which was full of people, and crossed to some empty benches in the corner. Lindsay and Matthew sat on one side while Lizzie Anne and Samuel sat across from them. By the time Katie reached the table, there was no room for her.

Lindsay frowned. "Oh, Katie." She squeezed over toward Matthew and patted a sliver of bench. "Sit here. I'll make room."

"I can make room too." Lizzie Anne also revealed a small section of bench that wouldn't be enough for even one of Katie's legs.

"That's okay." Katie glanced around the room and spotted her sister Nancy sitting with some of the younger girls. "I'll go sit with Nancy. I'll see you later." She forced a smile and turned to go.

"Katie, no!" Lindsay called. "We can make room."

"Really, I don't mind." Katie waved and then crossed the room to her sister's table. "May I join you?" she asked Nancy.

"*Ya!*" Nancy said, scooting over for Katie. "Sit down. We were just discussing how cute Andrew Smucker is."

"*Danki.*" Katie sat on the bench and glanced back toward her friends as they laughed and talked together without her. She moved closer to Nancy, trying in vain to ease the hollow feeling in the pit of her stomach.

⟡

"I can do this," Lindsay muttered as she sat next to Daniel in the buggy. She stared at the bishop's large white house and sucked in a breath. "I can do this," she repeated. "I know I can."

Daniel smiled. "*Ya*, you can do it, and I'll go in with you to give you support."

"*Danki*," she said. Seeing the bishop's house caused her to doubt herself and wonder if she should just go to the youth gathering without meeting him first. She was thankful her uncle insisted on supporting her through this important meeting.

Lindsay climbed from the buggy and then headed up the porch steps toward the bishop's front door with Daniel. She'd spoken to the bishop numerous times since coming to live in Bird-in-Hand, and he'd always been pleasant during their brief encounters. However, now she was going to ask permission to enter into something sacred. Lindsay touched her prayer covering and then smoothed her black bib apron over her best purple frock. She had tried to look her best for this very important meeting. Mustering all of her confidence, she knocked on the door and mentally rehearsed what she'd told Daniel and Rebecca she'd say.

The door swung open revealing Bishop Abner Chupp dressed in black trousers, a brown shirt, and suspenders. His gray hair matched his long beard, and the wrinkles on his ivory face suggested he had to be close to his eighties.

"*Wie geht's*, Abner," Daniel said.

"Hello," Lindsay said.

"*Gut* evening," Abner said. He glanced between Daniel and Lindsay with a confused look in his small brown eyes. "Is everything okay at your farm?" he asked Daniel. His expression turned to worry. "Is Rebecca doing well today?"

"She's doing quite well, *danki*." Daniel pointed to the row of four rocking chairs by the porch railing. "May Lindsay and I speak with you for a moment?"

"Of course." Abner stepped onto the porch and made a sweeping gesture toward the seating arrangement. "Please have a seat."

Lindsay sank into a chair and took a deep breath while meeting the bishop's curious gaze. She turned toward Daniel, and he nodded with a reassuring expression that told her to begin talking.

"*Danki* for talking with us this evening," Lindsay began. "I recently went to Virginia to take care of *mei aenti* Trisha who had broken her *beh*."

Abner fingered his beard. "*Ya*, I'd heard that. How is she?"

"Better," Lindsay said. "She's walking with a special cast now."

"That's *gut* news," Abner said. "Praise God."

"*Ya*." Lindsay cleared her throat. It was time to get to the real purpose of her meeting with the bishop. No more small talk. "Before I left for Virginia Beach, I wasn't certain where I belonged."

"Where you belonged?" The bishop shook his head. "I don't understand. Do you mean where you're supposed to live?"

"Partly that." Lindsay folded her hands in her lap. "What I mean is, I didn't know if I should be in the Amish or the English world. *Mei schweschder*, Jessica, was constantly pressuring me to go back to school and join her at college, but that never felt right to me. However, I wasn't ready to be baptized either." She paused to gather her thoughts. "But after spending several weeks back in Virginia Beach, I realized I belong right here." She looked at her uncle, who smiled. She was thankful he was sitting next to her.

Abner nodded. "I see. I'm glad God put that in your heart and you listened to Him."

"He did put it in my heart, and I heard Him loud and clear." Lindsay agreed with an emphatic nod. "I've come to accept that although *mei schweschder* and I had the same parents, we're very different. She's living a life meant for her, and this life here is meant for me." She tapped the chair as she spoke.

"*Gut*. That's very nice to hear." The bishop glanced at Daniel. "I'm certain you, Rebecca, and the *kinner* are glad Lindsay is staying."

"We are," Daniel said. "She's a part of our family, and we love having her with us."

"*Danki*." Lindsay said. Seeing her uncle's smile gave her the burst of confidence she needed to continue with what she wanted to say. She looked at Abner. "I want to be baptized with *mei freinden*."

The bishop's bushy gray eyebrows flew to his hairline. "Lindsay, you've missed too many lessons to make up at this point." His expression softened. "You can join another class with a neighboring district next year. I'll speak to the bishop if you'd like me to."

She shook her head. "I'd prefer not to wait on this, Bishop. It's very important to me."

"I realize that, but it will still be important to you next year." He fingered his beard. "It wouldn't be fair to the rest of the class after all of the lessons they've had."

"Oh, I know that." She sat up straighter. "I'll make up all of the lessons."

"I know Lindsay will keep her word and make up all of the lessons," Daniel chimed in. "And I'm certain you remember you helped *mei bruder* Timothy's wife, Miriam, make up her lessons and allowed her to be baptized with a class that had begun before she joined them."

"*Ya*," Lindsay said. "I'll do exactly as *mei aenti* Miriam did. I'll come over and meet with you whenever it's convenient for you, and I'll do whatever I need to do. It means that much to me."

The bishop paused for a moment with a thoughtful expression. "Why do you want to be baptized, Lindsay?"

Lindsay glanced at her uncle, and he nodded with another encouraging expression. She then turned back to the bishop. "I want to be baptized so I can live the life I believe God wants me to live. Being Amish is what I'm meant to be." She thought of her experience volunteering at the nursing home. "While I was staying with my aunt and uncle in Virginia Beach, I volunteered in a nursing *heemet* on Saturdays as part of a church project. During my time there, I met an Old Order Amish woman from

Pennsylvania who'd had a stroke and could only speak *Dietsch.* Her name was Mrs. Fisher."

She pointed to her chest. "I was the only person who could communicate with Mrs. Fisher. She fell and I was there to help her tell the nurses she'd hurt her *beh.*" Tears filled her eyes. "And I helped her write a letter to her estranged *dochder* in California before she passed away unexpectedly."

"I'm *froh* you were there to help her, Lindsay," Abner said with a sympathetic expression. "You were a blessing to her."

"*Danki.*" Lindsay sniffed and swiped her fingers over her tears. "I did what I felt God wanted me to do, and I came to realize my being Amish is the most important part of my life." She folded her hands as if pleading with the bishop. "Please let me join the current baptism instruction session. It would mean so much to me and *mei freinden.*"

The old man rubbed his beard and looked out past the porch.

"Please, Bishop Chupp," she added. "I promise I'll attend the lessons, and I'll do my very best to get caught up with the current class. I'll be ready when the baptism day arrives."

Meeting her gaze, compassion glimmered in the bishop's eyes. "You're absolutely certain about this, Lindsay?"

She nodded. "There's no doubt in my mind."

"This is a very serious decision," he said. "It's not one to be taken lightly. Once you've joined, you're in for life."

"I know," Lindsay said. "My mom made *mei aenti* Rebecca our guardian because her heart was still here even years after she left the community to marry my dad. I feel I'm closer to her now that I'm here. That's not why I want to join the church, but it gives me extra comfort in making this decision. I know in my heart it's the right time for me to make the commitment to Christ and my community."

"Abner," Daniel began. "Rebecca and I each have talked to Lindsay about this, and we've discussed it at length with each other as well." He placed his hand on Lindsay's shoulder. "Rebecca and I both feel Lindsay is serious in her commitment to the church. If I didn't feel this decision was right for her, I wouldn't be here supporting her and talking to you right now."

Lindsay smiled at her uncle. She was so thankful for his words of support.

Abner was silent for a moment. "Next week we'll begin your instruction," he finally said to Lindsay. "Be here next Monday at six."

"I will! *Danki!*" With her own hands trembling with excitement, Lindsay stood and shook his hand.

"*Danki*, Abner," Daniel said. He also shook the bishop's hand. "This means a lot to our family."

"*Gern gschehne*," the bishop said.

He and Daniel made small talk about the weather before Daniel started down the porch steps. "*Danki* again, Abner. I appreciate your time with us."

"*Danki* so much," Lindsay repeated. She started toward the buggy, her heart pounding with excitement.

"*Gut nacht*," Abner called after them.

Lindsay waved to Abner and then continued toward the buggy. She climbed in next to her uncle and smiled at him. "*Danki* for bringing me here, *Onkel* Daniel. And *danki* for all you said to the bishop. I don't think I could've done this without you."

"*Gern gschehne*," he said, gripping the reins. "I think it went very well. Now let's get you to the youth gathering."

"I'll see you later tonight," Lindsay said as she climbed out of the buggy in Lizzie Anne's driveway.

"Have fun," Daniel said.

"I will," Lindsay replied. "I'll get a ride *heemet* with Samuel and Katie." She rushed toward the barn. She couldn't wait to tell her friends the news. She'd left a message for Matthew earlier in the day telling him she was going to meet with the bishop before the youth gathering and found him waiting for her outside the barn.

He raised his eyebrows in question as she approached, and she couldn't stop a smile from appearing on her face.

"Wie geht's," Matthew called. "From the excited look on your face, I guess your meeting with the bishop went well?"

"It did," she said, her voice bubbling with her excitement. She clasped her hands together. "I can't believe it! He said yes! He gave me permission to make up the discussions I've missed, and I'll be baptized with *mei freinden.*"

"That's *wunderbaar,* Lindsay." Matthew chuckled. "You're really that surprised?"

"Of course I am." Lindsay turned toward him. "He said I can make up the classes beginning next week Monday." She shared the conversation she'd had with the bishop, and Matthew listened with interest.

"I'm so *froh,*" Matthew said. "What *wunderbaar* news."

"Do you think I said the right things?" Lindsay asked, hoping for his approval.

Matthew's face assumed a serious expression. "Lindsay, I've figured out a couple of things about you since we became *freinden.*"

She held her breath.

"First of all," he began, "you're very, very smart. And you're always genuine. I don't think you have a dishonest bone in your body. So please stop doubting yourself because I could never doubt you."

Speechless, she nodded.

"Now," he said, gesturing toward the barn door. "Let's go see our *freinden* before we miss the whole event."

"That sounds like a *wunderbaar* idea," Lindsay said as they began to walk toward the barn door, where voices rang out in High German while the youth members sang hymns from the *Ausbund*.

They stepped into the barn and Lindsay glanced around, finding Katie, Lizzie Anne, and Samuel sitting together on a bench. Lindsay dropped down next to Lizzie Anne, while Matthew sat beside Samuel.

"You look awfully excited, Lindsay. What's going on?" Lizzie Anne asked with a grin.

Katie leaned toward Lindsay. "That's what I was going to ask."

"I went to see the bishop," Lindsay said looking between her friends. "And I'm joining your baptism class."

Both of her friends pulled her into a hug at the same time. Lindsay smiled and spotted several people turning around to see what the fuss was.

"We're attracting attention again," Lindsay said.

"I don't care," Katie said, smiling. "I'm glad you made this decision. It will be nice for us all to join the church together."

"I agree," Lizzie Anne chimed in. "This is how it should be."

"*Ya*," Lindsay said, pushing her ribbons behind her shoulder. "It is."

"This is *wunderbaar gut*," Lizzie Anne said. "We're all going to be baptized together. Can you tell me about your conversation with the bishop? I know it's very personal, but I'm really surprised you went to see him. Would you mind telling us?"

"*Ya*, I can tell you," Lindsay said with a shrug. "I'm not embarrassed. He was very nice."

"Let's go outside and talk so we don't disturb anyone," Katie suggested.

Katie stood with Lizzie Anne and Lindsay outside the barn while they listened to the story of Lindsay's visit to the bishop.

"That's *wunderbaar!*" Katie said, clapping her hands together. "I'm so glad you went to visit him."

"*Ya!*" Lizzie Anne hugged Lindsay again. "You were very brave."

"I'm thankful *Onkel* Daniel went with me," Lindsay said. "He really gave me strength. He also said some really nice things that I believe helped the bishop decide to let me make up the discussions. I couldn't have done it without *Onkel* Daniel." She gestured toward Matthew and Samuel, who were standing together and talking several yards away. "Look at them. Isn't it funny how Matthew and Samuel are good friends like you and I are, Lizzie Anne?"

Katie felt herself bristle at the comment. "Am I invisible?" she asked, forcing a laugh to try to make it sound like a joke.

"No," Lindsay said quickly. "I'm sorry, Katie. I didn't mean to make it sound like you weren't here. I was just saying it's funny how Samuel and Matthew are good friends, and Lizzie Anne and I like them. That's all I meant."

"*Ya,*" Lizzie Anne chimed in. "The three of us are best *freinden*, like always. Best *freinden* forever."

"I just need to find a *bu* to like, *ya?*" Katie asked.

"*Ya!*" Lindsay and Katie said in unison.

Lizzie Anne pointed at a group of boys standing over by the fence. "How about Rueben? He's nice."

Katie scrunched her nose and shook her head. "No, he's too hyper. He never sits still and he twitches."

"How do you know he twitches?" Lindsay looked confused.

"I sat next to him in school, and his leg was always bobbing up and down. It was like he had too much nervous energy." Katie frowned. "Trust me."

Lindsay laughed.

Lizzie Anne pointed to another young man. "What about Jason? He's handsome, no?"

"No," Katie said. "Talks too loud. He used to give me a head-ache in school."

Lizzie Anne and Lindsay both laughed.

Lizzie Anne gestured toward another young man. "Joey is nice. He always smiles at you."

Katie's expression transformed to disbelief. "Joey? His sus-penders are always crooked."

"What?" Lindsay asked with surprise. "Are you serious, Katie? That's ridiculous." She nodded toward another boy. "What about Merv? He's really nice."

Katie shook her head. "He always misses a snap on his shirt." She pointed toward the group. "And don't even mention Titus. His one boot is untied. I'm surprised he hasn't fallen yet tonight."

Lindsay and Lizzie Anne burst into laughter, and Katie couldn't help but join in. Oh, how she loved these fun moments with her two best friends! She wished they would last forever.

"You are too picky, Katie Kauffman," Lizzie Anne said, slap-ping Katie's arm. "You'll never find a *bu* if you have such high standards."

Katie shrugged. "I just know what I don't like."

"I don't know if you'll find any *bu* as perfect as you expect," Lindsay said, wiping her eyes from laughing so much.

"I don't know either." Katie frowned. *Does that mean I'll wind up alone?*

⁌⁌⁌

"I had a lot of fun tonight," Lindsay said while riding next to Katie on the way back to her house later that evening.

"I did too," Katie said. "I'm so glad you had a good visit with the bishop. It will be nice to have you in baptism instruction with us."

Samuel guided the horse into Lindsay's driveway. "You two and Lizzie Anne better behave at those classes. You do realize it's serious, *ya?*" He smiled. "I'm only joking. I think it's great you'll all be baptized together."

"*Ya,*" Lindsay said. "*Danki* for the ride. Drive safely *heemet.*"

"*Gern gschehne,*" Samuel said. "Tell *Aenti* Rebecca and *Onkel* Daniel hello for us."

"*Gut nacht,*" Katie said, hugging Lindsay. "Talk to you soon."

Lindsay climbed down from the buggy and waved before entering the house. She retrieved a flashlight from the shelf by the door and used it to guide her up the stairs. She spotted a light under Rebecca's door and continued down the hallway toward it. She gently tapped on the door, hoping her aunt and uncle were still awake.

"Come in," Daniel called softly.

Lindsay gingerly turned the knob and pushed the door open, finding her aunt and uncle propped up in bed while reading. "Hi."

Rebecca's eyes lit up as she closed her Christian novel. "Lindsay! I'm so glad you're *heemet.* I heard it went well with the bishop."

"I'm sorry, Lindsay, but I couldn't wait to tell Rebecca the *gut* news." Daniel placed his Bible in his lap. "I hope you're not disappointed in me."

"I'm not disappointed," Lindsay said. "I'm glad you told *Aenti* Rebecca."

"Come here, *mei liewe.*" Rebecca reached over and took Lindsay's hand before pulling her into a hug. "I'm very glad the bishop agreed to allow you in the class. I know this is very important to you."

"I told Rebecca how mature you were," Daniel said. "We both agree you'll do fine with the makeup sessions."

"*Danki.*" Lindsay sat on the edge of the bed. "I was *naerfich.* But the bishop was very understanding and he listened to everything I had to say."

"Your words were perfect," Daniel said with a solemn expression. "You showed him you were serious."

"*Danki*. I also appreciated everything you said too, *Onkel* Daniel. You were a source of great strength to me." While tracing a leaf on the flowery design of Rebecca's quilt, Lindsay wondered what her mother would say about her decision to become Amish. In her heart, she felt her mother would be supportive. Glancing up, she found Rebecca yawning while cupping her hand to her mouth. "I should let you rest."

"No, no." Rebecca shook her head and yawned again.

Daniel touched Rebecca's hand. "I believe our niece is right, *mei liewe*. Your exhaustion is written all over your face."

"And your yawns," Lindsay added with a smile.

Rebecca nodded. "I guess you're both right."

"You know we are." Daniel placed his Bible on his nightstand. "We should all head to bed."

Lindsay stood. "*Gut nacht. Danki* for your help with my decision."

"You made the decision," Daniel said with a knowing smile. "We just listened while you talked yourself through it."

Rebecca nodded. "That's the truth."

"*Gut nacht*," Daniel said. "We'll see you in the morning."

Lindsay stepped out into the hallway and gently closed the door behind her. After sneaking in to kiss her cousins, she headed to her room. Sitting on her bed, she blew out a deep breath and then silently thanked God for the blessings in her life.

5

The following evening, Lindsay was tucking Emma into bed when she heard Daniel call her name. Rushing down the stairs, she found Daniel and Matthew standing in the kitchen.

"Matthew," she said, breathless from hurrying down the stairs. "What a surprise. Is everything okay?"

"*Ya*," Matthew said. "I was wondering if we could speak on the porch for a few moments."

Lindsay glanced at Daniel, who nodded.

"A few minutes will be fine," Daniel said.

"*Danki*, Daniel," Matthew said. He opened the back door, holding it for Lindsay.

Lindsay stepped out onto the porch and sat on the porch swing, smoothing her dress and apron over her legs. She touched her headscarf, hoping it was straight. "What brings you out here, Matthew? I wasn't expecting you tonight."

"I felt like we didn't get much time to talk last night." Matthew lowered himself onto the swing next to her. "It was noisy at the youth gathering, and Lizzie Anne and Katie wanted to spend time with you." He reached into his pocket. "I made something for you today. Hold out your hand."

She opened her hand and he placed a small wooden heart in her palm. "Oh, Matthew." She ran her fingers over the smooth piece of wood. "I love it." She smiled up at him. "*Danki*."

"It has two meanings. It represents my heart, and I thought it was symbolic of what you're about to do."

"What do you mean?" she asked, rubbing the heart with her fingertips.

He pointed at the heart. "You're going to be baptized and give your heart to Jesus."

Lindsay smiled. "That's exactly right. *Danki*."

"Are you *naerfich*?" he asked.

"Oh *ya*," she said. "This is such a huge commitment. I know it's right for me, but I hope I can live up to the community's expectations."

"You will." Matthew leaned back on the swing. "You're too hard on yourself." He looked up toward the sky. "It's a *schee* night. Look at the stars."

"They're lovely." Lindsay gripped the heart and studied the stars. "I used to sit on the back porch with my dad and watch the stars when I was younger."

"Did you?" Matthew looked surprised. "You never told me that."

Lindsay shrugged. "It's just a memory from my childhood." She shook her head while thinking back to her childhood days. "When I was really young, I used to make a wish on the first star I'd see. Isn't that silly?"

Matthew smiled. "I think a lot of little girls do that, *ya*?"

Lindsay nodded and thought of her father again. "I loved spending time with my dad. He and I used to like to go on the back porch to watch thunderstorms. Whenever I see a thunderstorm, I think of those times. I miss him."

"I'm certain you do," Matthew said. "I miss *mei mamm* and the happy memories I had of *mei dat* before he left us. But God gives us those precious memories to help us through the hard times."

"What do you miss most about your *mamm*?" Lindsay asked.

Matthew rubbed his chin, considering the question. "I miss our talks the most. We'd always talk while we drove to church. *Mei dat* was a good listener when I was young before he changed and decided he was unhappy living the Amish life."

"I know how you feel." Lindsay frowned. "I miss talking to my parents too." She studied his handsome profile. "Did you feel different after you were baptized? Did you feel reborn in your faith?"

"Absolutely," he said with a serious expression. "I'm certain you will too."

"*Ya*." Lindsay stared at the stars and silently marveled how much she enjoyed sitting with Matthew. "I imagine it was difficult for you to move here with your *mamm* and leave all of your *freinden* back in your former community."

He nodded. "*Ya*, but everyone was so welcoming here. It quickly felt like *heemet*."

"I understand," Lindsay said. "I felt the same way when Jessica and I came here."

"And now you're taking the final step to become Amish," Matthew said, his smile returning. "Have you shared the news with Jessica?"

"*Ya*." Lindsay slipped the heart into the pocket of her apron. "I was pleasantly surprised. She was supportive."

"*Gut*." Matthew patted the arm of the swing. "It's time she accepted your decisions."

"I know." Lindsay looked toward the stars. "I'm so *froh*. Things are working out the way I'd hoped. Soon I'll truly be a member of the community I love."

"You're already a member in my eyes." Matthew's expression was serious. "I look forward to the day you're baptized, Lindsay."

Before she could respond, the back door opened with a squeak, revealing Daniel. "It's getting late. I think you should be heading *heemet*, Matthew. Work comes early in the morning, *ya?*"

"*Ya.*" Matthew stood. "*Danki* for the reminder." He shook Daniel's hand. "*Danki* for allowing me to visit with Lindsay for a short while. I'll see you at work tomorrow."

"You drive safely. See you tomorrow." Daniel glanced at Lindsay. "It's bedtime, Lindsay." He stepped back into the kitchen and closed the door.

Lindsay smiled at Matthew. "I'm so glad you came to visit tonight." She pulled the wooden heart from her pocket. "*Danki* for the lovely gift."

"*Gern gschehne.*" He smiled. "I'm glad I got to see you." He pointed to the heart. "Take *gut* care of my heart, Lindsay." He then loped down the steps toward his waiting buggy.

As his buggy bounced down the driveway toward the road, Lindsay smiled. Her heart fluttered as she wondered how her relationship with Matthew would change once she was baptized and allowed to date.

⦿≫⦿

For the next six weeks, Lindsay attended baptism classes at the bishop's house on Monday and Thursday evenings and also before the church service every other Sunday. She felt her heart swell with love for the Amish culture every moment of her lessons. The more she learned about the traditions, the more she knew she was meant to become an official part of the community.

Finally, the day arrived. Lindsay's hands trembled as she sat on a bench near the front of the room during a regular Sunday service, which was being held in her aunt Sarah Rose's and uncle Luke's house. The walls downstairs had been moved to make room for rows of benches. More than one hundred members of her church district were there for the service. Today was the day she would be baptized and truly become Amish. Her heart thumped in her chest and her eyes filled with tears.

Earlier that morning, Lindsay and her baptism classmates had met with the ministers one last time while the congregation began singing hymns. After their meeting, they filed into the church service together, first the young men and then the young women. They had taken their seats on the benches reserved for them, divided by gender as their elders were, at the front of the congregation near the ministers.

"Are you okay?" Lizzie Anne whispered while sitting next to Lindsay.

"You don't seem like yourself," Katie chimed in from the other side of her.

"I just wish *Aenti* Rebecca were here," Lindsay said as Katie took her hand.

"I miss her too," Katie whispered. "But you know the doctor said it's not safe for her to get up. She's thinking of you and praying for you right now. Just remember the rest of your family is here, including *Onkel* Daniel."

"She's right," Lizzie Anne whispered. "You can tell her all about it later."

"Shh," Katie warned. "It's time for the service to begin."

Lindsay and her classmates bowed their heads and covered their faces with their hands, a symbol of their willingness to submit to God and the church.

She did her best to concentrate through the two sermons based on the Book of Acts, but her mind buzzed with thoughts of how much her life would change once she was a member of the church. She would participate in the fall Communion service coming next month. It felt so right, her heart soared.

Glancing to her right and left, she found her best friends staring at the minister with serious expressions. She inwardly smiled to herself and silently thanked God for her special friends and for the opportunity to share this important day with them.

Once the sermons ended, the deacon left the room to retrieve the pail of water and a cup.

"Go down on your knees before the Most High and Almighty God and His church if you still think this is the right thing to do to obtain your salvation," Bishop Chupp instructed Lindsay and the rest of the candidates.

Once on her knees, the bishop stood by Lindsay first. She held her breath with anticipation. The moment had come.

"Can you renounce the devil, the world, and your own flesh and blood?" the bishop asked.

"*Ya*," she said, her voice a quavering whisper.

"Can you commit yourself to Christ and His church and to abide by it and therein to live and to die?"

"*Ya*," she whispered.

"And in all the order of the church, according to the Word of the Lord, to be obedient and submissive to it and to help therein?"

"*Ya*," she said.

Lindsay closed her eyes and tried to calm her heartbeat as the bishop moved to Lizzie Anne. Once he was finished asking the questions of each candidate, he directed the congregation to stand. He read a prayer from the traditional Swiss Anabaptist prayer book before the congregation sat again.

The bishop, his wife, the deacon, and his wife stood before Lindsay. The deacon's wife removed Lindsay's prayer covering. Lindsay's body shook anew as the deacon poured water into the bishop's cupped hands before it dripped onto Lindsay's head. The water was cool and refreshing. She truly felt reborn!

Bishop Chupp then extended his hand to Lindsay and she rose. She closed her eyes while he recited a prayer. "May the Lord God complete the good work which He has begun in you and strengthen and comfort you to a blessed end through Jesus Christ," he said. "Amen."

The bishop's wife kissed Lindsay as a symbol of the "holy kiss" before Lindsay was given her prayer covering, which she placed back on her head.

Lindsay closed her eyes and prayed while the baptism was completed for the rest of the candidates. She prayed for Rebecca, Jessica, the rest of her family, and her friends who were also baptized today. When the process was complete, the bishop reminded the congregation to be obedient.

⊘⇜⊘

Once the service was over, Lindsay greeted her friends and family members and accepted their handshakes and words of encouragement. She was now a member of the church. Her eyes filled with tears as she thought of her mother, and she wondered if her mother had felt this same elation when she'd been baptized so many years ago.

"Congratulations," Matthew said as he approached. He held out his hand, and she shook it.

"*Danki,*" Lindsay said. "It's really overwhelming. Just like you told me, I feel like I've been reborn."

He hooked his thumbs around his suspenders. "I remember that feeling. It's like a brand-new beginning, a new chapter in your life."

"*Ya,*" Lindsay said. "That's exactly right."

Katie walked up and pulled Lindsay into a hug. "This is the best day of my life. I'm so *froh* we could be baptized together. It was perfect!"

"I agree." Lindsay smiled at her friend. "I can't wait to tell Rebecca all about it."

Lizzie Anne joined them and pulled them both into a group hug. "We did it."

Daniel stepped over to Lindsay and touched her arm. "I'm so *froh* for you, Lindsay. Welcome to the church."

"*Danki.*" Lindsay gave him a quick hug. "I'm so glad you could be here."

"I am too," he said. "You know Rebecca wishes she could be

here. I'm thankful *mei mamm*'s neighbor was able to help out with the *kinner* so I could attend and represent Rebecca and myself and our support of your new life in the church."

"I know," Lindsay said. "I'm glad you could share this special day with me."

Daniel greeted Lizzie Anne and Katie before moving on to talk to another relative.

"We'd better help serve the meal," Lindsay said before turning to Matthew. "We need to help the rest of the women set up lunch."

"I know," Matthew said. "I'll see you in a little bit."

"Okay," Lindsay said before turning to walk with her friends to the kitchen. She nodded greetings to relatives and friends as she passed.

Lizzie Anne leaned in close. "Now you and Matthew can really date!"

Lindsay's stomach fluttered at the thought. "I'm not in any rush."

Lizzie Anne stopped Lindsay by grabbing her arm. "You don't have to rush, Lindsay. Just take your time. Samuel and I are getting to know each other slowly, and it's been a lot of fun." She grinned. "I'm sure you and Matthew will have a lot of fun too. Just be yourself and see where your heart leads you."

Lindsay couldn't stop her smile. "You sound like you've fallen in love with Samuel Kauffman. As *mei schweschder* would say, you've got it bad."

Lizzie Anne laughed. "I guess I do."

With a grin, Katie shook her head. "You two are *gegisch*. We need to serve lunch so we can eat. I'm starving."

Lindsay looped her arms around Lizzie Anne's and Katie's shoulders. "This has been one of the best days of my life. Let's go get some lunch."

Later that afternoon, Matthew glanced out at the porch and spotted Daniel standing with his brothers, Timothy and Robert. He sidled up to the group and nodded a greeting to Timothy and Robert. "I'm sorry to interrupt," he said. "Daniel, may I speak with you for a moment?"

"Of course." Daniel nodded toward the pasture. "Would you like to go for a brief walk?"

"That would be *wunderbaar*," Matthew said. He followed Daniel down the steps. "I wanted to talk to you about a personal matter." He swallowed and hoped he would choose the right words. "It's something I've been considering for a while now."

Daniel frowned. "This sounds like something serious. Are you unhappy at the furniture store?"

"No, no." Matthew shook his head as they approached the barn. "I'm perfectly *froh* at work. It has nothing to do with that." He looked back and saw Lindsay stepping out onto the porch, and he gestured toward the barn. "Could we please go inside the barn?"

Daniel shrugged. "That would be fine."

They stepped into the barn and Matthew took a deep breath.

"What's on your mind, Matthew?" Daniel asked. "You look *naerfich*."

Matthew nodded. "I am."

"Go ahead," Daniel said. "You know you can talk to me about things."

"*Danki*," Matthew said. "I want to ask your permission to date Lindsay. I really care about her, and I've enjoyed getting to know her since I moved here. Now that she's baptized, I'd like to ask her to be my girlfriend."

Daniel smiled, and Matthew felt a weight lift from his shoulders.

"I knew this day would come." Daniel shook Matthew's hand. "You have my permission. I trust you with her."

"*Danki,*" Matthew said with a smile. "I will treat her very well, Daniel."

❧

Lindsay spotted Elizabeth on the porch and rushed over to touch her arm. "I was looking for you."

"Lindsay." Elizabeth took her hand and steered her away from the group of friends who had surrounded her. "I wanted to speak with you too." She pulled her into a hug. "I'm so *froh* you've joined the church. I'd hoped this was the path the Lord would choose for you." She looked down at Lindsay's green dress. "You look so *schee*. Is this a new frock?"

Lindsay ran her hands down her dress. "I've been working on it for a few weeks. I made it special for today."

"You positively glow." Elizabeth touched her cheek. "This was the right choice for you."

"*Danki.*" Lindsay fiddled with the ties to her prayer covering as her thoughts moved to Rebecca. "I can't stop thinking about *Aenti* Rebecca. I wish she'd been here."

Elizabeth's expression was sympathetic. "I know you wanted to share this moment with her, *mei liewe,* and I know she wishes she'd been here. But she was thinking of you and praying for you today. I'm certain her heart is full of joy. You and your *schweschder* are like her *dochdern,* and your decision to stay and join the church has given her more joy than she can ever express to you. Even though she couldn't be here today, she's celebrating with you in her heart."

Lindsay sighed. "I know you're right, but I just wish *Aenti* Rebecca and Jessica could've been here to celebrate with us in person."

"Lindsay, you know things don't always work out the way we

want them." Elizabeth sat on the porch swing and patted the spot next to her. "Sit, *mei liewe*. Remember that verse from Joel that the bishop read?"

Lindsay lowered herself next to Elizabeth and nodded.

"It tells us, 'Be glad, people of Zion, rejoice in the Lord your God, for he has given you the autumn rains because he is faithful. He sends you abundant showers, both autumn and spring rains, as before.'" Elizabeth touched Lindsay's hand. "Even though Jessica and Rebecca weren't here physically, they were with you in your heart. Like your parents always are."

Lindsay gently pushed the swing back and forth. "What do you think my mom would think about me joining the church?"

"What do you mean?" Elizabeth looked confused.

"She joined the church and then she left to marry my father," Lindsay said. "Would she be *froh* for me today?"

Elizabeth paused, considering the question. "You never would've come here if your parents hadn't died, so it's a complicated question. However, your *mamm* chose Rebecca as the guardian for your *schweschder* and you, which means there's a reason why you're here. Therefore, I think she would be very *froh* to see how you've grown, matured, and also assimilated into the community here. That makes me believe she wanted you here so she could provide the best life for you and your *schweschder*, if you each chose to take it."

Lindsay smiled. "I was hoping you'd say that."

Elizabeth laughed and hugged Lindsay again. "Are you heading *heemet* now? It's getting late."

Lindsay nodded. "*Onkel* Daniel should be around here somewhere."

"There he is," Elizabeth said as she stood. "He's over by the barn talking to Matthew."

"Oh," Lindsay said, looking to where her uncle and Matthew stood together. "I wonder what they're talking about."

"Why don't you go find out?" Elizabeth asked.

"That's a *gut* idea." Lindsay stood. *"Gut nacht."*

Lindsay left the porch and walked toward her uncle and Matthew. She approached and overheard them talking about the weather.

"I guess it's time to go," Daniel said. "I need to hitch up the horse."

"I'll help you," Matthew said.

"No, no," Daniel said with a smile. "You go on and say *gut nacht* to Lindsay while I hitch it up."

"Okay," Matthew said. *"Danki."*

Lindsay thought she saw a private expression pass between her uncle and Matthew, and she wondered what it meant.

"Let's go for a walk," Matthew said as Daniel walked away.

"That sounds nice," Lindsay said, falling into step with him while they walked toward the pasture.

"It was a nice day, *ya?*" Matthew finally asked.

"Ya, it was nice," Lindsay said, fingering the wooden heart she'd kept in her pocket for the baptism.

"What were you and Elizabeth discussing on the porch?" he asked.

"I told Elizabeth I wished *mei aenti* and *schweschder* could've been here today, and she reminded me they were all celebrating with me from afar even though they couldn't be here."

He nodded. "That's very true."

"I also asked her if she thought my mom would be happy for me today, and she said that she thought my mom would be *froh* that I've made a life in this community."

"I agree." Matthew smiled. "I'm very *froh* too."

"So we can be *froh* together," Lindsay joked.

"I'd like that very much." He looked serious and Lindsay's skin tingled.

She asked him about work, and they talked about their upcoming week as they stood by the fence. She wished the evening could last a few more hours. Being in his company was relaxing, fun, and exciting all at once. She spotted her uncle leading the horse and buggy toward the fence. "I guess I better go." She gestured toward the buggy. "The horse and buggy are ready."

"Lindsay," Matthew said, "wait. I need to ask you something."

Her heart pounded in her chest as she met his serious gaze. "*Ya?*" she asked.

"We've been spending a lot of time together lately, *ya?*" he asked.

She nodded.

"And we have a *gut* time when we're together, *ya?*" he asked, his expression anxious.

"Always," Lindsay said.

"I was wondering if maybe you'd consider ..." he paused. "Would you be my girlfriend?"

Lindsay couldn't stop her grin. "I'd love to."

"*Gut.*" A nervous smile crossed his face. "We'd better get you to the buggy before Daniel gets impatient."

"Did you think I'd say no?" she asked with surprise, walking beside him toward her uncle.

"I hoped you wouldn't," he said.

"*Gut nacht,*" Lindsay said when they reached the buggy. "I hope you have a *gut* day tomorrow."

"I hope the same for you," Matthew said. "I'll talk to you soon. *Gut nacht.*"

Climbing into the buggy, she couldn't stop her pulse from pounding or her smile from deepening. This had been the best day of her life.

Daniel sat beside her and took the reins. Still smiling, Lindsay waved at Matthew as the buggy bounced down the driveway toward the road.

CHEESE CUPCAKES

12 cupcake foils
1 can of cherry pie filling
12 vanilla wafers
2 eggs
¾ teaspoon vanilla
4 3-ounce packages of cream cheese
¾ cup sugar

Place vanilla wafers in the bottom of each cupcake foil. Beat cream cheese, eggs, sugar, and vanilla. Fill each cupcake foil 2/3 full with mixture. Bake at 325 degrees for 20 minutes. Remove cakes and let stand 25 minutes before topping with pie filling. Refrigerate for at least 90 minutes.

6

The following Saturday, Katie sat on the floor and pushed a toy train toward Daniel Junior. He grinned and pushed it back. With a squeal, Emma launched herself across the floor, intercepting the train before it reached Katie's legs. Katie laughed while Daniel Junior frowned.

"Did you want the train, Emma?" Katie asked in *Dietsch* while picking up the toy. "Can you ask for it?"

Emma held out her hand and grunted while Daniel Junior continued to glower.

"She's not going to ask for it," Junior said. "She only talks when she wants to. She's very stubborn."

Katie smiled at Junior. "Would you please share with your *schweschder?*"

"*Ya,*" Junior said. "You can use it."

"I think it's nap time," Lindsay announced as she entered from the kitchen, crossed the family room, and picked up Emma, who bellowed in protest. "You know the routine."

Katie stood and reached for Daniel Junior's hand. "May I walk upstairs with you?"

"*Ya,*" he said, taking her hand.

While holding Emma in her arms, Lindsay smiled at Katie. "I appreciate all you and Lizzie Anne are doing for me today. It helps to have you here with the *kinner* while Lizzie Anne and I do some cleaning."

"*Gern gschehne,*" Katie said. "I'm glad we can help. It was fun too. I love spending time with you and Lizzie Anne."

Lizzie Anne appeared from the kitchen holding a tray of food for Rebecca. "I have Rebecca's lunch ready. I'll bring it to her."

Katie followed Lindsay up the stairs with Daniel Junior in tow. After tucking him in his bed, she stepped out into the hallway and headed to Rebecca's room. Stepping through the doorway, Katie found Lizzie Anne sitting on Rebecca's hope chest while Rebecca sat propped up in bed eating from the tray on her lap.

"Katie," Rebecca said. "Come in."

Katie sank into a chair next to the bed. "How are you feeling?"

Rebecca nodded while chewing her turkey sandwich. "I'm feeling pretty well today, *danki*. I just wish I could've helped you *maed* clean the house with Lindsay. I appreciate all you're doing for us."

Lindsay appeared in the doorway. "We had a *gut* time. Lizzie Anne and I scrubbed the kitchen floor and bathroom while Katie played with the *kinner* and fed them lunch."

"Many hands make light work," Lizzie Anne sang with a smile.

"That's very true," Katie chimed in. "*Mei mamm* uses that expression all the time."

"I'm glad to have the help." Lindsay lowered herself onto the end of the bed. "I can't possibly get it all done alone. I'm always worried the *kinner* will hurt themselves if I leave them alone."

"That's true. I worry when they are alone too." Rebecca placed her sandwich on the plate. "I'm so glad you are here to help. It's frustrating being stuck in this bed."

"But the doctor said . . ." Lindsay began.

"I know. I know." Rebecca sighed.

Katie smiled at her aunt.

"I need to hear some *gut* news," Rebecca said. "Tell me what's new with you *maed*." She swiped the napkin across her lips and glanced at Lizzie Anne. "How is your family? I miss coming to church and seeing everyone."

"Everyone is fine." Lizzie Anne's lips turned up in a wide grin.

"What's that expression for?" Lindsay asked, facing her.

Katie raised her eyebrows. "You look like you have some exciting news."

"I sort of have a secret." Lizzie Anne's cheeks glowed cherry red. "And Katie's right. It's something really exciting."

Lindsay gasped. "You need to tell us," she said. "You can't keep this secret now. That would be teasing."

"Well," Lizzie Anne began, studying her black bib apron, "Samuel asked me something last night."

"What?" Katie asked. "What did *mei bruder* ask you? He asked you to be his girlfriend, *ya?*"

Lizzie Anne shook her head.

"Oh my!" Lindsay shot up from the bed. "He asked you to marry him?"

Lizzie Anne nodded, and Lindsay launched herself toward Lizzie Anne, nearly knocking her off the hope chest as they hugged and squealed.

"But I thought you were going to take it slow," Lindsay said when she'd calmed down. "That's what you told me Sunday after the service."

"He changed his mind." Lizzie Anne laughed. "I'm just as surprised as you are."

"Wait a minute," Katie began, trying to comprehend this development. "Samuel asked you to marry him? How can this be?" She rolled the information through her mind, trying to make sense of it all. *Samuel didn't discuss this with me. Why would he make a decision like this without telling his family?*

"I know you weren't expecting this, Katie," Lizzie Anne said, her eyes filling with tears. "But it's all true. He asked me to marry him, and he wants to get married this season."

Katie glanced at her aunt, who looked as surprised as Katie felt. "Congratulations," Rebecca said. "When were you expecting him to propose?"

Lizzie Anne wiped her eyes while Lindsay sat next to her and looped her arm around Lizzie Anne's shoulder.

"Not this soon," Lizzie Anne said. "Like I said, I was completely surprised."

"Don't you think you're a little young?" Katie asked. "I mean you're only eighteen. Where are you going to live? It's not like he's built a *haus*."

"He's already thought of that." Lizzie Anne's expression darkened a little as if the question stung. "We're going to live in the apartment attached to your parents' house until we have our own place. Your *dat* is giving Samuel land, so we can build on the other side of the pasture."

Katie stared at her. "Samuel discussed this with *Dat* already?" *How could he tell* Dat *and not me?*

Lizzie Anne nodded. "*Ya*, he did. He wanted to have it all set before he asked me."

"Does *mei mamm* know too?" Katie asked.

Lizzie Anne shrugged. "I guess so. I'm not really sure."

But neither of my parents told me. Katie shook her head with disbelief. "I'm really shocked."

"Katie," Lizzie Anne said, looking hurt. "Aren't you excited? We're going to be *schweschdern*! We'll be living together until Samuel and I have our own place!"

"This is *wunderbaar gut*," Lindsay said, hugging Lizzie Anne again. "I'm so excited for you. Are you getting married in November or December?"

"*Mei mamm* and I were talking about that last night." Lizzie Anne angled her body toward Lindsay. "We have to get out the calendar and talk about it. I think we're going to discuss it more tonight."

"You have a lot of planning to do," Rebecca said. "It's a very exciting time. I'm so happy for you and Samuel."

"*Danki,*" Lizzie Anne said with a grin. "I'm so *froh.* I feel like I'm dreaming."

Katie tried to force a smile. However, the idea of her best friend and her brother getting married in a couple of months made her feel confused. It was all happening so fast. She knew she had to stay positive, though. She was happy to hear Lizzie Anne would be her sister, and she did think Samuel and Lizzie Anne made a good couple. They complemented each other.

"I have news too," Lindsay said with a smile. "Matthew asked me a question too."

Rebecca looked concerned. "What did he ask you, Lindsay?"

Lindsay clasped her hands together. "He asked me to be his girlfriend."

Lizzie Anne squealed and hugged Lindsay. "That's so exciting! You'll be the next bride, Lindsay."

"Let's slow down," Rebecca said, grimacing. "There's no rush. Let Lindsay and Matthew get to know each other better, Lizzie Anne. They didn't grow up together like you and Samuel did."

"That's a *gut* point," Lizzie Anne said.

Katie smiled and folded her arms across her apron. "I'm so happy for you, Lindsay. I'm not surprised. I thought he was only waiting for you to be baptized before he made it official."

Katie watched and listened while Lizzie Anne talked about the upcoming wedding and how much she had to plan. She turned to Rebecca and found her aunt studying her while she broke apart a homemade pretzel. "Can I get you anything, *Aenti?*" she asked. "Do you need more water?"

Rebecca shook her head. "No, dear. I'm fine."

Katie stood. "May I get you a slice of chocolate oatmeal cake? I brought a freshly baked one this morning. *Mei mamm* did some baking yesterday and told me to bring you one."

Rebecca smiled. "That's so kind of her. I'd love a piece."

Katie placed Rebecca's glass on the nightstand beside her and handed her the plate for the pretzel before lifting the tray. "I'll go get you a piece of cake." She turned to her friends. "To celebrate your exciting news, I'll make some chocolate chip *kichlin*. I have a new recipe I put together which includes some nuts along with the chocolate chips."

"Sounds *gut. Danki*, Katie," Lizzie Anne said with a smile while Lindsay nodded.

❧

When Katie arrived home later that afternoon, she found Samuel in the back pasture hammering a post into the ground as part of the fence repair. She approached him, relieved to find him alone. She felt disappointment and hurt bubble up inside her as she stood in front of him. "Hi," she said.

"Hey." Samuel dropped the mallet onto the ground and yanked off his work gloves. "Did you just get *heemet* from *Aenti* Rebecca's?"

Katie leaned against a stable fence post. *"Ya."*

"How is she?" he asked as he lifted a jug of water.

"Doing well." She folded her arms over her apron and watched him drink from the jug.

"Did you have fun?" He placed the jug on the ground and wiped his glistening forehead with a rag.

"I did. I helped clean, and I baked some *kichlin*." Katie paused and studied him, wondering how long he'd been keeping the secret from her.

"What?" He looked confused. "You look upset."

She gestured toward the pasture behind him. "Is this where you plan to build your *haus*?" When he didn't answer she pressed on. "Are you fixing the fence in preparation for the *haus*? *Dat*'s helping you get the land ready, *ya*?"

"Lizzie Anne told you." He frowned. "And you're upset you didn't know first."

"*Ya*, Lizzie Anne did tell me, and I'm upset the news didn't come from you." Katie stood up straight. "How long have you known you were going to propose? Better yet, how long have *Mamm* and *Dat* known?"

"*Mamm* doesn't know," he said. "You and I both know *Mamm* couldn't keep a secret if her life depended on it. She's ruined Christmas surprises more than once."

"Only *Dat* knows?" Katie asked.

"*Ya*." He wiped his brow with the back of his hand.

She considered his words, feeling childish and hurt at the same time. "Why didn't you tell me too?"

He grinned and shook his head. "You're one of Lizzie Anne's closest *freinden*. How could I trust you to keep it to yourself?"

"How could you not?" Katie pointed to her chest. "I've trusted you so many times in the past, Samuel. Remember when I was struggling with whether or not I should write Lindsay and tell her how *grank Aenti* Rebecca was? I needed someone's advice, and I came to you. No one else—just you, Sam."

He shook his head. "This is different."

"How so?" She challenged him with a glower.

"This is a life-changing step I'm taking with the *maedel* I love, Katie. It's not the same as trying to figure out whether or not you should go against an elder." He shook his head with disbelief. "Why are you even upset with me? You were going to find out eventually."

"But Lizzie Anne is one of *mei* best *freinden*, and you're *mei bruder*. Plus, you're going to be living in our house. This affects me."

"But it's my life." He pointed to his chest. "This isn't about you. It's about me and Lizzie Anne. Besides, she already told you. You have no reason to be upset. So you found out a day after she did." He shrugged. "What's so bad about that?"

Katie frowned while he put his gloves back on. She couldn't understand why her brother didn't feel the need to apologize. Why didn't her feelings matter?

"Why aren't you *froh* for us?" Samuel asked as he lifted the mallet. "I thought you were excited Lizzie Anne and I were together."

"It seems like you're moving awfully fast."

He raised his eyebrows. "You think so?"

She nodded. "She's only eighteen."

"And she'll be nineteen in January," he said. "I'm almost twenty-two."

"*Mamm* and *Dat* were older when they were married." Katie leaned back against the fence. "Why do you need to rush into this when you don't even have a *haus*? Why do you want to bring your bride *heemet* to your parents' *haus*?"

He frowned. "You're awfully judgmental."

"No, I'm not." Katie lifted her chin in defiance. "You asked me what I thought, and I told you. I didn't mean to upset you."

Samuel eyed her with suspicion. "Actually, I think you did. It seems like you are being spiteful because you're upset I didn't tell you first."

"That's not true." But she knew her brother was right; she just wasn't about to admit it. She was hurt, and it caused her to say unkind things.

"Katie!" Her father's voice boomed from across the pasture. "Your *mamm* is looking for you!"

"I'll see you later," she said before she jogged back toward the house. She didn't like how mean she was being to her brother, but she knew why she had said those hurtful things to him. For the first time, she felt alone while her two best friends moved on with their lives.

7

Monday morning, Katie pushed the broom around the front area of the bakery, moving it past the small tables and display carousels as if she were navigating a maze. She hummed to herself while remembering the hymns she'd sung during the singing last night. When she'd found there wasn't any room on the bench for her to sit with Lizzie Anne and Lindsay, Katie had chosen to sit with Nancy and her friends for a good portion of the evening. Later on, Lindsay had come and asked her why she wasn't sitting with her and Lizzie Anne. When Katie told her that there wasn't any room, Lindsay had insisted she join them and had made room.

Fetching the dustpan from the floor, Katie felt disappointment nip at her. Although she was happy to sit with her friends, she couldn't stand being the fifth wheel as their relationships with their boyfriends blossomed.

She pushed the thought aside while sweeping up the dirt from the floor into the dustpan. Once the dustpan was full, she crossed to the trash can and dumped it in before returning to the broom in the center of the room. A truck rumbled into the parking lot outside, and Katie wondered who could be arriving so early in the morning.

Elizabeth crossed into the front of the store from the kitchen and smiled. "They're here. Eli said they'd be here early."

"*Daadi* is here?" Katie asked, leaning the broom against the doorframe. "Who else?"

"I'm not sure which carpenter he brought with him." Elizabeth headed out the front door and onto the porch that surrounded the bakery.

Katie stood by the large windows at the front of the bakery and spotted her grandfather, Eli, and Jake Miller walking from Jake's pickup toward the porch where Elizabeth stood. Jake was clad in work boots, jeans, a button-down, green shirt, and a baseball cap.

After a brief conversation on the porch, Elizabeth entered the bakery, followed by Eli and Jake. Katie stood by the window and leaned on the broom while her grandparents moved past her.

"*Wie geht's,*" Eli said with a wave.

"I'm fine, *danki,*" Katie said. "How are you, *Daadi?*"

"I'm well." Eli followed Elizabeth over to the counter in front of the entrance to the kitchen.

"This is where I'd like the new display cases." Elizabeth made a sweeping gesture and explained how she'd like the new cabinets.

Jake sidled up to Katie. "*Wie geht's?*"

"Hi, Jake," Katie said. "How are you?"

"I'm well." He smiled. "Looks like we're going to be seeing a lot of each other."

"Oh?" she asked with surprise. "Why is that?"

"Remember that cabinet project I told you about a while back?" Katie nodded.

Jake jammed a thumb toward her grandparents. "Today we start it. Your grandfather thinks business will start slowing down, so we can start it now and finish before spring."

"Oh." Katie smiled. "That's *wunderbaar gut.* The bakery could use a little bit of a facelift. It certainly stays too busy to do it in the summer."

Jake crossed his arms over his chest. "I heard congratulations are in order."

"*Ya.*" Katie frowned and nodded, thinking of her brother and the awkward conversation they'd shared two days ago.

Jake looked surprised. "Oh. I said the wrong thing. I'm sorry. I thought baptism was an important occasion. I'm sorry."

"Oh no. I'm the one who's sorry," Katie said, feeling her cheeks burn with embarrassment. "I thought you were talking about something else. You're right. I was baptized, and it is an important occasion. *Danki* very much."

"You're welcome." He smiled again. "I know being baptized is a sacred moment. I'm certain it was a very special day for you."

"It was," she said.

"I've often wondered about the Amish baptism," Jake said. "I wish I could come to one."

"Really?" Katie was surprised. "Why would you want to come?"

He shrugged. "I've always been interested in the Amish customs. After all, my grandparents are Amish and my mother used to be before she met and married my father."

Katie pointed toward his shirt. "You almost look Amish with your button-down shirt."

"Yeah, but my jeans and ball cap ruin the look, huh?" He grinned, and she laughed.

"*Ya,*" she said. "You're right."

"Jake," Eli called. "Let's cut the chatter and start unloading supplies. *Mei fraa* is anxious to get her new cabinets installed."

"I'm ready when you are, Eli," Jake said. He started for the door and then stopped and faced Katie. "Do you have the chocolate chip cookies you promised me?"

Katie gestured toward the kitchen. "I can whip some up."

"Really?" He looked impressed and then suddenly doubtful. "Or will you just grab some from the shelf and pass them off as your own."

She frowned. "You don't trust me, Jake Miller?"

"Jake," Eli said as he stood at the door. "We're here to work, not beg for *kichlin*. *Kumm*." He started for the truck, letting the door slam behind him.

Katie grinned. "Beg for *kichlin*," she repeated with a chuckle.

Jake wagged a finger at her. "They better be your *kichlin* and not someone else's."

She crossed her heart. "You have my word."

"Good." He winked and then headed out the door.

"Katie," Elizabeth called, "please finish the sweeping."

"*Ya, Mammi*." Katie turned and found her grandmother frowning. "What?" She glanced around the bakery. "Did I do something wrong?"

"No. I just need you to finish up your work out here and then continue with your baking for the day." Elizabeth headed back toward the kitchen.

"I will, *Mammi*." Katie gazed out the window toward Jake's truck and smiled. It was nice to have a new friend.

⁂

Katie slid chocolate chip cookies onto a plate and then glanced up at the clock, finding it was almost noon. With the plate in one hand and her lunch bag in the other, she crossed the kitchen to the office where Elizabeth sat at the desk examining a ledger.

"*Mammi*," Katie began, "I'm going to take lunch."

"I'll join you," Amanda, her cousin, called from the other side of the bakery.

"I will too," Ruthie chimed in.

Elizabeth pointed at the cookies. "Katie, did you make those for Jake?"

"No. I made them for everyone. I'm going to bring some out for *Daadi* and share them with Amanda and Ruthie during lunch too." Katie glanced at the plate and breathed in the scent of the chocolate chips, causing her stomach to growl.

"*Gut.*" Elizabeth's expression softened. "Just remember you need to be careful, Katie. Jake is Mennonite."

"I know, but he's *mei freind, Mammi.*" Katie turned toward the door. "After lunch I'll start on a peach cobbler." She moved through the doorway and found Eli and Jake working together to take apart the existing display cabinets. A pile of wood and tools sat behind them.

Jake looked over. "Do I smell chocolate chip cookies?"

"I made them for you and *Daadi.*" Katie moved the plate back and forth. "Don't they smell *gut?*" He reached for the plate, and she snatched it back from his reach. "You both need to take a break for lunch before you can have one."

"What time is it?" Eli asked, wiping his hands on a rag. "Is it lunchtime already?"

"It's noon." Katie handed her grandfather a cookie. "Have one, *Daadi.*"

Eli grinned at Jake. "*Freindschaften* have priority." He bit into the cookie and nodded with approval. "*Appeditlich.*" He started toward the kitchen. "Lunchtime. Enjoy a break."

Jake wiped his hands on a rag. "Let me wash up and then get my lunch out of the refrigerator in the kitchen. Eli said he set it in there for me earlier."

Katie gestured toward a small table on the porch beyond the window. "Want to eat together on the porch? Amanda and Ruthie are going to eat out there too."

"That sounds nice." Jake started toward the kitchen area. "I'll be out soon."

Katie moved to the porch and sank into a chair at a small metal table. She looked back toward the door just as her cousins came out.

"What a *schee* day," Amanda said as she sat across from Katie.

"*Ya,*" Ruthie agreed. She sat beside Katie and placed her brown lunch bag on the table.

Jake reappeared with a lunch bag and two cups of water. He

lowered himself into the chair across from Katie and looked around the porch. "This is a nice venue for lunch." He placed a cup of water in front of Katie and she thanked him.

"*Ya,*" Amanda said. "I love eating out here."

"I agree." Katie smiled and then bowed her head in silent prayer. Once she finished her prayer, she opened her lunch box and pulled out lunch meat, cheese, and homemade bread.

"So about those cookies ..." Jake opened his lunch bag. "I think you've made me wait long enough."

Katie touched her chin. "Hmm. I don't know." She pointed toward his ham sandwich. "You need to eat your lunch first," she teased.

He raised an eyebrow. "But your grandfather got to try one before he ate his lunch."

"Let him have one," Ruthie said in Jake's defense as she lifted her sandwich. "He and *Daadi* have been working hard on those cabinets."

"*Ya,*" Amanda chimed in. "They have."

"Fine. *Mammi* wouldn't be happy to see me let you start with dessert, but here." She handed him a cookie. "Enjoy."

He took a bite, closed his eyes, and grinned. "Your brother is right. You truly are a good baker."

"*Danki,*" she said.

"She's one of the best," Ruthie said between bites. "I always seem to burn things, but Katie never does."

"*Appeditlich.*" Jake finished the cookie in a few bites.

Katie shook her head and then bit into her sandwich. "You sound like a true Amish person."

"*Danki.*" He lifted his cup. "I've heard the language from my grandparents my whole life. And you know I hear it at work too."

"Have you ever been to a church service?" Amanda asked as she bit into her sandwich.

"I've been a few times."

"Could you understand the ministers?" Ruthie asked.

"I didn't understand every word, but I got the gist of it." He placed his sandwich on his napkin and took another cookie.

Katie was curious about Jake's experience with the Amish culture. "Did you enjoy the service even though it's different from what you're used to?" she asked.

"Yes, I did." He finished his second cookie. "These are too good to waste."

"They won't go to waste," Amanda said. "I'm going to have to grab some before you finish them all." She took a few and placed them on her napkin.

"I'll try a couple too." Ruthie took two and broke one in half before biting into it. "These are *gut*, Katie. They taste a little different than usual. Did you change the recipe?"

"*Ya*, I did try something new as an experiment," Katie said. "I'm working on some new versions of old recipes."

"I like this recipe," Ruthie said. "You did a *gut* job."

Katie took a cookie and bit into it. "Not my best, but not bad either."

Jake finished chewing and looked surprised. "So you can do even better?"

"I think so." Katie finished the cookie. "I guess creating the perfect recipe is something you always strive for. I guess it's an analogy for how we live our lives. We're always trying to improve ourselves and be more like Jesus."

"Wow," Ruthie said. "I've never thought of it that way."

"I hadn't either." Amanda nodded. "I like that."

"I do too." Jake looked impressed. "That's deep, Katie Kauffman."

Katie swatted at him with her hand. "Don't make fun of me."

"I'm not." He looked serious. "That was a very profound statement."

Katie studied him with disbelief. No one had ever called her profound or deep. Jake was different from any boy she'd ever had as a friend.

"So Jake," Ruthie said, "tell us about yourself. What did you do over the weekend?"

Jake rubbed his clean-shaven chin and considered the question. "Let's see. I cleaned the house, mowed the yard, worked on a project in my garage, and went to church on Sunday."

"Really?" Katie pulled an apple from her bag and wondered if all Jake ever did was work. "Did you do anything fun?"

"Yeah." He shrugged. "I had dinner at my grandparents' house Saturday night, and I met my parents at church yesterday. That was pretty fun." He lifted his sandwich. "How about you, Katie?" he asked.

"I spent Saturday at *mei aenti* Rebecca's helping Lindsay with my cousins." She pulled out a knife and began slicing the apple.

"I bet that was fun," Amanda said before eating another cookie.

"It was," Katie said. "Lizzie Anne and Lindsay cleaned, and I took care of the *kinner*. I even did some baking, which you know is my favorite pastime. It was fun."

"How was Rebecca doing?" Jake asked.

"She's doing well," Katie said. "She's anxious to get out of bed, but she knows that the best thing she can do is rest."

"I can't imagine how difficult it is, but I'm glad she's doing fine," Amanda said.

"I know. I am too. I was worried for a while." Katie handed Jake and each of her cousins an apple slice.

"Thanks," Jake said, taking the slice. "How's your brother Samuel doing?"

Katie's eyes widened with surprise. *Does he know Samuel is engaged to Lizzie Anne?* "He's fine. Why do you ask?"

Amanda turned to Ruthie and asked about another couple

in their youth group. They launched into a conversation about a couple Katie didn't know well.

Jake shrugged in response to Katie's question. "I haven't seen him much lately." He popped the apple slice into his mouth.

Katie studied her napkin and considered telling Jake and her cousins the news she'd heard.

"Katie?" he asked. "Is something bothering you?"

Katie placed her knife on the napkin next to the apple slices and considered her answer. She studied Jake's concerned expression and felt the urge to be honest.

Since her cousins seemed to be occupied with their own conversation, Katie felt comfortable telling Jake the news about her brother and Lizzie Anne. "Samuel proposed to Lizzie Anne Friday night," she said softly so her cousins wouldn't hear her spoil the secret.

Jake looked stunned. "He did?"

"*Ya.*" Katie nodded. "They want to get married this season. I heard him talking to my parents last night. They're considering December."

"Oh." Jake nodded slowly. "That's pretty quick, don't you think?"

"It's very quick," Katie said, still keeping her voice soft. "I don't understand what the rush is. Lizzie Anne is only eighteen, and he's twenty-one. I said that to him, and he was very defensive." She lifted her cup of water and took a sip.

"I imagine he didn't like that too much," Jake said. "Is he building a house for her?"

"They're going to move into the apartment my parents have attached to our *haus*," Katie said, handing him another apple slice. "My grandparents on *mei mamm*'s side lived there a long time ago. Eventually Samuel is going to build a *haus* on our property for them, but who knows how long that will take. Why do they have to get married now? Why can't they wait a year and build the *haus* first?" She paused when she realized she was committing a sin. "I'm sorry. I shouldn't be judging them. You must think I'm terrible."

His smile was sympathetic. "No, I don't. I actually had the same thoughts you did."

"You did?" she asked with surprise.

"Yes, I did." He ate the apple slice. "It seems a little hasty, but I guess love can be like that."

Katie shrugged. "I guess so, but I really can't relate. I guess Lindsay and Matthew are next."

Jake looked surprised. "Did Matthew finally ask her to be his girlfriend?" he asked Katie.

"Yes," she said. "I'm happy for them both, but I can't really relate, you know?"

He looked sympathetic. "I know the feeling all too well."

"You do?" she asked.

He nodded. "I've never been good at relationships."

"I've never had one." She attempted to be positive and smiled. "I guess it will happen when it's meant to, right?"

"Of course it will. You can't rush love. I found that out the hard way."

Katie studied his frown and wondered if he was talking about Jessica. She glanced at her cousins who were still discussing their youth group friends. "How long have you been working at the furniture store?" she asked.

"A very long time," he said. "I started working there over the summer when I was around eleven."

"Really?" Katie asked. "You were very young."

He nodded while chewing a cookie. "I was very young, but I was determined to be a carpenter like my grandfather. I started working in his shop with him when I was around five. It's what I've always wanted to do."

"I know the feeling." Katie sipped some water. "I always

wanted to work in this bakery like *mei mammi*. There's no other place I'd rather be."

He lifted his cookie. "And you're a very talented baker."

The door to the bakery opened with a squeak, revealing Eli. "All right, you four," he called. "Lunch hour is over. Let's get back to work."

Katie stood and gathered up their trash. "I'll take care of this."

"Thanks," he said. "I had a nice time, ladies. Thank you for inviting me to your lunch party." He picked up his lunch bag. "I'm going to toss this in my truck. I hope your afternoon goes well."

"Yours too," Katie said.

"Work hard, Jake!" Ruthie said with a laugh. "*Mei mammi* wants those cabinets done."

"*Ya*," Amanda agreed with a chuckle.

Katie walked with her cousins back into the kitchen. Her aunt Kathryn approached as Katie approached her workstation.

"Can you possibly whip up some cheese cupcakes?" Kathryn asked. "I just got a phone-in order for two dozen. You can make a peach cobbler later, *ya*?"

"Of course." Katie tossed out the trash and placed her lunch bag under her workstation. She smiled while she started collecting the ingredients for the cheese cupcakes. She had enjoyed having lunch with her cousins and Jake and was happy she could count Jake as a new friend.

Lemon Sponge Pie

1 lump of butter the size of a quarter
1¼ cups sugar

Cream together and then add:
3 tablespoons of flour
2 egg yolks
1 tablespoon of lemon juice
1 cup milk

Mix and then add 2 egg whites, beaten stiff. Bake at 450 degrees for 10 minutes and then at 350 degrees for 35 minutes.

8

L ater that evening, Jake dropped his keys into the small bowl by the front door before kicking off his work boots. He then glanced around the small lower level of his side of the two-family house he rented from his uncle and wondered if this was what was to become of his life. When he'd rented the house six years ago, Jake had believed it would be temporary. He assumed he'd eventually meet someone, get married, and settle down on a few acres in the surrounding area. Those dreams, however, hadn't become a reality.

Passing through the small family room, Jake stepped into the kitchen and opened the freezer. Spotting a stack of frozen pizzas, he grabbed one from the top and placed it on the counter. He looked at the instructions and then snickered to himself. He'd made so many of these pizzas he knew the instructions by heart; reading them had just become part of his mundane routine. He flipped the stove dial to preheat the oven to four hundred degrees and retrieved a baking sheet from the drawer under the oven.

After fetching a can of Coke from the refrigerator, Jake sat on the small sofa in the family room and flipped through a hunting magazine while waiting for the oven to beep. He turned the page, glancing at an article about a man who'd shot a huge buck, and tried to read the words, but his thoughts were still back at the bakery with Katie Kauffman.

He'd tried all afternoon to keep his thoughts from returning to Katie, but he couldn't derail his one-track mind, which focused only on her honey-blonde hair, sky-blue eyes, and captivating smile. He'd known Katie all his life, since his grandfather and her grandfather had gone into business together before she was born. She'd always been a sweet girl, offering a kind greeting and small talk whenever their paths crossed. However, something had changed when he'd talked to her today. It was as if she'd suddenly grown up and blossomed into a beautiful young woman with a kind heart.

But she's Amish ...

The thought had echoed in the back of his mind all day. He knew any chance of a relationship with Katie was impossible. Amish were only permitted to date and marry other Amish, unless they wanted to be shunned. He was certain Katie would want to stay with her community, otherwise she wouldn't have been baptized with her friends.

Besides, why would she like me?

The stove beeped, indicating it had reached the required temperature. Jake moved to the stove, unwrapped the pizza, placed it on the baking sheet, and slipped it into the oven.

After setting the timer, he returned to the sofa and his drink. He popped open the can, which fizzed in response. He sipped the carbonated liquid and stared at the magazine. The words were meaningless while he continued to think of Katie's pretty smile. He shook his head with disgust as his inner voice chastised him. *You're just setting yourself up for heartache if you continue to think about her!*

The phone rang, causing Jake to jump up and trot back to the kitchen. He grabbed the receiver and held it up to his ear. "Hello?"

"Jake?" a familiar voice said.

"Yes, this is he," Jake said, trying to figure out who the caller was. The voice was female, but who did it belong to? For a split second he hoped it was Katie but he quickly dismissed the thought, knowing it was a silly notion. "Who is this?"

"You don't recognize my voice," she teased. "Has it been that long?"

"I can tell you how long it's been once you tell me who you are." He paused and then it hit him like a ton of bricks. "Jessica? Is that you?"

"In the flesh," she said, and then chuckled. "Can you believe it? I finally got up the nerve to call you."

"Wow." He ran his hand through his short, dark hair. "I have to admit I'm a little surprised. How long has it been? Five months?"

"It's been almost six actually." Jessica clicked her tongue. "I'm a lousy friend."

"I'm sure you've been busy." He sat on a chair at his small, round table. "How was New York?"

"I worked fifty to sixty hours per week at the internship," she said. "It was a whirlwind. I made quite a bit of money, but I didn't get to enjoy much of the city."

"Oh." He ran his finger over the wood tabletop while he listened. "I bet you got a lot of experience, though."

"I did. My résumé will look fantastic, but it was hard work."

"Are you back at school now?"

"Yes, I am," Jessica said. "I'm pulling eighteen credits this semester. My friend Kim says I like to torture myself. I guess that's true. I went from a stressful internship to a stressful semester back at school. My life consists of stress and more stress."

He shook his head. "Why do you punish yourself, Jess?"

"I don't know. That's something I need to figure out," she said. "But I want to hear about you. How are you doing, Jake?"

He shrugged even though she couldn't see him. "I'm the same as always. You know me. I like things simple. I go to work at the furniture store and then come home. Not much else."

"Huh." She paused for a beat. "I just wanted to tell you I've been thinking of you."

"You have?" he asked, trying in vain not to sound as surprised as he was.

"I was going through a box, and I found some photos from when we went to the beach last year with a few of my friends," she said. "That was fun."

He shook his head. Why was she rehashing old memories? *We haven't even spoken in six months, but now she wants to bring up the day they spent at the Virginia Beach Oceanfront more than a year ago?* "Jess, I don't know what you want me to say."

"You don't have to say anything," Jessica quickly added. "You said it best when I was there last spring—we're stuck in a holding pattern because neither of us will ever bend. You want to stay in Lancaster and work at the furniture store, and I want to finish college and get a job with a big accounting firm. I know that."

"Exactly," he said.

"But we're still friends, right?" she asked.

"Yes." He placed his elbow on the table and rested his forehead in the palm of his hand. "We're friends."

"I'd like to see you when I come to visit," she said.

"When are you planning to come?"

"Probably over the holidays," Jessica said. "I'm super busy with classes and projects, so I won't have time before then."

She made small talk about the weather and her roommate's boyfriend in New York. When the oven timer finally rang, Jake popped up from the table and moved to the stove.

"What's that noise?" Jessica asked.

"My dinner," he explained, balancing the phone on his shoulder and pulling the baking sheet from the oven with the help of an oven mitt.

"What are you having tonight?" she asked.

"Pizza," he said as he placed the baking sheet on the stove.

"Extra pepperoni." The warm fragrance of the pizza wafted up to his nose. "Yum."

"Gourmet frozen pizza." She snickered. "Your favorite."

"That's correct." He retrieved a cutting board and pizza cutter. With the help of a spatula, he slid the pizza onto the board and began to slice it. "Want a piece?" he joked while continuing to balance the phone on his shoulder.

"No, thanks. I'll let you go."

"All right," he said, slipping two slices onto a paper plate.

"It was great talking to you," Jessica said.

"You too." He carried his plate to the table and sat down.

"I'll talk to you soon," she added.

"Sounds good."

"Good-bye," she said.

"Bye." He hung up and then shook his head. After offering a prayer, he bit into the hot pizza.

That same evening, Katie rolled another pretzel and placed it on a baking sheet. She couldn't stop the smile that had taken over her lips after the lunch she'd shared with Jake and her cousins. For the first time in months, she felt happy—truly and completely happy. She was filled with excitement thanks to her new friendship with Jake Miller.

"What are you doing?" Nancy asked, crossing the kitchen.

"Making pretzels," Katie said as she rolled more dough.

"Why are you baking tonight?" Nancy looked confused. "Don't you do that all day at the bakery?"

"I don't make pretzels at the bakery." Katie placed another unbaked pretzel on the baking sheet. "Want to help?"

Nancy grinned. "*Ya!* I love to make pretzels."

The back door opened, and Samuel stepped in from caring for the animals. "What are you two doing?"

"Making pretzels," Nancy said, rolling more dough. "It was Katie's idea."

"Why are you doing that now?" Samuel asked as he kicked off his work boots. "Isn't that a Saturday project?"

Katie shrugged. "I just felt like baking. You know it's my favorite thing to do."

"Are you going to save me one?" Samuel crossed to the stove. "They look *gut*."

"*Ya*, but I need to take some to work." Katie arranged another pretzel on the sheet. "It's a surprise."

"A surprise?" Samuel looked intrigued. "And who is going to be surprised?"

"Jake." Katie rolled more dough. "And also Ruthie and Amanda."

"Jake Miller?" Samuel asked, looking even more intrigued.

Katie nodded while continuing to shape a pretzel.

"You're making pretzels for Jake Miller?" Samuel asked again, his eyes wide with interest.

"What was that?" their mother inquired as she entered the kitchen from the family room.

"Katie's making pretzels to bring to Jake Miller tomorrow," Samuel repeated.

"Is that true, Katie?" Sadie asked.

Katie nodded. "I'm making them for Jake and also for Ruthie and Amanda. The three of us had lunch together today, and we had a really nice time."

"Oh." Sadie stood before her with a confused expression. "I thought you were working at the bakery tomorrow. Are you going to the furniture store?"

Katie ignored the curious expressions she could see her siblings shooting her. "Jake and *Daadi* are working at the bakery. They're building new display cabinets for *Mammi*. He had lunch with us today, and I wanted to bring him a surprise tomorrow when we eat together. Jake told us he only eats frozen pizza for supper. I thought it would be fun to bring something in for a special lunch-time treat."

"Do you like him?" Nancy asked with a big grin.

"No. I mean, I like him, but he's *mei freind*," Katie said. "We talked today and—"

"Katie," Sadie interrupted. "Why would you make him a surprise? He's a Mennonite *bu* who works for your *daadi*. It's not appropriate."

"We're *freinden*," Katie repeated, wishing she'd kept her mouth shut about Jake. She'd never expected this much fuss over homemade pretzels. "We simply had lunch with my cousins and talked on the porch a bit. I made chocolate chip *kichlin* to share with him, *Daadi*, Amanda, and Ruthie today, and everyone loved them. I thought it would be nice to bring him, Ruthie, and Amanda a couple of pretzels tomorrow."

Grimacing, Sadie shook her head. "Katie, that's inappropriate. He's Mennonite." She leaned forward and lowered her voice. "If your *daed* heard you were making special goodies for a Mennonite *bu*, he would be very upset." She wagged a finger at Katie. "You're a baptized *maedel* now. You know better than this."

Katie lifted her arms with frustration, causing flour to sprinkle down toward the floor like confetti. "I'm making them for everyone at the bakery, *Mamm*. Besides, I can't have *freinden* who aren't Amish?"

Sadie shook her head. "Having *freinden* is one thing, but having lunch and baking for a Mennonite *bu* is something completely different." She pointed toward the pretzels. "You may bake these, but don't bring them just to Jake. You can share them with everyone at the bakery."

Katie nodded. "I know, *Mamm*. I already told you I was going to share them with everyone."

Sadie glanced at Nancy. "You're going to help your *schwesch-der* finish this up?"

"*Ya,*" Nancy said. "Then I'll bathe Aaron if you need me to."

Sadie shook her head. "I'll do it." She started toward the doorway and then glanced back at Katie. "I mean it about the pretzels. You don't want your *dat* to hear about this."

Katie nodded with a frown. Why couldn't her mother understand she and Jake simply liked to talk, and that was it? Besides, they weren't even having lunch alone.

When her mother disappeared, Katie turned to Samuel. "Did you see Lizzie Anne today?" she asked. "I heard you tell *Mamm* you might try to stop by Naomi's to see her."

Samuel leaned against the counter and folded his arms over his chest. "I did. She's doing well. She's enjoying babysitting for her sister, and she's looking forward to the birth of her new niece or nephew pretty soon now."

"Did you discuss the wedding?" Nancy asked, placing another pretzel on the sheet.

"We did. We're looking at the second week in December." He grabbed a chocolate chip cookie from the jar by the sink and bit into it.

"Oh, dear," Nancy said with a gasp. "That doesn't give you very long to plan. That's less than three months away."

"I know, but that's what Lizzie Anne wants." He straightened and walked toward the family room. "Let me know when the pretzels are done."

Katie shook her head once he was out of earshot. "I can't believe they want to get married so quickly. What's the hurry?"

Nancy grinned. "I think it's romantic."

Katie snorted. "You're *gegisch.*" She gestured toward the pretzel dough. "Let's finish these up so we can get them in the oven."

9

The following day at noon, Katie sat next to Jake at the same table on the porch. The new bakers, including Hannah, Fannie, and Vera, who were all in their mid-twenties, sat at the same table but talked among themselves about their husbands and the weather.

"How's your day going?" Katie asked Jake while opening her lunch bag.

"It's going well." He pulled his bologna sandwich from his lunch bag. "How about yours?"

"Fine. I brought a surprise for everyone." She retrieved a half dozen homemade pretzels from the zipper storage bag she'd packed in the bottom of her lunch bag. "I made these last night. I'd hoped to bring more, but my siblings enjoyed them more than I'd expected they would." She placed them in the center of the table, and Hannah thanked her while taking one.

"Enjoy them," Katie said. She bowed her head in silent prayer. When she looked up, she found Jake holding a pretzel.

Jake smiled. "This is so nice of you. I don't know what to say."

"*Danki* will suffice." Katie said. "I had fun making them. Nancy helped. I love baking with *mei schweschdern*. I'm hoping to teach Janie how to bake this year. She's starting to show an interest, and it's fun teaching her."

"I've noticed that you like spending time with your family," he said.

"Oh *ya*." Katie couldn't stop her smile. "I love being a part of a big family. I hope to have a big family myself someday." She nodded toward his pretzel. "I hope you like it. I thought you might enjoy a change from frozen pizza."

"You're right," he said before taking a bite. "Katie, these are outstanding. Thank you so much." "You're welcome." She placed a few pieces of lunch meat on a piece of bread along with some cheese.

"How's the project coming along?" Katie asked. "I saw you and *Daadi* have one cabinet disassembled." She took a bite of her sandwich.

He nodded. "It's coming along fine. I just hope the construction isn't too intrusive for the customers."

"Oh, not at all." Katie wiped a napkin across her mouth. "It's been fine. I ran the front earlier, and no one seemed annoyed by the construction noise. You and *Daadi* are very conscientious. If nothing else, the Englishers enjoy seeing an Amish carpenter and his apprentice at work."

"Apprentice?" Jake asked with feigned offense. "You do realize I'm a true-blue carpenter, don't you?"

"Oh, I'm sorry." Grinning, Katie held up her hand. "I didn't realize I was in the presence of a real carpenter." She laughed. "I'm only teasing you. I'm certain you're a *wunderbaar gut* carpenter." She studied his face. "Do you want to work at the furniture store for the rest of your life?"

"I do." Jake pulled another piece off of his pretzel.

The other bakers were engrossed in a conversation about shoofly pie.

Jake leaned over the table toward Katie. "How about you?" he asked. "What do you want to do for the rest of your life? Continue working here with your family?"

Katie glanced down at her sandwich. "I really want what every Amish girl wants—a family." She looked up at him and he smiled. "I want a farm like my parents have, and I want a big family. It's my dream to be like *mei mamm*, you know? Marry and raise *mei kinner* in the Amish faith, hopefully in this district alongside *mei freindshaften* and *mei freinden*. Family is very important to me."

"That makes sense." He took another pretzel. "How was your evening? Did you do anything else other than make *appeditlich* pretzels?" He held a pretzel out to her. "Would you like one?"

She shook her head as she chewed her sandwich. "Thank you, but I had one last night. Actually the pretzels took up most of my evening." She remembered her conversation in the kitchen with her siblings. "Oh, I did find out something interesting."

"What was that?"

"Samuel said he and Lizzie Anne want to get married the second week in December."

Jake's eyebrows shot up to his hairline.

"I had the same reaction when he told me." Katie paused as two customers walked by the table and entered the bakery. "That doesn't give them much time."

"No, it sure doesn't. But if that makes them happy, then who are we to judge, right?"

"You're right." She sipped from her cup of water and tried to look excited for them. "I'm certain they will be very happy together. They do get along well, and I think they're very much in love. And, of course, I'll love having Lizzie Anne as *mei schweschder* since she's one of *mei* best *freinden*."

Jake didn't look convinced. "Is something bothering you? You look like you're a little down."

Katie sighed. "It's just kind of difficult to watch *mei freinden* move on while I'm stuck in the same place." She forced a smile. "But I'm very happy Lindsay and Matthew are dating and Sam and Lizzie Anne are getting married. How could I not be happy for them, right?"

He looked sympathetic. "It has to be difficult watching your friends' lives change while yours is still the same."

"It is, but I wish them well." Katie needed to change the subject. "How was your evening?" she asked.

He shrugged. "The usual. I ate frozen pizza and read a magazine. After that, I did a load of laundry and then headed to bed early."

Katie frowned. "Another frozen pizza?"

He laughed. "You're appalled, right? I bet you eat a square meal every night."

"No, no," she said quickly. "To each his own." She wished she could make him supper sometime, but she knew her mother wouldn't approve. If she was upset over pretzels, she would definitely lose her temper if Katie asked to invite Jake over for a meal. "That's all you did? Just frozen pizza, a magazine, laundry, and bedtime?"

He paused, then looked as if he remembered something. "I also received an unexpected phone call."

"Oh?"

"Jessica called me for the first time in nearly six months." Jake shook his head and sipped his cup of water. "I was surprised, to say the least."

"How's she doing?" Katie asked.

"She's fine. She's busy at school."

"That's nice." Katie bit into her sandwich and wished she had the nerve to ask what happened between him and Jessica. "Is she coming to visit soon? I'm certain Lindsay would love to see her."

"She said she wants to come for the holidays. She won't have time to come visit before then."

"Oh." Katie finished her sandwich while contemplating Jessica. "You'll be *froh* to see her, *ya?*"

He nodded, considering the question. "It would be nice to see her again. We were close friends for four years."

Curious, Katie wondered about his relationship with Jessica.

"But my feelings have definitely changed," he continued. "She and I are just too different. We have different goals in life, and you can't build a relationship when your hopes and dreams are worlds apart."

"That makes sense," she said. "I assume her goal in life is to live and work in a big city with a fancy job, *ya?*"

"That's right. Our lives would never mesh." He shook his head. "The last time we talked we had a disagreement. But we both knew we could never be together. After all, I'm Mennonite, and she's not. Our lives are just too different."

"I see what you're saying," Katie said. "Even so, you cared for each other, and it must have been difficult for you both to accept when the relationship ended."

"It was at first, but we both had to move on. Tell me what you're working on today," he said, changing the subject. "What's on your baking agenda this afternoon?"

Katie rattled off the list of items she planned to bake and the other chores she had to complete before the bakery closed. The conversation turned to the weather, and soon Katie realized that the lunch hour had flown by.

"I guess we'd better get back to work before we get ourselves fired." Katie started collecting the trash. "I enjoyed lunch again today."

"I did too," he said. "The pretzels were the best part."

Katie dropped the trash into a nearby can and then collected her lunch bag and cup. "I'm glad you liked the pretzels. I'll have to think of something else to make for you tomorrow."

"No, no," Jake said. "Don't do that. I don't expect you to bake for me every day."

"Ladies," a voice called, "I need you in the kitchen, please."

Katie turned and found her grandmother watching them. "We're coming now, *Mammi.*" She met Jake's gaze. "I'll see you later."

"Absolutely," he said with a smile. "Thanks again."

Katie walked back to the kitchen alongside the other bakers.

⁓⁓⁓

Friday afternoon, Katie stood in the bakery kitchen and mixed cookie dough while listening to the sound of rain pounding on the roof above her. Glancing at the clock, she realized it was almost time to head home. She still needed to check the supplies in the back pantry before she left. She grabbed a notepad and pen from the counter and rushed out of the kitchen to a large walk-in pantry located by the office.

Stepping inside, she made a list of which supplies were running low, including oil, flour, sugar, and sprinkles. It took a while, and when she walked back to the kitchen, she found it empty.

"Hello?" she called. "*Mammi*? *Aenti* Kathryn? Ruthie?" She wondered if everyone was out in front of the bakery waiting for the van. When she stepped over toward the counter, her foot slipped on a puddle of water, and she screeched as she fell onto her bottom.

Jake rushed into the kitchen. "Katie?" He held his hand out to her. "Are you okay?"

Katie laughed despite her sore tailbone. "I sort of slipped. I guess someone splashed water on the floor earlier while washing dishes." She took his hand, and he lifted her to her feet as easily as if she were weightless. "Thank you."

"You're welcome." He let go of her hand and looked at her curiously. "What are you doing here? Everyone else left."

"What?" Katie shook her head in disbelief. "They're all gone?"

"Yes." He nodded. "I think they left about ten minutes ago. You didn't see them go?"

"No," Katie said, gesturing toward the hallway off the

kitchen. "I was in the pantry doing a supply inventory. I was supposed to do it earlier, but I got sidetracked with baking." She bit her lower lip. "I don't understand. Why would they leave me?"

"Maybe they thought you had a ride," he suggested. "I'm certain it had to be a mistake."

"But I didn't tell anyone I had another ride *heemet* today, and I always go in the van." Katie glanced out the window toward the blowing wind and rain. "What am I going to do? I guess I can call the phone shanty at *mei haus* and see if Samuel can come get me."

Jake paused, as if he were debating something. "I can give you a ride," he finally said. "As long as it doesn't get you in trouble."

Katie hesitated, remembering both her mother's and Elizabeth's warnings about being friends with Jake. The perception of her alone with a Mennonite boy could be negative for both Katie and her family. "I don't know if that's a good idea."

"I don't want you here alone. Is it okay if I wait with you until Samuel comes?" Jake offered.

"Let me see if I can reach him at the house." Katie walked to the front of the bakery and picked up the phone. She dialed the phone in her family's phone shanty, and her heart sank when she reached the voice mail instead of a live person. She left a quick message and then called the furniture store, again reaching the voice mail.

She walked back into the kitchen and found Jake standing by the counter. "I couldn't reach anyone at *mei haus* or the furniture store, and it's pouring outside like a monsoon. I don't know what to do, Jake."

"Let me finish picking up out front, and then I'll lock up the front like I told your grandmother I would. I'll be right back." Jake disappeared through the doorway.

Glancing around the kitchen, Katie blew out a sigh as she

picked up a stack of stray pans that had been left near her workstation. Never had she'd imagined she'd find herself alone at the bakery with Jake Miller. What if word got back to her father that she was alone with him? Katie would be in deep trouble for certain.

In an attempt to burn off her nervous energy, she washed the pans, put them away, and straightened the counters. She then swept the floors and checked to be sure the gas lamps were off in the office. She fetched the keys from her grandmother's desk and returned to the kitchen to find Jake leaning against the counter and smiling. She'd never noticed how handsome he was until that moment. The thought caused her to feel flustered and embarrassed.

"I took my tools to my truck," he said, standing up straight. "I'm ready to go when you are."

"Wunderbaar gut," she said, crossing the kitchen to retrieve her lunch bag and small tote. "I'm ready." She followed him to the back door, which he held open for her. *"Danki."* Standing under the overhang, she pulled the door closed and jammed the key in. When it refused to turn, she jiggled it. "I don't understand it. This key never gives me a problem," she muttered. "Why isn't it moving?"

Jake held out his hand. "May I try?"

She yanked the key out of the lock and handed it to him. "Here you go."

Jake slipped the key in the lock and turned it with ease. He then handed it back to Katie, and she shook her head with amazement.

"You just didn't have that special touch." He motioned toward the truck. "Ready to run through the rain?"

Katie hesitated as worry gripped her. "This is a bad idea. I should go call the phone at *mei haus* again and see if I can reach Samuel."

Jake shook his head. "No. It's raining like crazy, Katie. It wouldn't even be safe for Samuel to come and get you in a buggy, and it would take him quite a while to get here."

"I don't know, Jake." She looked up at him. "I'll be disobeying *mei daed* if I get in the truck with you. Waiting for Samuel seems to make more sense."

"Katie, please listen to me," he began. "Your family is probably worried sick about you since you didn't arrive home on time and it's storming out. The sooner I get you home, the sooner they'll know you're safe. Trust me on this."

She bit her lower lip and then nodded. "You're right. Let's get to *mei haus* as soon as we can."

He gestured toward her bags. "Do you want me to carry those for you, so you can run without balancing the bags?"

"No, *danki*," she said, shaking her head. "I can run." Katie sprinted across the parking lot, dodging two large puddles on the way.

When she reached the passenger side of the pickup truck, Katie climbed in, placing her bags on the floorboard. She shivered and ran her hands over her soaked dress while wondering how she would make her parents understand she had no other alternative ride home.

Jake jumped in the driver's side and brought the engine to life. "I can't believe how hard it's raining. I wonder if we'll have some flooding."

She cleared her throat and hugged her arms to her chest.

He kept his eyes trained on the road before him. "I'm sorry they left you behind. If I'd known, I would've told your aunt to wait."

"*Danki.*" She glanced away, hoping he wouldn't see the anxiety she was certain was apparent on her face.

They drove in silence for several moments. The only sounds were the roar of the engine, the rain beating on the windshield and roof, and the jingling of Jake's key chain as it hit the steering column. She tried to think of something to say, but her only thoughts were about how her parents would react when she arrived home in Jake Miller's truck.

"Katie," he began, "I really enjoy spending time with you."

"I enjoy spending time with you too," she said, watching the trees rush by out the window. "But I—"

"Wait," he said. "Please let me finish. I don't want to make you feel uncomfortable." He gave her a sideways glance. "I realize we're walking a fine line between two worlds, and I know what difficulties that can cause for you. The last thing I want is to make trouble for you."

She faced him, and the sincerity in his expression filled her with warmth despite her anxiety. "You don't make me feel uncomfortable, Jake. In fact, I feel more comfortable with you than with some of the *buwe* in my district I've known my whole life."

He smiled. *"Danki."*

"I know we're walking a fine line, but we can have lunch together every once in a while and talk as long as we're with my cousins or the other bakers, right?" she asked.

"My father once told me his relationship with my mother began with an innocent lunch date." He slowed down as the truck reached the road leading to her farm. "I'm afraid friendship may lead to problems for you if word got around that you're spending time with a Mennonite boy."

"Why can't I have *freinden* who aren't Amish?" Katie couldn't stop her disappointed frown.

"You can," he said with a shrug. "My mother keeps in contact with many of her school friends. But they're females, Katie. Unfortunately, there's a difference. Perception is a problem. Remember when Jessica and Lindsay first came to live with Rebecca?"

Katie nodded. "Of course I do."

"Jessica found herself in a bit of trouble because of how she was perceived," he said, frowning. "I don't want that to happen to you. I'll worry about what people might say or think every time we're together. I know my mother's family wound up divided when my parents fell in love. It only got worse when my mother left the church and became Mennonite so she could marry my father."

He steered onto her driveway, and Katie felt her worries churn in her stomach. Soon her family would know she'd ridden home with Jake. "I have a difficult time believing our friendship is a sin," she said, speaking quickly.

"Katie, it's more complicated than that. Your community has certain rules you need to abide by, and I respect that." Jake gripped the steering wheel. "But I promise I'll always be your friend, whether we have lunch together or not."

Katie spotted her youngest siblings, Linda and Aaron, looking out the family room windows. "Oh no," she said. "They saw the truck."

"You'd better go." Jake frowned. "I'll see you Monday."

"*Danki* for the ride." She gathered up her lunch bag and tote before hopping out of the truck.

He smiled. "*Gern gschehne.*"

Katie stepped away from the truck and ran through the cold rain toward her back door.

Chocolate Whoopie Pies

Cookie Halves:
   ½ cup vegetable shortening
   1 teaspoon baking soda
   1 cup brown sugar
   ¾ cup cocoa
   2 eggs
   ½ cup milk
   1½ cups flour
   1¼ teaspoons vanilla
   ½ teaspoon salt

Cream shortening, sugar, and eggs. Add vanilla. Then add milk with dry ingredients. Drop by the spoonful onto baking pans. Bake at 350 degrees for 10 minutes.

Filling:
   2 egg whites
   2¼ tablespoons milk
   2 teaspoons vanilla
   1½ cups shortening
   4 tablespoons flour
   1 lb. powdered sugar

Beat egg whites until stiff. Add vanilla, flour, and milk. Beat well and add shortening and powdered sugar. Spread between cookies. Makes two-dozen whoopie pies.

10

Katie rushed through the splashing raindrops toward the back of the house. Fear gripped her as she reached for the cold doorknob. Although she had enjoyed having a few moments to talk to Jake, she knew the repercussions could be serious.

"Katie!" Janie pushed the back door open and stepped out onto the porch. "How was your day?"

"*Gut*," Katie said as she touched her little sister's headscarf. "How was yours?"

"*Gut*." Janie took Katie's lunch bag from her hands. "I'll carry this for you."

"*Danki, schweschder*," Katie said as they stood together on the back porch. "What did you do today?"

"I helped Nancy scrub the floor in the bathroom, and we also swept the *schtupp*," Janie began. "And then we did a little bit of weeding in the garden, but we didn't finish since it started to rain. Maybe you can help us tomorrow if it dries enough overnight? *Dat* says it shouldn't rain too long. We're going to plant the new flowers once the beds are weeded."

"I'd love to help," Katie said, wrenching open the back door and holding it for her sister. "We'll work on that tomorrow for certain if it's not too muddy." She followed Janie into the kitchen and found her father glaring at her while he sat at the table. Her hands shook with worry as she hung her tote bag on a peg by the back door. *"Wie geht's, Dat?"*

He turned his glare to Janie. "Go into the *schtupp*, Janie. *Now."*

"Ya, Dat," Janie said. She rushed through the doorway, dropping the lunch bag in the process.

Katie's heart thudded in her chest as she stared into her father's angry eyes. *"Was iss letz?"*

"I believe you know what's wrong, Katie Joy," Robert said.

Katie glanced toward the doorway where her mother stood frowning back at her. Her mother shook her head with disappointment, and Katie quickly turned her gaze down to the floor.

"Katie Joy!" Her father's voice boomed, causing her to jump. "Look at me when I'm talking to you, *dochder."* He pushed the chair back, the wood scraping the floor with a foreboding din.

She turned her eyes on him but hunched her shoulders in humiliation. *"Ya, Daed,"* she whispered, her voice thick.

"I began worrying about you when you were more than twenty minutes late, but the fact that a strange pickup truck and driver brought you *heemet* makes the situation much more infuriating," he began.

"I missed my ride," Katie began, wishing her voice sounded more confident. "I went into the pantry to do inventory for *Mammi*, and when I came out, everyone was gone. Jake Miller brought me *heemet*. You know him, *Dat*. He's not a stranger." She hated hearing her voice so thin and shaky.

"Jake Miller?" Her father looked surprised. "That Mennonite *bu?"*

"Ya," she said. "He's Elmer Yoder's grandson. He's a close family *freind*. He's not just some stranger."

"That's not the point, Katie!" Her father wagged a finger a millimeter from her nose. "Why didn't you ride *heemet* with your *aenti* like you do every day?"

Katie bit her lower lip and glanced at her mother, who continued to look disappointed. "I told you I missed my ride. I called the phone shanty and the furniture store, but no one answered. I didn't know what else to do. Jake is working at the bakery right now—he's helping *Daadi* build new display cabinets for *Mammi*—and he was the only one left in the bakery. He offered to take me *heemet*. I had no other choice."

"How could you miss your ride?" he asked, looking suspicious. "You went into the pantry and no one saw you? That's preposterous!"

"It's the truth," Katie said, feeling irritation bubble up inside her. "I don't know why *Mammi* thought I had gone already. I didn't sneak into the pantry. I looked at the clock and thought I had ten minutes before the van came."

"Stop!" her father bellowed. "I've heard enough. No *dochder* of mine is going to go around begging *buwe* for a ride *heemet*. It's improper, inappropriate, and embarrassing for the family. Do you know what people will say about you, Katie? Have you thought about that? Or were you only thinking of being alone with a *bu*?"

Angry tears pooled in the corners of Katie's eye, and she brushed them away as she stared at her father in disbelief. How could he be cruel enough to accuse her of acting inappropriately? Didn't he know her at all? Katie had always followed the rules, and she would never deliberately embarrass her family.

"Well?" Robert asked. "What do you have to say for yourself? I asked you a question."

"I thought you wanted me to be quiet," Katie replied, wiping more tears.

"I want to know what you were thinking." He gestured with his hands for emphasis. "Why did you assume staying late to be alone with a *bu* in the bakery and then riding alone in his truck was okay? What went through your mind?" He pointed toward her head. "What's going on in that brain of yours, Katie Joy?"

"I had no choice, *Dat*," she said, hoping her voice would sound more confident despite her tears. "I was stranded without a ride, and I couldn't reach anyone on the phone. It's pouring rain, and it's a long walk *heemet*. What else could I have done?"

Her father shook his head. "You should have tried to call again. Did you try to call one of your *onkels*? You know everyone's number in our family." He looked disgusted. "How could you even consider being alone with a Mennonite *bu*? What's gotten into you?"

Katie wanted to tell her father that Mennonite or not, Jake was a nice young man. She wanted to tell him that she was allowed to have friends who weren't Amish and that she was old enough to make her own decisions about her friends.

But she couldn't speak. The lump swelling in her throat prevented any words from escaping her mouth.

Her father spat out his words. "You're not to leave this *haus* except to go to work and church for a month."

"A month?" Katie's words returned with a squeak. "I can't leave the *haus* for a month because I was stranded at work with no way *heemet*? That's completely unreasonable!"

"What? You'd like it to be longer?" Robert nearly shouted.

"No," she whispered.

He pointed toward the doorway. "Go to your room. I don't want to look at you."

Katie moved to the doorway and then broke into a run when she hit the stairs. She burst through the doorway to her room, slammed the door shut behind her, and hurled herself onto her bed, sobbing into her pillow. How could her father treat her this way?

Rolling to her side, Katie wiped her eyes and sniffed. The squeak of her door opening announced a visitor.

"Go away." Katie's voice croaked.

"Katie," her mother's voice said. "I would like to speak with you for a moment."

Sitting up, Katie hugged a pillow to her chest.

Her mother sat on the bottom corner of the bed, which squeaked under her weight. "I worried that you liked Jake." Sadie shook her head and touched Katie's leg. "You realize your behavior could result in a bad reputation. Is that what you want when you go to youth gatherings? Do you want the *buwe* to point at you and accuse you of improper behavior?"

"I don't understand why *Dat* is so angry. I was stranded without a ride. It's not my fault *Aenti* Kathryn left without me." Katie sniffed and hugged the pillow closer to her body. "I didn't do anything improper. Besides, I don't understand how having a *freind* is improper. Is being someone's *freind* truly a sin? If so, then where is the Bible verse that states it?"

Her mother glowered. "You know better than that, Katie. You're baptized now, and you know the rules we live by." She pointed to Katie. "You chose to become a member of this community and pledge your heart to God. Don't act as if you're surprised by your *dat*'s reaction to seeing you come *heemet* in a strange boy's truck."

"He's not a stranger. He's a close family *freind*." Katie cleared her throat, hoping to dissolve the lump.

"Katie," her mother began, "I think you consider him as more than a *friend*. You don't bake for *freinden*."

"I didn't bake for only Jake," Katie said, her body trembling. "I brought pretzels in for everyone at the bakery. I shared them with Jake, Hannah, Fannie, Vera, and the rest of the bakers."

Sadie's countenance transformed into a sympathetic expression. "I know you're anxious to find the right *bu*, and you will. Take your time, and let God guide you to him."

"I don't see why I can't be Jake's *freind*. Where's the sin in that?" she whispered.

"Are you saying you want to be shunned?" Sadie leaned in close. "Your *daed* would be very upset if he heard you say that."

Katie wanted to tell her mother not to tell him, but she knew her attitude would be construed as defiant. Instead she rolled onto her side. "I think I want to just rest for a while. Please close the door on your way out."

"Katie Joy." Her mother's voice was authoritative.

Katie sat up. *"Ya, Mamm?"*

"Are you considering leaving the faith?" Her mother looked worried and upset at the same time. "If you are, then you need to let me know so I can prepare my heart."

"No." Fresh tears streamed down Katie's hot cheeks. "I'm not planning on leaving the faith. I love my family too much."

"Gut." Looking relieved, Sadie stood. "Supper will be ready soon."

Katie watched her mother leave and close the door behind her. She had no appetite after the two emotional conversations with her parents. She rose, removed her prayer covering, and returned to her bed, snuggling under the covers. She couldn't stop her tears or her disappointment in her parents. Closing her eyes, she sobbed herself to sleep.

⟡

Katie awoke to a knock on the door. "Come in." Her voice croaked the words. Sitting up, she rubbed her eyes.

The door opened with a loud squeak and she gazed at Samuel, who was standing in the doorway holding up a plate of food.

"Ready to eat?" he asked, stepping over the threshold. "You missed supper. We had chicken and dumplings tonight. Your favorite."

"I'm not hungry." Katie folded her arms over her chest. "I've lost my appetite."

Samuel crossed the room and held the plate in front of Katie, causing her stomach to rumble. "Are you certain you're not hungry?" He moved the plate back and forth. "It's still warm."

She took the plate and fork. *"Danki."* After a silent prayer, she dug in, enjoying her mother's delicious food. "It is *gut*."

Samuel sat in a chair next to the bed and watched her eat. She waited for him to make a comment, but he was silent until her plate was clean.

"Jake Miller, huh?" Samuel finally asked. "Why?"

Katie frowned and placed the plate and fork on the night-stand. "Did you come up to lecture me? If so, I've already heard it all from *Mamm* and *Dat*. I'm finished with listening to lectures today."

He crossed one leg over the other and rested his hands on his knee. "I'm not here to lecture you, but I'm trying to understand."

"He gave me a ride *heemet*, because I was stranded at the bakery. We're just *freinden*." She studied her brother. "I don't know why *Mamm* and *Dat* are making such a big deal about this. I tried to call both the phone in the shanty and the furniture store. My only other choice was to walk *heemet* in the pouring rain."

"But you should've known *Dat* would go off the deep end," Samuel said. "Do you want to be shunned?"

"Of course I don't." She moved to sit on the edge of the bed facing him. "I just want to be his *freind*."

"You've really upset *Dat*," Samuel said.

"Today wasn't planned, Sam," Katie said. "I'm telling you the truth when I say I was stranded. I'm telling the truth that I walked back into the kitchen from the pantry and everyone was gone. I wonder if they thought you'd picked me up like you did the day you went to see *Daadi* for fence supplies." She shook her head. "I wish you'd believe me. My choice was to ride *heemet* with Jake or walk in the pouring rain."

Samuel nodded. "I believe you, Katie, but I get the feeling you like him as more than a *freind*."

"I like talking to him," Katie said, shrugging. "He's really nice. I wish I could get to know him better." She paused for a moment. "Samuel, what would you do if you were me?"

He shrugged. "I don't know what to tell you. My future *fraa* is a baptized member of the community. We don't have to worry about our relationship causing any problems for us. You won't be able to have a life like that with him unless you leave the faith. Is that what you want? You know *Dat* would never accept you if you left."

"You're right," Katie said. "*Dat* is not like Jake's *grossdaadi*."

"No, he's not." Samuel shook his head. "It wouldn't be like Jake's situation where his *mamm* and grandparents worked things out even though she was shunned."

"And I don't want to leave the faith," Katie said. "My heart belongs to this community."

"I know." Samuel frowned.

"I can't be *freinden* with Jake," Katie said the words slowly as the reality filtered through her. "I guess I knew that all along, but I didn't want to accept it."

"I know you're unhappy, and I'm sorry for that," Samuel said. "But you'll find happiness here. I know it. You just may have to wait a while until you find the right person."

Katie sighed. She couldn't imagine meeting anyone who would make her feel like she did with Jake. Conversation was so easy with him. It was as though they connected on a deeper level than she'd ever connected with anyone else. But now she had to walk away from him and act like they were never friends. How could she ever do it?

"I need to just keep my distance from him and hope someday he'll understand," she said.

Samuel stood and grabbed the plate and fork from the end table. "I'm sure he'll understand. He knows the rules we live by." His expression was serious. "You need to convince *Dat* you won't disobey him again so you can go back to the youth gatherings."

"Why does it matter if I go to the gatherings?" she asked with a frown. "You're with Lizzie Anne, and Lindsay is with Matthew. It doesn't matter if I'm there or not. When I am there, I hang out with Nancy and her *freinden* now. I'll never meet anyone new hanging out with them."

"I doubt you'll meet *anyone* with that kind of attitude." He started toward the door. "I just wanted to bring you something to eat. I felt bad that you missed supper."

Her expression softened as guilt rained down on her. "I'm sorry. *Danki* for supper."

Katie watched him leave silently and wondered if her brother was right. Did she have a poor attitude, and was it her fault she never connected with anyone in her community? Even if it were true, she still couldn't shake the feeling that Jake was supposed to be her friend since they got along so well. How could she look for someone else in her community when she was wishing she could get to know Jake Miller better?

Peanut Butter Pie

8 ounces of cream cheese
½ cup peanut butter
1 cup powdered sugar
8-ounce package of whipped topping

Mix cream cheese and powdered sugar. Add peanut butter and mix well. Fold in whipped topping. Put in baked pie crust and refrigerate 90 minutes.

11

Jake couldn't get Katie out of his mind all evening. The image of her running through the rain toward the back door of her house had haunted him since he'd dropped her off. Instead of going straight home, he'd driven around for more than an hour, thinking of her and wondering what she'd faced when her father found out Jake had driven her home.

Guilt nipped at him when he thought of the punishment she'd have to endure alone. Jake wished he could've stood by Katie and defended her actions to her father, but he knew the idea was preposterous. Katie was Amish, and he was Mennonite. He had no right to even think about her as more than a friend, but he couldn't stop the growing feelings he had for her.

As he motored down the street, he glanced toward the turn that led to Katie's farm and he steered onto that road. He wasn't certain why he was going that way, but he felt the urge to do it. When he reached Katie's house, he slowed down, staring at the building and wondering which bedroom was hers. Was she asleep? Was she thinking of him?

Jake looked next door to the farm where Matthew lived with his sister and her family. He spotted the barn door leading to Matthew's shop was open and a faint light spilled out onto the rock driveway. He turned into the driveway and slowly drove up it. He parked by the barn and hopped out of the truck, noticing the rain had stopped.

Matthew met him by the barn door with a surprised expression. "Jake." He shook Jake's hand. "What brings you here tonight? I wasn't expecting you."

"I was in the neighborhood and saw your light," Jake said. "I hope it's okay."

"Of course it is." Matthew gestured toward the house. "Would you like a drink?"

"No, no." Jake held up a hand in protest. "I won't bother you for long. I just wanted to say hello. I was out driving around, and I thought I'd stop by and see if you were up. How are you doing?"

"Fine. Would you like to have a seat in the shop?" Matthew motioned toward the barn where a lantern sat just inside the door. Jake assumed it was the light he'd seen from the street.

"That would be nice." Jake followed Matthew to the back of the barn where a small area had been converted into a shop. He spotted a couple of workbenches, two stools, and a collection of tools. An unfinished bookshelf sat in the corner awaiting stain. A line of lanterns had been placed on the workbench and illuminated the entire area. The heaviness of sawdust, the pungent odor of stain, and the sweet smell of wood filled Jake's lungs. It was the same fragrance he'd become accustomed to when he began working with his grandfather. It smelled like home. "What are you working on?"

"A surprise for Lindsay." Matthew ran his hands over the hope chest that sat on the bench in front of him. "This was *mei mamm*'s. I am going to sand it down, stain it, and replace the hardware as a Christmas gift for her."

"It's beautiful." Jake ran his fingers over the wood. "Cedar, right?"

Matthew nodded. "*Mei mamm* loved this hope chest. She told me to give it to someone special when the time was right."

Jake smiled. "Lindsay will be very happy this Christmas."

"I hope so." Matthew hopped up on a stool and motioned for

Jake to sit. "I miss our conversations at the store. How are the display cabinets going at the bakery?"

"They're going well." Jake climbed onto the other stool. "We've gotten the old ones disassembled, and we're designing the new ones. Elizabeth seems quite pleased with them."

"That's *gut*." Matthew pulled out two bottles of water from a cooler nearby. "I just remembered I'd brought these out earlier. Have one." He handed one to Jake.

"Thanks," Jake said. "How's the entertainment center coming along?"

Matthew sipped his water and then raised the bottle as if to toast. "It finally went *heemet* with the customer last Friday. I was certain I was going to work on that piece of furniture until the day I was buried, but I got it all done. The customer was very happy, which was a plus."

Jake sipped the drink. "That's always great news. You don't want any complaints."

"No, I don't." Matthew drank more water and wiped his mouth with the back of his hand. "What seems to be on your mind, *freind*? You look like you want to discuss something."

Jake fingered the cool bottle while considering his words. He couldn't stop thinking of Katie and what she was going through in her house tonight. He wondered about the Amish life and the rules by which they lived every day. "What's it like being an Amish man?"

Matthew looked surprised by the question. "What do you mean?"

"Did you ever feel like you were missing out on anything?" Jake asked.

Matthew rubbed his chin. "You mean like modern conveniences, such as a car, electricity, and a cell phone?" He shook his head. "I was never interested in having those things."

"Never?" Jake asked. "Not even when you were young?"

"No." Matthew smiled. "You can't miss what you've never had, *ya*? It would be different if I had those modern things and then gave them up to become Amish, like Lindsay did."

"Very true." Jake placed the bottle on the workbench. "Did you ever go through *rumspringa*?"

Matthew shrugged again. "Not to the extent some of *mei freinden* did. I didn't go to wild parties or move out into an apartment and buy a motorcycle. But I spent time with *mei freinden*. We had some late nights and we listened to music, but that was it. I was baptized very young."

"How young?" Jake asked.

"Sixteen."

"And you never had a second thought?" Jake asked.

Matthew shook his head. "Not one regret or second thought."

"That's astounding," Jake said. "You knew in your heart you were meant to be Amish. God put the feeling there without any doubts."

Matthew was silent for a moment. "I'll be honest with you, Jake." He leaned his arm on the workbench. "*Mei daed* left the faith and abandoned my family, so I've seen firsthand how painful it can be when someone leaves under bad circumstances. I was determined to follow the opposite path from the one he chose to take, which is why I was baptized so young."

"I didn't know that," Jake said with surprise. "I knew you had a rough time at home, but I had no idea your father walked out on you. That had to be devastating."

"It was." Matthew sipped his bottle of water. "But a lot of good came out of it. I'm glad *mei mamm* and I moved here and I met everyone." He grinned. "Especially Lindsay. And I'm really happy she joined the church."

Jake smiled. "I know you are."

Matthew's expression became serious. "Samuel came over tonight to talk, and he shared that Katie got a ride *heemet* with you today."

"He knew about it?"

"The whole family knows." Matthew frowned. "Apparently she got into a lot of trouble because of it. She's not permitted to leave the house except for work and church for a month now."

Jake groaned. "Oh no. That's what I was afraid of. I'm certain her father was really upset."

Matthew grimaced. "He was more than upset. Sam used the word conniption when he described the scene. It was bad."

With dread filling him, Jake ran his hand over his face. "It couldn't be avoided. I would never do anything that would risk Katie's relationship with her family. She was stranded at the bakery after everyone else left, and she couldn't reach anyone else for a ride home. I had a really bad feeling about it, but it wasn't like I could let her walk home in the pouring rain. What else could I do, Matthew?"

"I'm sure she'll be okay, but I would imagine she has to steer clear of you." Matthew finished his bottle of water and tossed it into a nearby trash can.

"Spending time with me will only make it worse for her." Jake shook his head. "Katie and I had lunch together at the bakery, and I have to admit I enjoy spending time with her."

"You know you can't be with her, right?" Matthew asked. "You're only going to make problems for her if you pursue her as more than a *freind*."

"I know, but I wish I could find a way to make it work with Katie," Jake said. "I care about her, and I wish we could be together."

"That's impossible. She's Amish, and you're not. To make matters worse, her father is very stern. The best thing you can do for Katie is stay away from her. She's baptized now, and she'll run the risk of being shunned if you try to be with her." Matthew looked at the clock on the bench. "I had no idea it was after ten. I better close up for the night. I have to get up early to care for the animals."

"I'm sorry for keeping you up so late." Jake hopped down and tossed his bottle in the trash can.

"Don't apologize. I enjoyed our talk." Matthew turned off all but one lantern and used it to guide them through the barn.

Jake stopped at the door and pointed toward the lantern there. "Why do you keep a lantern here?"

Matthew laughed. "It's to help guide *mei schweschder* if she comes out looking for me. She tends to trip and fall a lot."

"Even if she has a flashlight?" Jake asked.

"Yes," Matthew said. "*Mei mamm* was a klutz too."

Jake chuckled and shook Matthew's hand. "Have a good night. Thanks for talking with me."

"Any time," Matthew said.

Jake stepped over to the truck and fished his keys from his pocket. "See you soon." He climbed into the driver's seat and rolled down the window.

"Oh, wait." Matthew stepped over to him. "Could you possibly do me a favor tomorrow?"

Jake shrugged. "Of course. What is it?"

"*Mei schweschder*'s refrigerator died today, and we were talking about going to look for one tomorrow. Could you possibly take *mei bruder*-in-law and me to the store?" Matthew leaned on the door. "I'd really appreciate it."

"Absolutely," Jake said. "I can be here around nine. Will that work?"

"That would be perfect," Matthew said. "I'll see you tomorrow. Good night."

"Good night," Jake said before starting the truck and backing down the driveway. As he motored toward his house, he thought of Katie and the horrible evening she must've endured with her parents. He wished he could make it all better.

Saturday morning, Katie leaned over and pulled more weeds. Her back ached from the action, and she had to strain to stop yawning. She'd spent most of the night staring at the ceiling and listening to her sister snore. Throughout the night, her mind raced with thoughts of her horrible discussions with her parents and the reality of never being able to enjoy a friendship with Jake.

"I'm so glad the ground was able to dry overnight. I think we're just about done," Janie said. "It looks really *gut. Mamm* will be pleased."

Katie nodded and pushed aside a stray lock of hair that had fallen out from under her headscarf. She was thankful for her mother that morning. Her mother had actually spoken to her while they'd eaten breakfast. On the other hand, her father had acted as if Katie were invisible during breakfast. Even when Katie asked him a question and tried her best to engage him in conversation with her, he looked away and spoke to someone else. It nearly moved Katie to tears, but she was determined not to show him how much he hurt her.

She briefly wondered if that was what it felt like to be shunned. If so, then she was certain she never wanted to endure that in her lifetime. Although it was painful to accept she could never be friends or anything more with Jake, she knew she couldn't face being invisible to her own family. She loved them too much.

"Katie?" Janie asked. "Are you awake?"

Katie glanced over at her sister, who was crouched by nearly a dozen pots of mums. "I'm sorry. What did you say, Janie?"

Janie motioned for Katie to join her on the ground. "Let's start planting."

"Oh," Katie said. "Right."

Nancy appeared next to them holding a trowel. "Need help?"

"*Ya,*" Katie said. "We can use all of the help we can get."

Her sisters began digging and placing the mums in the ground, and Katie assumed the task of covering the mums with soil. While her sisters discussed the mums' beautiful fall colors, Katie continued to think about her predicament with her father.

She was covering the last mum when she heard voices behind her. Turning, she found Samuel talking with Matthew and Jake in the driveway. Although Jake looked handsome, she wished he were dressed like her brother and Matthew.

If only he were Amish, all of these problems would evaporate. If he were Amish, we could be freinden, *and no one would tell us we were wrong.*

She pushed the thoughts aside and looked back at the flowers. When she felt someone staring at her, she glanced back toward the driveway and spotted Jake's intense stare.

"What are you looking at?" Janie asked.

"She's looking at Jake Miller over there by Matthew and Samuel," Nancy said while wiping her hands on her apron.

Katie bit her lower lip.

Janie hopped up. "I'm going to go wash my hands and fill the watering can. I'll be right back with some water." She rushed off toward the house, leaving Nancy and Katie sitting alone by the flowerbeds.

"You know you can't talk to him," Nancy whispered. "If you do, *Dat* will only get angrier, and you'll get in more trouble. Is that what you want?"

"No," Katie said. "But I need to tell Jake that's why I am avoiding him."

"I can go keep *Dat* busy in the barn while you run over and you can say what you have to say to Jake," Nancy offered. "But hurry, I don't know how long *Dat* will stay in the barn."

Katie smiled. "You would do that for me?"

Nancy shrugged. "Why not? You'll owe me one someday when I want to go talk to a *bu*." She looked toward Jake. "Go before he heads *heemet*."

Katie squeezed her sister's arm before jumping to her feet. *"Danki."*

"Don't thank me yet. It might not work." Nancy frowned. "If you get caught ..."

"I won't get caught." Katie rushed toward the driveway, and the three men all shot her questioning glances. After sharing an intense stare with Jake, she continued over the property line through a stand of trees, heading toward Matthew's barn.

Standing by the barn door she suddenly felt silly. What if Matthew's sister, Betsy, came outside? What excuse could Katie possibly use for why she was standing by the barn looking stupid? Maybe she could say she needed to borrow something, like apples for making an apple pie? But would Betsy even believe Katie needed apples?

"What are you doing?" a voice behind her called.

Katie turned and found Jake coming toward her with a concerned expression. "Jake!" She rushed toward him. "I had to see you."

He glanced behind him toward her father's barn, which stood behind the trees separating the two properties. "This isn't a good idea. Matthew and Samuel told me you got in a lot of trouble yesterday."

"But I have to talk to you." She stood in front of him. "I can't see you anymore. *Mei dat* has forbidden it, and I can't risk making him even angrier. I needed a chance to tell you I'm going to miss talking to you."

"I'm going to miss you too," he said. "I'm very sorry your father was so angry. It's all my fault."

"No, it's not." She shook her head. "You were just helping me get *heemet* in the rain. I disobeyed *mei dat* by being alone with you and got what I deserved."

Jake frowned. "No, you didn't. You didn't deserve it at all."

He shook his head. "I want to be your friend, but I can't risk your getting shunned. I don't want to be the reason you get into more trouble with your father."

"I don't want to be shunned. I love my family too much. The mood in our house is already too difficult to bear. *Mei dat* wouldn't even talk to me this morning at breakfast. I feel as if I'm already invisible, and I haven't even been shunned." Scowling, she shook her head. "We're going to have to pretend we're not *freinden*. It's going to be so difficult, Jake."

"I know." He took a step back and motioned toward her house. "You'd better go. I'll see you Monday at the bakery."

"But we can't eat lunch together anymore, not even with my cousins," she warned him. "We have to keep our distance."

"I know." He gestured toward her yard. "I don't want you to get into more trouble."

"Good-bye, Jake," she said.

Jake climbed into his truck, and Katie began to trot through the trees toward the barn. Her feet hit the grass on the other side of the property line as Jake's truck came to life in the driveway. She started across the yard just as her father stepped out of the barn and shot her an accusing look.

"Where were you, Katie?" he demanded as he charged toward her. "Why were you over at Betsy's *haus*?"

"I needed to go speak to Betsy," she said, her voice trembling under his glare.

"What did you need to ask her?" He folded his arms over his wide chest as he towered over her.

"I asked her if she had any apples," she said, her voice a mere whisper.

"Why did you need apples while you were planting mums in the garden?"

"I was going to make you a pie later," she said. "Your favorite —apple pie."

Robert looked past her toward where Samuel and Matthew stood watching with uncomfortable expressions. "Didn't I see that Mennonite *bu* over with your *bruder* earlier?"

Katie hesitated, her heart thudding in her chest. She shouldn't lie to her father. Not only was it a sin, but she'd only get caught in it later on, which would make things worse.

"You don't know the answer?" He looked past her. "I'll find out then. Samuel! Matthew!" he bellowed. "Didn't I see that Mennonite *bu* here earlier?"

Katie faced her brother and Matthew as she held her breath. *This is it. Starting right now, I'm going to be stuck at home for the rest of my life.*

"You mean Jake Miller?" Matthew asked.

"*Ya,*" Robert said. "That *bu*. Elmer's grandson."

"He was here earlier," Matthew said. "He came to help me move a refrigerator."

"I helped too," Samuel chimed in. "But Jake's gone now."

Katie bit her lower lip as her father's accusing eyes turned back to her. She knew she was in for it again; it was all her fault. When was she going to stop making stupid choices?

"You weren't going over to see Betsy about apples, were you, Katie Joy?" he asked.

"No," she said. "I wanted to tell Jake I couldn't be his *freind* any-more. That's it, *Dat.* I wasn't trying to disobey you, I was simply—"

"You were simply disobeying me again!" His voice roared like thunder. "When will you learn?" He gestured toward the house. "Go! I can't trust you at all. You're to stay in the *haus* until further notice. And I'm going to talk to your *mammi* and tell her to watch over you at the bakery. You won't leave the bakery under any circumstance, and you're to stay away from that Mennonite *bu*."

"But *Dat*, I—" Her voice squeaked as tears rolled down her cheeks.

"This conversation is over," he said, interrupting her again. "You're not being truthful, and you disobey me over and over again. Go now before I drag you into the house myself."

With her tears flowing, Katie fled into the house, through the kitchen, and up the stairs, dodging siblings and her mother on the way. When she reached her room, she collapsed onto the bed and prayed for the Lord to give her a sign as to how she should handle her difficult father.

"Katie," Nancy's voice rang out over her prayers. "Katie, I'm so sorry. I tried to keep him in the barn."

"I know you did." Katie sat up and swiped her fingers over her fresh tears. "I never should've involved you."

"It's okay." Nancy sat on the end of their bed. "I can't imagine how hard it is for you to like a Mennonite *bu.* I feel so bad for you."

"Danki." Katie forced a smile. "You're very thoughtful, but I got myself into this mess."

Nancy shook her head. "No, you didn't. You didn't mean to like him. It just happened, *ya?*"

"Ya." Katie sniffed. "It did. I never realized how kind he is until he came to work at the bakery. But we're not allowed to like someone who isn't Amish unless we leave the church. It doesn't seem fair. Why can't we care about someone who isn't like us?" She blew out a sigh. "I know the answer to that. It's because we're all supposed to be loyal to the church and our community. I know what will happen if I keep disobeying *Dat.* I'll be shunned, and I don't want that. Having *Dat* ignore me at breakfast was enough to show me I need to be obedient from now on." She shivered as more tears flowed from her eyes. "But I'm going to miss Jake so much. It's just not fair, Nancy. I want to be his *freind.*"

"Oh, Katie." Nancy moved closer and hugged her. "I hate seeing you cry like this."

Katie leaned into her younger sister's shoulder. "Why does this have to hurt so much?"

"I don't know." Nancy rubbed her back. "I wish I could fix it for you. You won't feel this way forever. I promise you. Someday you'll meet a nice Amish *bu* who will love you and make you *froh*, Katie. I know it in my heart."

Katie closed her eyes. "*Danki*, Nancy. You're a *gut schweschder.*"

Frosted Carrot Bars

Bars

    4 eggs
    2½ teaspoons cinnamon
    1 cup brown sugar
    1 cup white sugar
    ¾ teaspoon salt
    2 cups sifted flour
    3 cups grated carrots
    1½ cups vegetable oil
    1½ cups shredded coconut
    2 teaspoons baking soda
    1¼ cups walnuts

Beat eggs until light. Gradually beat in sugar. Add oil and flour sifted with baking soda, cinnamon, and salt alternately. Mix well. Fold in carrots, coconuts, and walnuts. Pour into 13x9x2 pan. Bake at 350 degrees for 30 minutes. Cut into bars. Allow to cool.

Icing

    1 tablespoon milk
    3 ounces cream cheese
    A pinch of salt
    1 teaspoon vanilla
    2½ cups powdered sugar

Combine until smooth. Spread icing onto cooled bars.

12

Katie was almost convinced Monday would never end. She'd been working in the kitchen since she'd arrived, and she hadn't set foot in the front area of the bakery. Knowing Jake was out there working was driving her to distraction, but she'd been aware of her grandmother's frequent glances throughout the day.

The whole situation was so embarrassing and heartbreaking that she didn't want to discuss it anymore. Yet she couldn't keep her thoughts from gravitating back to Jake Miller no matter how hard she tried to think of anything else. However, she was determined not to disobey her father.

"Katie," her grandmother called. "It's nearly one o'clock. You may go eat your lunch now, *mei liewe*."

"*Danki*," Katie called. After cleaning up her workstation, she retrieved her lunch box and headed out to the bench by a little playground. She prayed and then pulled out her turkey sandwich. She watched her younger cousins play while she ate. She wished she had someone to talk to, but she knew it was best she stay alone with her thoughts.

Katie was finishing her sandwich when her grandmother sat down beside her.

"Your *dat* came to visit me yesterday," her grandmother said. "I'm sorry he was so upset with you over the weekend."

"*Danki*," Katie said, wondering what her father had said to her grandmother. How serious was the conversation?

"I defended you," Elizabeth said.

Katie studied her grandmother's face. "Why would you defend me?"

"Because I felt your *dat* was overreacting a bit." Her grandmother patted Katie's lap. "You had no choice but to get a ride *heemet* from Jake on Friday. It was my fault for not realizing you were still in the bakery. I thought you'd gotten a ride with Samuel again. The whole situation was an honest mistake that was blown out of proportion, but my son is very stubborn and very strict. It made me recall the heartache *mei freind* endured when she fell in love with the Mennonite *bu*. I wanted to try to soften the blow for you as much as I could."

"*Danki*." Katie studied her grandmother's expression. "I never said I was in love with Jake. He and I are simply *freinden*. I enjoy talking to him, and I think he likes talking to me too."

Elizabeth smiled. "I'm not blind. I see how you and Jake look at each other, and I know there are feelings blossoming between you two." Her expression then became grave. "I promised your *dat* I would watch out for you and keep you and Jake apart as much as possible. I need to keep that promise, Katie. You know that."

"I know." Katie pulled an apple out of her lunch bag and studied it for a moment while contemplating her grandmother's words. "What happened to your friend who fell in love with the Mennonite *bu*?"

"She was shunned, Katie. She left the community and married him." Elizabeth took Katie's hands in hers. "Katie, you're *mei grossdochder*, and *Ich liebe dich*. Of course I'm going to wish you a life of happiness. However, I've seen a situation like this end badly."

"What do you mean?" Katie tried to contemplate her grandmother's words. "How can falling in love end badly?"

"The repercussions of leaving the community will be difficult to manage, *mei liewe*." Her grandmother squeezed her hands. "Could you really handle walking away from your family and *freinden* who love you so much? And how would you feel breaking your parents' hearts?"

Katie swallowed as the reality of what she was doing trickled through her. "I see what you're saying and what the results of my actions could mean." She pulled her hands back. "I promise I won't disobey *mei dat*, and I won't talk to Jake ever again."

"I just want you to be careful with your heart." Elizabeth pointed toward Katie's chest. "I know how sweet and sensitive you are, and Jake is a very nice *bu*. However, you need to think about what the consequences could be if you allow yourself to be swept away in the moment without a care in the world."

Katie thought of her two best friends and frowned. "It's not easy being the only one without a boyfriend when Lizzie Anne is getting married and Lindsay is dating Matthew."

Her grandmother's face assumed a sympathetic expression. "I know that has to be difficult, but your time will come. Have patience and faith." She suddenly brightened. "Remember the verse from the service last week?"

Katie shook her head. "Which one?"

"It was from the second of Thessalonians, verse sixteen," Elizabeth said. " 'May our Lord Jesus Christ himself and God our Father, who loved us and by his grace gave us eternal encouragement and good hope, encourage your hearts and strengthen you in every good deed and word.' Keep that in mind, Katie. Always keep your faith and hope. Your time will come when it's right. You're very young. You don't need to fall in love at eighteen, even though your friends have."

"*Ya*," Katie said. "I know."

Elizabeth waved to a few of Katie's cousins who were climbing the jungle gym and laughing. "I remember when you were out there playing. It's amazing how quickly *mei grandkinner* are growing up. Soon you'll be married and having *kinner* of your own. It will happen in God's time."

Katie frowned at the thought. Would she ever find an Amish boy to love?

Her grandmother looped her arm around Katie's shoulders. "I wish I could take your sadness away. You're so young, and you have your whole life ahead of you. Don't let this situation color the rest of your youth, Katie."

Katie bit into the apple. She knew her grandmother meant well, but the words seemed meaningless in her disappointment. All she knew was she and Jake had to go their separate ways and pretend they were never friends.

Elizabeth stood. "I'm going to go start making sandwiches for the *kinner.*"

"Do you need help?" Katie asked, wiping her hands with a napkin.

"No, *danki.*" Her grandmother smiled. "You enjoy your lunch. I'll take my break when you come back in."

Katie finished the apple, wrapped the apple core in her napkin, and pulled out a zipper storage bag filled with frosted carrot bars she, Janie, and Nancy had made Saturday. She glanced toward the parking lot and spotted Jake sitting on the tailgate of his truck and eating lunch. She wondered if he missed her as much as she missed him. He turned toward her, and their gazes locked. She wished she could speak to him, but she'd heard her father's rules loud and clear. The last thing she needed to do was disobey him and have the word get back through one of her relatives.

When she could no longer take the pain of staring from afar, Katie turned back toward the playground and wondered what she could do to make this day end faster.

By Friday, Katie was tired of spending her days stuck in the kitchen at the bakery. Although she loved to bake, she was ready to venture outside of the hot kitchen for a change of scenery.

At noon, she crossed to her grandmother's office and found her sitting at her desk. *"Mammi?"* she asked as Elizabeth looked up from her ledger. "I was wondering if I could go for a walk during my lunchtime today."

Placing her pen on the desk, Elizabeth looked curious. "Why do you want to go for a walk, Katie Joy?"

Katie leaned on the doorframe. "Janie's birthday is next week, and I was thinking about heading to the fabric store. I'd like to make her a new dress as a special gift."

"That's very nice," Elizabeth said, smiling. "Did you want to go now?"

Katie nodded. "Walking in the nice cool air sounds like a *gut* break from the hot kitchen."

Elizabeth motioned toward the door. "Go on. You can eat your lunch when you get back."

"Danki." Katie nodded at her aunts and cousins and the other bakers as she crossed the kitchen and grabbed her cloak from the peg by the back door. Pulling on her cloak, Katie crossed the parking lot and noticed Jake's pickup truck wasn't parked among the tourists' cars. She wondered why he was absent from work and hoped he was okay.

She started down Gibbons Road and hugged her cloak closer to her body while thinking of Jake. She'd missed talking to him all week, and she wondered if he missed her as well. Did he think of her as a good friend too? She contemplated if Nancy and her grandmother were right and she would meet and fall in love with an Amish man someday. But how could she possibly forget her special friendship with Jake Miller, even if it had lasted only a short time?

Pushing the thoughts of Jake away, Katie walked down the road and thought about her little sister's birthday. She contemplated what color fabric she should get for Janie's dress. Her little sister loved the color pink, but she thought she should get a more traditional color, such as cranberry or maybe purple.

"Hey!" a voice called, interrupting her thoughts of her sister's gift.

Katie looked behind her and spotted three young men following her. They each were clad in stained, ripped jeans and dirty denim jackets. Their long, greasy hair fell past their shoulders. Two carried beer bottles while the third held a fancy cell phone.

Assuming they weren't speaking to her, Katie turned her gaze toward the road ahead of her. An uneasy feeling gripped her, and she picked up her pace, wishing she'd asked Amanda or Ruthie to walk with her to the store.

"Hey, Amish girl!" one of the men yelled. "We want to ask you a question."

Oh no. They are *talking to me!* Katie walked faster, hugging her cloak closer to her body. *Only two more blocks, and I'll be at the fabric store. I can make it!*

"Wait up!" one of the men yelled.

Katie heard footsteps rushing up behind her, and she considered running to the corner. However, a strong arm grabbed her and spun her around, forcing her to face the three men. Her heart thudded in her chest as they sneered at her.

"You know, it's rude to ignore someone who's talking to you," the tallest of the men, who was holding a beer bottle, said. "We were calling you."

"What do you want?" she asked, her voice a strangled whisper.

"We just want to ask you a question," the second man said. He reached over and touched the tie to her prayer covering. "Where do you get these pretty bonnets you Amish chicks wear?"

Katie stepped away from his touch. "We make them."

"How do you make them?" the third man asked. He smiled, revealing yellowed, chipped teeth.

"We make them by hand," Katie said. "Now, if you'll excuse me. I must go." She turned.

"Wait," one of the men said, grabbing her arm with a forceful grip that made her wince. "We're not done." He threw down his beer bottle, which smashed into pieces by her black sneakers.

Katie's stomach lurched as the man stood close to her. His breath smelled of onions, and she feared she might vomit from the stench. "Please let me go," she said.

"No," he said with an evil grin. "We want to take your photo." He nodded toward the short man. "Hank has an iPhone, and we want to get a photo with you so we can prove to our friends we really met a pretty Amish chick today."

"It's against my religion to have my photo taken," she said, her voice quaking with fear. "Please let go of me. You're hurting me."

Hank held up his phone. "Be a nice girl. Just let me get a photo with you."

"Let go of me!" Katie called, tears pooling in her eyes. "I have to go!"

"Come on, babe," the third man said, throwing his beer bottle into the street. "Why don't you have a little fun with us."

Katie tried to pull away from them, but the man was still holding onto her wrist, and the third grabbed her prayer covering, yanking it off her head and causing her to yelp as the pins and ribbon were ripped from her hair.

"Stop!" she yelled, tears spilling from her eyes. "Let me go!"

"Let's see your dress, babe." The man who was holding her wrist looked at his friend. "Help me get her cloak off, Nick."

"Stop!" Katie screamed as the two men held her and pulled

off her cloak. "Please! Let me go! Stop it, please!" Her sobs cut off her voice as they threw her cloak to the ground and began to paw at her dress. She prayed someone would come and help her. Why hadn't she asked one of her cousins to walk with her to the store? How long would this nightmare go on?

"Are you getting this on video, Hank?" the first man asked with a grin. "Look at her pretty dress. Do you make your clothes yourself too?" He grabbed at her waist, and her dress tore with a loud rip.

"Please stop!" she pleaded with them. "Let me go."

"What's your name, babe?" the first man asked, pulling her to him. "You're awful pretty for an Amish girl."

A horn blasted and a dark-colored pickup truck slammed onto the sidewalk less than a foot from where Katie stood, struggling to get away from the groping men.

"Get away from her!" a voice hollered. "Go now! I'm calling the police!"

Katie's heart swelled with relief as Jake approached with a fierce expression and a two-by-four in his hands.

Glowering, Jake held the board like a baseball bat. "I mean it!" he bellowed. "Let the girl go now!"

The men scattered, and Jake tossed the piece of wood into the bed of his truck. Katie launched herself toward Jake, wrapping her arms around him and burying her face in his shoulder while she sobbed.

"Katie," he said, running his hand over her hair. "Are you okay?"

She swallowed deep breaths and tried to regain her composure. "Jake," she finally said, holding onto him for comfort. "I was so scared. I didn't know what they were going to do to me. I'm so glad you came along when you did."

"I know," he said softly, holding her close. "I couldn't believe my eyes when I saw them." Putting his fingers under her chin, he tilted her face so that she looked right into his deep blue eyes. "I'm so glad I had to get supplies this morning, and I'm thankful there was a back-up at the store. If I hadn't arrived when I did, I don't know what would've happened to you, Katie." He shook his head, his expression serious. "I don't know what I'd do if something happened to you."

"Katie Kauffman!" a voice bellowed behind her.

Katie looked behind her and spotted Bishop Chupp sitting in his buggy by the side of the road. "Bishop Chupp," she said, pulling away from Jake and stepping back. "I was—"

"Get in the buggy, child," the bishop said. "I need to take you *heemet* right this minute."

Katie looked at Jake, and he nodded.

"Go," Jake said. "I'll go tell Elizabeth and Eli what happened."

"*Danki,*" Katie whispered.

"Go," Jake repeated. "Now."

Katie climbed into the buggy next to the bishop and hugged her arms to her trembling body. Reaching up, she realized her prayer covering was gone. She wondered if her cloak and prayer covering were lying on the sidewalk near where she'd been accosted. Her body shuddered as she thought of the three men who'd groped her. What would've happened if Jake Miller hadn't come along? The thought caused her to feel queasy.

"Bishop," she began. "Jake Miller had just saved me from three men who—"

"There's no need to explain yourself, Katie," the bishop said, keeping his eye on the road as he guided the horse. "I know what I saw."

"I'm telling you the truth," Katie began. "Three men had surrounded me." She pulled at her ripped dress and her tears began anew. She sniffed and swiped her hand over her face, but the bishop kept staring straight ahead as if she were invisible. Why didn't he believe her?

They drove in silence the rest of the way to her house. When the buggy came to a stop, Katie walked slowly behind the bishop as they entered the house, where her parents and her younger siblings sat at the table eating lunch.

"Katie," her mother said with a gasp. "What happened to your dress? Where's your covering?"

"Bishop Chupp?" her father asked. "What's going on? Katie, why aren't you at work?"

The bishop gestured toward the family room. "May I speak to you alone, Robert?"

Katie touched her mother's hand. "I was attacked by three men," she whispered, hoping not to scare Janie. "Jake Miller saved me."

Her mother looked confused. "What? I don't understand."

"Go get changed," her father said before following the bishop into the family room.

"Go," her mother said. "Get changed. We'll talk later."

Her mother trailed behind her father, and Katie stared after her in disbelief. Didn't her mother care Katie had just been hurt by three men?

Katie hurried up the stairs to her room. Staring at her disheveled reflection in the mirror, she dissolved in sobs.

13

Jake watched Katie drive off in the bishop's buggy, and his body shuddered with a mixture of anger and regret. He wished he'd arrived at the scene earlier. His stomach soured at the thought of those three disgusting men touching Katie. Why hadn't he left the wood supply sooner? He was just glad he was able to stop the incident before it had become even more grim.

Glancing around, Jake found Katie's prayer covering and cloak on the ground. He retrieved them and then climbed into this truck. He had to get to the bakery and tell Elizabeth and Eli what had happened. Speeding toward the bakery, he thought of Katie and the fear he'd seen in her gorgeous blue eyes when he'd driven up. Holding her in his arms and comforting her was the greatest feeling he'd ever experienced. He knew one thing for certain—he'd wanted to comfort her and take away her pain. More than anything, he wanted to be with her. If he could only find a way . . .

Jake steered into the parking lot, pulled into a spot near the front entrance to the bakery, and slammed the truck into park. Grabbing his keys, he raced up the front steps and into the bakery.

"Jake!" Eli called with a smile. "Did you get the supplies?" The older man's smile faded. "What's wrong, son?"

"I need to speak to you and Elizabeth alone right away." Jake started for the kitchen.

"Oh, dear," Eli said. "This sounds serious."

"It is." Jake stepped into the kitchen and nodded at the curious stares the bakers aimed at him and Eli.

"She must be in her office," Eli said, walking beside him. "I think today is her paperwork day."

Jake followed Eli into the office, where Elizabeth sat at her desk writing in her ledger. She looked up as Jake closed the door behind him.

"Eli. Jake," Elizabeth said. "What's going on?"

"I need to speak to you both," Jake said. "It's very important."

"Have a seat." She pointed toward two chairs in front of her desk.

Jake sat on the chair beside Eli and took a deep breath, hoping to calm his still-frayed nerves. "I stopped to get supplies this morning," he began, "and as I was driving in, I saw Katie in distress by the side of the road."

"What?" Elizabeth asked. "What do you mean? She left here to go to the fabric store about thirty minutes ago."

"How was she in distress?" Eli asked.

"Three men accosted her about a block from here," Jake said. "I was able to scare them off."

"What?" Elizabeth stood, her eyes filling with tears. "They hurt my Katie?"

"She's okay," Jake said, motioning for her to sit down. "I stopped them before they could do more than take her covering and rip her dress."

"Oh no," Elizabeth said. "Poor Katie."

"Where is she?" Eli asked.

"Abner Chupp came along as I was comforting her, and he drove her home." Jake stood. "I have her prayer covering and cloak in my truck. I was going to take them to her house for her."

"Would you take us to her?" Elizabeth asked. "I want to go see her and make sure she's okay."

"Of course." Jake stood. "I rushed here as soon as she left with Abner."

"*Danki,*" Elizabeth said. "I'll go tell everyone we have to run an errand, and we can go to Robert's right away. We shouldn't tell anyone what's happened to Katie. I'm certain she's very upset about it, and she won't want people asking questions or spreading the news about it."

"I agree," Eli said while Jake nodded.

As Jake walked through the bakery toward his truck, he prayed Katie was okay.

☙❧

Katie changed into a clean dress before fixing her hair and putting on another prayer covering. She heard the clip-clop of hooves and glanced out the window as Abner's horse and buggy disappeared from her driveway. Her stomach tightened as she wondered what Abner had told her father about seeing her with Jake. She prayed her father would allow her to explain what had happened on the street corner. Surely, her father would thank Jake for saving her instead of chastising him for hugging her.

After rinsing off her tear-streaked face with the water from the washbasin in her room, Katie headed down the stairs and into the kitchen, where her parents stood talking.

"Where are the *kinner*?" Katie asked.

"I sent them outside so we could talk to you about your behavior," her father said, frowning. "I can't believe that less than a week after I punished you for seeing Jake Miller, you disobeyed me again."

"I didn't disobey you," Katie began. "I was walking to the store to get some fabric to make a dress for Janie for her birthday, when three—"

Robert held up his hand. "I'm tired of your excuses, Katie. I don't know what else to do aside from sending you away. It seems you can't stay away from this *bu*. I need to do something to prevent you from seeing him at all."

The back door opened, and her grandparents stepped in.

"Katie!" Her grandmother rushed over and hugged her. "Are you okay? Jake told us what happened."

Katie nodded, her eyes filling with fresh tears. "I'm okay."

"Here," Elizabeth said, handing Katie her cloak and prayer covering. "Jake found these for you."

"*Danki*," Katie said, placing the cloak and covering on a kitchen chair. Her body quaked as she thought of the evil men again.

"I want that Mennonite *bu* fired!" Robert bellowed. "I'm tired of him tempting my Katie Joy."

"No," Katie said, moving her hands over her cheeks. "Don't fire him. I'll stop working at the bakery. Maybe I'll help *Aenti* Rebecca, and Lindsay can go back to the bakery."

"But you love the bakery," her mother said with a frown. "Why would you quit the bakery for that *bu*, Katie?"

"You can't fire him," Katie said, looking at her grandfather. "Remove me from the bakery instead."

"You still defend that *bu*, Katie Joy?" Robert said, scowling. "What will it take to make you forget him?"

"He saved me, *Dat*," Katie said, nearly spitting the words at him. "Why won't you listen to me? I was in grave danger, and he saved me from it."

Her father shook his head. "He's Mennonite, Katie. Abner Chupp said you could be shunned from what he saw on the corner." He looked at Eli. "I want the *bu* fired, *Dat*. This has gone on long enough."

"How can I fire him?" Eli asked. "His *grossdaddi* is part owner in the furniture store. That's a preposterous notion."

"No one will be fired, Robert," Elizabeth said, her expression stern. "This is ridiculous." She turned to Eli. "I will make certain Katie and Jake don't interact at the bakery at all. I can keep my bakers busy if need be. Besides, the project is coming along quickly, *ya*?"

Eli nodded. "*Ya*. We should be done soon."

"Fine," Robert said. "I don't want any contact between them. If there's contact, then there will be more punishment, Katie. As of right now, you're only to leave the *haus* for work and church. Indefinitely."

Katie's heart ached as she studied her father's angry expression. Why didn't he see she was telling the truth? Why didn't he care about her feelings?

"Go to your room, Katie Joy," her father said. "I don't want to see you the rest of the day."

With tears in her eyes, Katie turned toward Elizabeth. "*Danki,*" she whispered.

"Go," Elizabeth said, handing her the prayer covering. "I'll hang up your cloak for you. I'll tell everyone at the bakery you're not feeling well. No one has to know what happened."

"*Danki, Mammi.*" Katie slowly climbed the stairs and wiped her tears from her cheeks. She wished she could start the day over and ask Amanda and Ruthie to go with her to the store. Or perhaps she never should've ventured to the store at all. Katie hung her covering on the peg by her bedroom door and crossed to her window, where she spotted Jake's truck idling in her driveway. Her heart warmed at the sight of him. Jake had brought her grandparents over to see her!

Placing her hand on the cool window glass, she wished she could go thank Jake again for saving her. Despite all of the emotional turmoil she'd suffered today, she knew one thing for certain—she was falling in love with Jake Miller.

⌒≈⌒

"How's Katie?" Jake asked as Elizabeth and Eli climbed into his truck as it sat in Robert's driveway.

Elizabeth frowned, and Jake's heart wrenched in his chest. *She's hurt worse than I imagined!*

"Robert wants you fired so you don't interact with Katie

anymore," Eli said. "Katie insisted I don't fire you, and she offered to quit her job at the bakery in order to save your job."

"She did?" Jake asked with surprise. "But she loves her job."

"I know," Elizabeth said. "I convinced my stubborn son to
allow you both to work there, promising to be certain you're
kept apart."

"I see." Jake nodded, hoping they couldn't tell his heart was
breaking.

Elizabeth's expression was sympathetic. "I know you care
about my granddaughter, but I need you to keep your distance.
I'm thankful you were able to save her today before she was
severely hurt, but I hope you realize how you can get her into
trouble with the church."

"I know." Jake sighed. "I would never do anything to hurt her."

"I know you wouldn't intentionally hurt her." Elizabeth
smiled. "You're a special young man, and she's a lovely young
woman. However, you're from different worlds."

"But we're very thankful for you, Jake," Eli said. "You came
along at the perfect time. God made certain you were there to
save our little Katie Joy."

"How is she?" Jake asked again. "Is she okay?"

Elizabeth frowned again. "She's okay physically, but I could
tell she was shaken up."

"And Robert made it worse." Eli looked disgusted. "Elizabeth
and I tried to talk some sense into him after Katie went up to her
room. But Robert is upset Abner Chupp brought her home and
said she could be shunned for hugging you in public. Robert convinced Abner not to shun her and promised to talk to her. Robert
told her she's not allowed to leave the house, and he wanted you
fired because the bishop came to see him about her behavior."

Jake's mouth gaped with shock. "Robert and the bishop
don't care that Katie was attacked?" he asked.

Elizabeth and Eli shook their heads in unison.

"They don't believe she was attacked," Eli said. "All they know is she was hugging you in public."

"You're saying they're more worried about her hugging me in public than the fact that three men accosted her in public?" Jake asked.

"*Ya,*" Eli said.

Jake ran his hands through his hair while contemplating the ridiculous actions of Robert Kauffman and Abner Chupp. "I can't believe it. Katie could've been in grave danger if I hadn't come along. It doesn't make sense to me that Robert would react like that to the news that his daughter had been attacked."

"I know," Elizabeth said. "However, he's her father, and there's nothing we can do other than abide by his rules."

"We'd better get back to work," Eli said.

Jake put the truck in gear and backed down the driveway, all the while wondering what he could do to find a way to be with Katie so he could protect her.

⎯⎯⎯ ⚭ ⎯⎯⎯

Katie sat on the grass Sunday afternoon and smoothed her hands over her apron. The sky was peppered with gray clouds, which seemed to mirror her dull mood. A slight chill in the air caused her to rub her hands over the long sleeves of her dark blue frock.

She'd struggled to concentrate on the service earlier this morning, but her thoughts were still on her failed relationship with Jake and the nightmarish memories of the men who'd accosted her Friday. The flashbacks had kept her up every night since the incident. The only person who had listened to her about the ordeal and who had offered comfort was Nancy. Katie was so thankful for her younger sister.

Her father avoided all contact with her at the house, and he wouldn't answer her when she'd tried to talk to him last night.

Her mother's reaction to her was also frosty as she offered one-word answers to Katie's questions. It seemed no matter how hard Katie tried, her parents were reluctant to listen to her explanation about what had happened Friday, and the whole situation caused her stomach to ache and her shoulders to tense.

Lindsay and Lizzie Anne continued their conversation about the evening's plans while sitting across from Katie.

"The gathering will be at Mary Elizabeth Zook's *haus* tonight," Lizzie Anne said, breaking an oatmeal cookie in half. "I'm so excited! Samuel is going to pick me up and take me. Is Matthew taking you?"

Lindsay nodded as she chewed a peanut butter cookie. "Ya. He said he's going to pick me up and take me heemet. I'm so glad we can ride together now. I enjoy having time to talk in the buggy."

Katie picked at a blade of grass and wondered if her friends realized they were ignoring her. Perhaps they were as insensitive as her parents.

"Katie?" Lindsay asked. *"Was iss letz?"*

Katie looked at her friends and debated what to share. "Nothing," she finally said. "Everything is fine."

Lindsay and Lizzie Anne glanced at each other.

"I'm sorry," Lizzie Anne said. "We didn't mean to leave you out of the conversation by talking about our boyfriends."

"No," Lindsay chimed in, shaking her head for emphasis. "We didn't at all, Katie. Please don't be upset."

"I'm not upset," Katie said, forcing a smile. "Why would I be upset?"

Lizzie Anne looked concerned. "You can ride with Samuel and me tonight to the youth gathering. I didn't mean to exclude you."

"Danki, but I can't go tonight." Katie yanked more blades of grass out and tossed them toward the toe of her black sneakers.

"What do you mean?" Lindsay asked, looking confused. "Why wouldn't you be able to go?"

"I'm not allowed to leave the *haus* except for church and work." Katie watched her best friends' eyes widen with shock.

"Why?" Lizzie Anne asked.

"What happened?" Lindsay asked.

"I don't even know where to begin," Katie said, shrugging. "I allowed Jake Miller to give me a ride *heemet* from the bakery last Friday when I was stranded without a ride, and *mei dat* was very upset I was alone with a Mennonite *bu*." She hugged her knees and stared at the ground as she spoke. "I was forbidden to see him. I made the mistake of sneaking over to Matthew's driveway to talk to Jake alone the next day. I only wanted to tell him I was forbidden from seeing him or talking to him. Unfortunately, *mei dat* caught me as I was coming back, and he was even more enraged. He asked *Mammi* to watch me at the bakery to be certain I don't even look at Jake Miller again."

"It's all because Jake gave you a ride *heemet*?" Lizzie Anne asked, breaking another cookie apart.

"There's more," Katie said with a lump swelling in her throat. "I avoided Jake all last week, as difficult as it was, and Friday I asked *Mammi* if I could walk to the store to buy fabric to make a dress for Janie for her birthday. While I was walking there ..." Her voice quaked as tears began to trickle from her eyes. She swallowed a deep, shuddering breath.

"Katie." Lindsay moved over, looping her arm over Katie's shoulder. "What's wrong, *mei liewe*?"

"Slow down." Lizzie Anne took Katie's hand in hers. "It's okay. Take your time."

Katie wiped away her tears with the back of her hand. Speaking slowly through fresh tears, she recounted the story of her attack, Jake's rescue, the bishop's interference, her parents' reaction to the incident, and her grandparents' visit. Her friends listened with their mouths gaping.

"Oh, Katie," Lindsay said, pulling her into a hug. "I'm so very sorry this happened to you. You must've been so scared."

Katie nodded while Lizzie Anne hugged her too.

"I don't understand your parents," Lizzie Anne said. "You needed their comfort more than anything, and they punished you instead. I'm so glad your *mammi* believed you."

Katie shook her head. "I don't know what I'd do without *Mammi* or Nancy." She gestured at Lindsay and Lizzie Anne. "Or you two."

"I don't understand." Lindsay looked confused. "Why don't your parents believe you?"

"Why do they think you would even imagine making up something so horrible?" Lizzie Anne chimed in.

"I don't know." Katie shrugged and pulled up more blades of grass. "I guess *mei dat* has lost all confidence in me since I disobeyed him by getting a ride with Jake and then speaking to him at Matthew's house after he told me not to. *Mei dat* is more worried about appearances than anything else, including my feelings or my safety."

"It doesn't make sense at all," Lindsay said, frowning. "You're his *dochder*, and you were hurt. You're what matters most, not what other people think about your behavior."

"I'm surprised at your *mamm*, Katie." Lizzie Anne shook her head with disappointment. "I know she can be strict, but why doesn't she believe you were attacked? Your dress was ripped. What more evidence does she need?"

Katie's lip quivered. "I don't know why she won't talk to me. Sometimes I think she goes along with *mei dat* to keep the peace between them."

"But your feelings should be more important," Lindsay said. "My mother always took time to listen to Jessica and me, even when we were in trouble. Besides, what's so bad about Jake driving you *heemet* when you're stranded?" She looked curious. "And why was he in the bakery in the first place?"

"Jake is working in the bakery now." Katie brushed a few

stray blades of grass off her apron. "He and *Daadi* are building new display cabinets. I had lunch with him and the other bakers a few times. The day I was stranded, *Mammi* thought I'd gotten a ride *heemet* with Samuel. I was taking inventory in the pantry, and when I returned to the kitchen, I realized everyone had left without me. The weather was bad, and no one was answering the phone. Jake insisted on driving me so I didn't have to walk in the rain. When I got *heemet, mei dat* was really upset. He called me disobedient and said I could wind up with a bad reputation if I kept behaving that way."

"You've been eating lunch with Jake?" Lizzie Anne asked between bites of cookie.

"Wait a minute. I'm confused." Lindsay held her hand up. "Do you like Jake Miller, Katie?"

Katie paused and studied Lindsay's curious expression. If she admitted her true feelings for Jake, would it cause problems between her and Lindsay since Jessica used to like him?

"You can tell us," Lizzie Anne said. "We won't tell your *dat*."

"You do like him, don't you?" Lindsay asked.

Katie nodded. "*Ya*, I do."

"Does he like you?" Lindsay asked.

"I don't know," Katie said. "I thought he did, but now I'm just so confused. We can't be together no matter what. We just have to pretend like we don't know each other at all."

"Oh, my." Lindsay looked stunned. "I had no idea you liked Jake."

"You can't tell anyone," Katie said quickly. "Please. I'm already in enough trouble. If word gets around about this, things will get worse for me."

"You can trust us." Lizzie Anne held out a cookie, and Katie took it even though she had no appetite. "I never imagined you would fall for Jake Miller. No wonder you have no interest in the Amish *buwe* in our district."

"It really doesn't matter if I like Jake or not. I'm stuck between a rock and a hard place." Katie's voice trembled, and she hoped she wouldn't cry again. "If I talk to Jake and word gets back to my parents, I'll wind up getting shunned, and I don't want that. It's painful enough as it is, and I miss Jake. I don't see how things could get much worse than this."

"I'm so sorry," Lizzie Anne said. "You must be heartbroken."

Lindsay shook her head, frowning. "I can't imagine how you feel."

"*Danki.*" Katie blew out a sigh. "Nancy and *Mammi* said I'll meet a nice Amish *bu* someday and fall in love, but I just don't believe that could ever happen. How will I ever find someone who is as nice and wonderful as Jake? It seems as if we have a special connection, and I've always believed you only find that once in your lifetime."

"I don't know," Lizzie Anne said, handing Katie another cookie. "But hopefully you'll find someone special. Don't give up hope."

Lindsay smiled. "I agree. You're *schee* and sweet, Katie. There's someone out there for you. I'm sure of it."

Lizzie Anne's eyes lit up. "Maybe after you're allowed to leave the *haus* again, we can go to a youth gathering at another district. My cousins are over in Lititz, and we can go there to see them. I imagine there are some nice and handsome *buwe* out there who'd love to meet you."

"That's a great idea, Lizzie Anne," Lindsay chimed, grinning. "We'll have fun going out there."

Katie sighed while her friends discussed the trip to Lititz. *But the only boy I want is Jake Miller,* she thought.

14

The following morning, Jake steered through the parking lot of the hardware store and merged onto the highway. He'd spent most of the weekend thinking about Katie and worrying about her. He couldn't erase the memory of the fear he'd seen in her eyes when he'd driven up to the scene of her attack. What if he hadn't made it there in time? The thought had haunted him all weekend—along with his frustration with Katie's strict father. How could a father be so cold as to not care when his daughter had been attacked?

Pushing the thought away, Jake glanced over at Eli in the passenger seat. He needed to get his mind focused on his job before he went crazy from frustration. "I think we have everything we need since I picked up the wood Friday."

The older man rubbed his long, graying beard and nodded. "*Ya*, I do think we're all set, at least for a few days." He grinned. "Until *mei fraa* changes her mind about the design again."

Jake nodded. "I guess all wives reserve the right to change their minds, right?"

Eli patted Jake's arm. "You're a smart young man. With that attitude, you'll make a *fraa* happy someday."

Jake forced a smile, but he couldn't keep his thoughts from turning to Katie. He turned to face the older man. "How's Katie doing?"

Eli frowned, and Jake's heart sank with worry.

"She seemed okay yesterday at church," Eli said. "Although I noticed she never once smiled. I'm afraid she's very unhappy and upset about what happened Friday."

Jake shook his head. "I can't even imagine how upset she is. She endured a lot."

Eli touched Jake's arm. "Elizabeth and I are so thankful you helped her, Jake. I know we've already told you, but you truly were an angel Friday. You saved our Katie's life."

Jake's stomach churned as he thought of the incident. He wished he could've done more to comfort Katie, but the bishop had ruined his chance to talk with her further. He knew more than ever that he cared for Katie. In fact, he loved her.

He hoped he could steal a glance at her when they arrived at the bakery. He knew he had to stay away from her in order to prevent more problems, yet he couldn't stop the feeling that he and Katie belonged together. How could Jake bridge the chasm that kept them apart? He needed to be with her. He wanted to protect her and care for her, but how could they ever be together when they lived worlds apart?

"Eli, how did you know you wanted to be baptized into the Amish faith?" Jake asked.

Eli rubbed his beard and considered the question. "I always knew it was something I wanted to do. God had put it in my heart when I was a young boy. Why are you asking, Jacob?"

Jake slowed at a stoplight before facing Eli. "I always wondered why my mother left the church. I know she met my father and converted when they decided to marry, but why did she decide not to be Amish when the rest of her family was?"

"I think that's a question for your *mamm* to answer," Eli said.

"That's very true. In fact, my parents invited me over for supper tonight, so I'll ask her when I see her." Jake paused for a moment and thought of his grandparents. "You've known my grandparents a long time, right?"

"*Ya*, that's true." Eli gazed out the window. "I believe your *daadi* and I were approximately ten or so when we met. Maybe even younger."

"How did my grandparents react when my mother left the church for my father?" The light turned green, and Jake accelerated through the intersection.

Eli was silent for a few moments. "They were very upset and disappointed."

Jake nodded, steering onto Beechdale Road.

"When a *kind* leaves the faith, the parents feel as if they don't know that *kind* at all," Eli continued. "The *kind* who leaves is not the *kind* they raised in the faith."

"My parents have a good relationship with my grandparents now," Jake said. "How did they come to work things out then?"

"The birth of you and your *bruder* helped," Eli said.

Jake let the words soak through him as he motored into the parking lot behind the bakery. He thought of his twin brother, Jeremy, who had died in a car accident when they were sixteen. He missed Jeremy every day of his life.

"My grandparents were a great source of strength for my parents and me when Jeremy died," Jake said.

"*Ya*, I bet they were." Eli nodded. "That was a difficult time."

"But I can see what you mean about how children helped to bridge the gap after my mother was shunned," Jake said.

"*Ya*," Eli agreed. "Your grandparents wanted to be a part of your life, and your parents wanted the same. It took some time, but they worked through it all. I've seen families that never heal, but thanks to their faith and God's help, your family did."

Jake silently considered Eli's words as he steered into a parking space at the back of the bakery and turned off the truck.

Eli patted Jake's shoulder again. "Now let's get this truck unloaded. We need to start working. Unfortunately, those cabinets aren't going to build themselves."

Jake hopped from the truck and stared toward the bakery

while thinking of Katie. Could he possibly steal a moment to speak to her without anyone spotting them together? He wondered how she felt about him. Did she feel anything for him? Was she, too, wondering what to make of this strong connection they shared?

"Jake?" Eli called. "You need to come help me. I'm an old man. Remember?"

"I'm coming, Eli." Jake jogged to the truck bed and tried to focus on hauling the supplies into the bakery.

Katie straightened the packages of cookies and cakes on the display in the front of the bakery. Her grandmother had asked her to complete her work up front before she began her morning baking duties, and Katie hoped she could finish setting out the fresh baked goods before Jake and her grandfather arrived from their supply run.

Although Katie hoped to see Jake, she knew it would be a bad idea. She'd be tempted to speak to him and run the risk of getting into more trouble. Yet she'd replayed the events of Friday frequently in her mind over the weekend, and she wanted to thank him again for saving her.

The squeak of the front door drew Katie's attention to the front of the bakery, where Eli and Jake were entering with a load of supplies. Her cheeks flamed when Jake met her gaze, and she quickly turned her attention back to the task of adding more packages of cookies to the display. She gathered the remaining chocolate chip cookies from the tray she'd used to carry the fresh baked goods from the kitchen and then placed them on the shelf.

"*Wie geht's,*" Eli called as he walked over to the cabinet. "How are you today, Katie Joy?"

"Fine, *danki,*" Katie said, while straightening the rows of chocolate chip cookies. "How are you, *Daadi?*"

"*Gut, gut,*" Eli said, placing the supplies on the floor. "I'm going to go say hello to Elizabeth," he said as he walked through the doorway to the kitchen.

Katie fixed the chocolate chip cookies and lifted the empty tray. As she turned toward the kitchen, she found Jake standing in front of her. Her heart thudded in her chest as they studied each other.

"Good morning," she mumbled, moving past him.

"How are you?" he called after her.

"I'm fine," she said, facing him. "*Danki.*"

"I've been worried about you," he said, his eyes full of concern.

"*Danki* for saving me," she said, gripping the tray in her fingers.

He shook his head. "You don't need to thank me."

Katie pointed toward the kitchen. "I have to go."

"I know." Jake nodded toward the new display cabinets. "I have to work too."

Katie rushed into the kitchen and dropped the tray on the counter with a loud clatter.

"Katie?" Amanda asked. "*Was iss letz?*"

"Nothing." Katie wrung her trembling hands together. "I'm fine." She stared down at her workstation and wished her body would stop quaking. For the first time since she'd begun talking to Jake, she felt awkward around him. When she'd looked into Jake's eyes, all she could think of was how he'd held and consoled her Friday. Why did things have to change between them? How would she ever recover from everything that had happened Friday?

Grabbing a cookbook, Katie flipped through the recipes, her hands still shaking with the confusing emotions that coursed through her body. She stared at the words in the book but couldn't comprehend them. The only thoughts in her mind were of Jake working in the next room while she wasn't permitted to even look at him.

A hand on her shoulder caused her to jump. "Katie?" her grandmother said. "Why don't you take a walk with me?"

Katie glanced up at Elizabeth and nodded. *"Ya, Mammi."*

Elizabeth placed her hand on Katie's arm and led her to the back of the bakery. After pulling on their cloaks, they walked together toward the parking lot. Katie studied Jake's truck while they walked toward the bench on the far end of the lot.

"You seem upset," Elizabeth said, placing her hand on Katie's shoulder again. "I wonder if you should go *heemet* and rest today. You went through a lot on Friday. I think you may have come back to work too soon."

"No," Katie said quickly, shaking her head. "If I go *heemet,* I'll only get into more trouble with *mei dat.* I can't endure any more stress at *mei haus, Mammi.* Please don't make me go *heemet.*"

Elizabeth grasped Katie's hand and shook her head. "No one is going to make you go *heemet,* Katie. It's okay if you stay, but I'm worried about you." She gestured toward the bench. "Have a seat and relax awhile."

Katie lowered herself onto the cool bench and stared at the bakery.

"Talk to me, Katie." Elizabeth took Katie's hand in hers.

Katie shook her head. "I'm so confused, *Mammi.*"

"Why are you confused?" Elizabeth asked, her expression full of sympathy. "You know you can tell me anything."

Katie stared across the parking lot toward Jake's truck while gathering her thoughts. "I have all of these conflicting feelings inside me, and I don't know what to do with them. I'm so angry with my parents. They won't listen to me, and they don't believe what happened on Friday. Lindsay and Lizzie Anne said they should believe me because I'm their *dochder,* and I agree.

But all *mei dat* cares about is how my behavior appeared to the bishop. What about how I feel?" She gestured to her chest. "Why don't I matter to my own parents?"

Elizabeth squeezed Katie's hand. "You do matter, Katie. Your parents aren't thinking clearly right now, but give them time. They'll realize how callous and wrong they've been, and they will apologize to you. I know in my heart that things will get better for you at *heemet*."

Katie sniffed and wiped her eyes. "To make matters even worse, I don't understand my feelings for Jake."

"What do you mean?" Elizabeth looked concerned.

"I just saw Jake, and it was so awkward." Her voice was thick with emotion as she spoke. "There's so much I want to say to him, and I know I can't talk to him. But, at the same time, I can't help how I feel about him."

"How do you feel about him?" Elizabeth asked.

Katie hesitated, afraid of the repercussions if she spoke the truth.

"Katie," Elizabeth began, "do you think you love him?"

Katie bit her lower lip.

Elizabeth shook her head. "We've already discussed this. You know you can't be with him."

"I know that, but I can't change how I feel," Katie said. "I wish I could turn my feelings off, but when I saw him, my heart began to race. I keep thinking we're meant to be together, as *narrisch* as it sounds." She frowned. "I don't even know if he cares for me, but I can't stop thinking of him."

"You're just upset." Elizabeth patted Katie's hand. "You've been through a very scary event, and all of your emotions are jumbled up. Just give yourself some time, and you'll realize you're just thankful Jake came along when he did on Friday." She stood and gestured for Katie to follow. "Why don't you come back into the bakery and take a break in my office? You can even read my Bible for a while. I'm certain it will give you comfort."

Katie followed her grandmother back to the bakery. While her grandmother discussed the pretty fall weather, Katie couldn't stop thinking about Jake. She was certain her feelings for him ran deeper than just appreciation and gratitude. She agreed with her grandmother that her feelings for him were a jumbled messed, but she doubted the feelings would subside after a few weeks.

Yet the problem still remained—although she loved Jake, she couldn't be with him. How would she cope with carrying around her broken heart?

15

As Jake slid his truck into reverse later that evening, he glanced toward the bakery and spotted Katie and her aunts and cousins climbing into the van to go home. He'd spent all day contemplating their brief conversation this morning and wondering what she was feeling. The conversation had been awkward and rushed, as if she couldn't get away from him fast enough. He'd hoped she was in a hurry because her grandfather was going to return to the room, and she wasn't permitted to speak to Jake, not because she didn't want to talk to him.

With a sigh, Jake backed out of the parking space and drove toward the exit. Why did their relationship have to be forbidden? His heart had nearly broken at the desperation in her eyes when she thanked him for saving her Friday. He wondered if she felt the same energy between them that he did.

Jake slowed at a stop sign and looked toward a farm on the corner where Amish children played on the driveway with a wagon. He contemplated what life would've been like if his mother had stayed in the faith. Obviously, he would never have been born, unless his father had converted instead of his mother. Would Jake have gone to school with the Kauffman children, including Katie?

He reflected on the conversation he'd shared with Eli earlier this morning. He longed to find out more about his mother's choice to leave the Amish church and how that choice affected his grandparents.

While he steered toward his parents' street, Jake wondered if his mother would tell him why she'd left the community. Was it only for love or was there something else? He needed to know why, and he planned to ask her when he joined his parents for supper tonight.

⌒∾⌒

Jake spooned a mound of mashed potatoes into his mouth later that evening. He found his cousin, Billy, who frequently visited his parents, and Billy's girlfriend, Heather, were also guests at supper tonight.

"Delicious, Mom." Jake smiled across the table at his mother. "This is a nice change from frozen pizza and TV dinners."

His mother chuckled. "You were always easy to please, Jacob."

"Actually, he's right," Billy chimed in. "Your food is always the best around." He turned to his girlfriend. "You agree?"

Heather finished chewing and swallowed another piece of her steak. "Absolutely, Mrs. Miller."

"How's work been, Billy?" Jake turned to his cousin next to him. "Are you staying busy at the body shop?"

Billy nodded and took a drink. "We've really gotten busy. Seems like a lot of folks are getting into wrecks lately. How's the furniture store?"

"It's been really good." Jake wiped his mouth with a napkin. "I'm working with Eli Kauffman at the bakery right now. Elizabeth wants some new display cabinets for the store area. She asked Eli to build some for her so she can spruce up the bakery for next spring."

"That sounds nice," his father, John, said. "Eli must think a lot of your work since he asked you to help him with the project and not one of the other carpenters."

"Thank you, Pop," Jake said. "This is what I've always wanted to do."

"Oh, I know." His mother, Anna Mary, smiled. "I remember you were always out in my father's shop helping him with a project or two. You loved going to his house. Sometimes you begged me to take you there after you got home from school."

Jake cut up his steak and thought back to those days. Even at the young age of seven, he knew he wanted to be a carpenter. While he continued slicing, he thought about his grandfather and wondered about his mother's decision to leave the Amish church.

He glanced up at his mother who was discussing a future shopping trip with Heather.

"Mom," he said after she finished her conversation, "I've been meaning to ask you something."

"What's that, dear?" Anna Mary asked before taking another bite of mashed potatoes.

"What made you leave the Amish church?" Jake asked.

His mother looked stunned by the question and nearly dropped her fork.

Beside her, John frowned. "I don't think this is an appropriate conversation to have now, Jacob."

"I'm sorry." Jake shifted in his seat and then glanced at Billy, who stared at him in confusion. "Have you gotten your Galaxie running yet? I know you wanted to work on the car once the weather cooled down a little."

"Yeah," Billy said. "I was going to start pulling the frame out from under it tomorrow if I can —"

"I'll answer the question, Jacob," his mother said, interrupting. "I'll tell you the reason."

The room fell silent, and Jake turned to his mother. "Thank you," he said.

"I left after I met your father," she said, smiling at his father.

"We fell in love and wanted to get married. The only way for me to marry him was to leave the church."

"That had to be a difficult decision," Jake said, placing his fork on the plate. "You must've mulled it over for quite some time."

Anna Mary nodded. "I did. I also talked to my grandmother about it."

"Your grandmother?" Jake asked. "You never told me that."

"I talked to her before I told anyone else in my family." Anna Mary put her hand on John's. "We both talked to her actually. We met her in secret one night. My parents didn't know anything about it. I'm certain they would've been upset I discussed it with her before I told them, but my grandmother and I were very close. I knew she would listen without getting too emotional before I finished explaining everything to her."

Billy looked just as intrigued as Jake felt. "What did she say?"

"My grandmother said she understood, but she was disappointed I wanted to leave. She said she knew love could make people do hasty things, and she told me to pray about it to see where God led me." Anna Mary paused to collect her thoughts. "I prayed about it." She glanced at John. "In fact, your father and I prayed about it together, and I kept coming to the same conclusion. I knew in my heart your father and I were meant to be together, which meant I needed to leave the church in order to be with him. I broke the news to my parents after reaching that conclusion."

"How did they take it?" Jake asked.

Anna Mary shook her head. "They were very upset. My mother cried, and my father was so upset he couldn't speak. They didn't understand how I could walk away from the only life I'd ever known. I tried to explain to them I would still worship the Lord, but I would do it in a different way."

"Did Pop go with you when you told them?" Jake asked.

"No, no," his mother said. "That would've made it worse. In

fact, they said your father and his family weren't welcome in their house. They didn't even come to the wedding."

"They didn't come to your wedding?" Heather asked, looking aghast. "How could they miss their daughter's wedding?"

"They'd shunned her," John explained. "It's a very complicated tradition, but it's meant to encourage those who have strayed to come back to the fold. Plus, they didn't agree with the wedding, so they couldn't attend and pretend they did."

"But they changed their minds eventually," Billy added, slicing up his steak. "You have a good relationship now."

"Jake is the reason we rebuilt our relationship with my parents," his mother said while grabbing a roll from the basket in the center of the table.

"That's what Eli told me," Jake said. "He said when Jeremy and I were born, we broke down the barriers between you and your parents."

"That's true," Anna Mary said, her eyes glistening with tears. "It's hard thinking back to those days since Jeremy is gone." She shook her head. "I know it's been a long time, but I'll always miss him every day."

Jake nodded. "I know. I miss him too." After a moment of silence, Jake continued, "Can you tell me what happened when you worked things out with Grandma and Grandpa?"

"Of course." She sniffed and wiped her eyes. "I went to visit my parents one day and told them I was expecting a baby. I didn't know at the time that I was going to have twins. I explained that I wanted them to be a part of the baby's life. My father resisted at first, but my mother cried and hugged me. She said she could never turn away her grandchild. It took some time to rebuild our relationship, but we did."

Jake contemplated her words. It had been painful for his mother to leave the faith, but what if the situation had been reversed? "What if it were the other way around?"

"What do you mean?" John asked, stabbing a slab of steak.

"What if someone wanted to join the Amish church? Would the church welcome them?" Jake lifted his glass of water.

"I don't understand," his mother said, looking confused. "People join the church all the time."

Jake sipped the water. "I'm talking about an outsider. What if someone who wasn't Amish wanted to become Amish?"

His parents glanced at each other.

"I don't know, son," John said. "I guess they would welcome him if his intentions were good and genuine. Why do you ask?"

Jake shrugged. "I'm just wondering what it would've been like if Mom had stayed in the Amish church and you had tried to join it."

Anna Mary chuckled. "I don't think that ever would've happened."

"You don't think I could be Amish?" John looked offended.

His mother shook her head. "You've always loved your vehicles and your other modern conveniences like indoor lighting. You wouldn't have done well as an Amish man."

"You wouldn't either," Heather said, nudging Billy with her elbow. "You like your car projects too much."

Billy nodded. "You're right. I wouldn't last a day without my sports car."

Jake watched his cousin interact with his girlfriend, and he wished Katie were there enjoying supper with his family. Why did their different faiths have to keep them apart?

"Time for dessert," Anna Mary said, standing up and gathering dishes. "Who wants apple pie and ice cream?"

⌒⥊⌒

That evening, Katie stared at the shadows the wind blowing the trees outside the window projected onto her bedroom ceiling. The strange shapes morphing above her seemed a fitting analogy for her life. In the past few weeks she'd gone from being certain of her place and future in the community to being confused and doubtful.

She rolled onto her side while contemplating her day at the bakery. When she'd talked to Jake in the bakery, she'd been rendered breathless while her body quaked. It was as if the energy between them was palpable and sparking in the air around her like lightning in a late summer storm. Had he felt it too?

The feeling had been so overwhelming it had frightened her and made her question what it all meant. This attraction was something she'd never experienced. Was it as strong as what her brother felt for Lizzie Anne or the connection Lindsay and Matthew shared?

Although Katie had felt comforted while reading the Bible in her grandmother's office, she had found herself mulling those questions over and over again during the remainder of the day. Her thoughts kept creeping back to the conversation she'd had with her grandmother last week when Elizabeth had told her about the woman who'd left the community to marry an *Englisher*. Was this the beginning of that life-changing road her grandmother's friend had taken? She remembered other stories about community members who had left. Was this how Lindsay's mother had felt when she'd met Lindsay's father at the market? Was it also how Jake's mother had felt before she converted and became a Mennonite?

Those thoughts led Katie to another nerve-wracking question: Was God telling Katie to break the vow she'd made to the church less than a month ago? No, she couldn't possibly leave. She loved her community and her family too much. Yet she couldn't stop believing she and Jake were meant to be together.

Due to her confusion and inner turmoil, Katie had remained in the kitchen as much as possible after seeing Jake. At noon, she'd taken her lunch bag outside to eat with her younger cousins, and she was thankful she hadn't run into Jake again. Yet, at the same time, she'd missed him and longed to see him. How could she avoid him and miss him all at the same time? Was this how confusing falling in love was?

Burrowing down into her pillow, Katie cupped her hands to her face and moaned. *I'm so confused!*

"Katie?" Nancy asked from her side of the double bed they shared. *"Was iss letz?"*

Tears pooled in Katie's eyes. "Nothing. Just go to sleep."

"You're not telling me the truth," Nancy said. "I can hear it in your voice."

Katie sniffed. "My allergies are acting up. I'm fine. Please go to sleep."

"Just tell me what's wrong, and I'll go to sleep."

"Fine," Katie said. "I'm upset about something." She sat up and considered how much to tell her sister. Although she trusted Nancy, she didn't want Nancy to feel obligated to tell their parents.

"What is it, Katie?" Nancy asked with impatience. "Just tell me. You can trust me."

"I can't tell you," Katie said, her voice trembling. "If you find out, you may feel you have to tell *Mamm* and *Dat*. I don't want you to be caught in the middle if anything happens."

Nancy sat up. "Is it that bad?"

"I don't know," Katie whispered. "I'm so confused."

"Then tell me what it is." Nancy leaned over and turned on the battery-powered lantern on her bedside table. The glow illuminated her blonde hair.

"I'm confused about my feelings." Katie picked at the pattern on the quilt in order to avoid her sister's probing stare. "I just don't know what to do about them because it's all so very jumbled up inside me."

"Is this about what happened Friday?" Nancy asked, looking concerned. "Do you need to talk about it some more?"

"No, it's not that, but *danki* for offering to listen." Katie leaned back against the headboard and drew her knees up to her chest. "It's about a *bu*. I talked to *Mammi* today, and she's warned me to be careful because this could cause more problems for me. But how can I deny how I feel? I've tried to forget him, but I just can't. I'm so confused I don't know what to do or how to feel."

Nancy looked confused for a moment and then her eyes flew open. "It's Jake Miller, isn't it?"

Katie nodded.

"Oh, Katie." Nancy shook her head and frowned. "You're already in so much trouble with *Mamm* and *Dat*. You have to try to let go of your feelings for him. I hate seeing you struggle with this."

Katie stared up at the ceiling, wishing it held the answer to her problems. "I don't know what to do now. I saw him today, and I was actually trembling. I've never felt that way before. It was so awkward and uncomfortable. I can't even explain it, and the feelings were so strong, Nancy. But, at the same time, I know we're not meant to be." She looked at her sister's intrigued expression. "But then I wonder if we are meant to be, would God lead me to Jake only to break my heart?"

Nancy grinned. "You're in love."

"And a lot of good that's done me." Katie frowned. "I'm more unhappy now than when I felt all alone. It was bad enough watching Lizzie Anne and Lindsay fall in love, but now I've found someone I care for and I'm miserable."

Her sister's smile faded. "Don't look at it that way. You never know. Maybe there's a way it can work out for you and Jake."

"How?" Katie asked. "The only way I can see that happening is if I leave the church and am shunned. I don't want to leave my family or the church. This is where I belong."

"Hmm." Nancy tapped her chin with her fingertip. "That's true."

"There's no other way." Katie shook her head. "It's hopeless."

Nancy yawned. "I don't know what to tell you. What did *Mammi* say?"

"She told me my feelings are all jumbled up because of the attack. She said once I sort through it all, I'll see I wasn't meant to be with Jake. She thinks I'll meet an Amish *bu* and be *froh*. But as much as I want to believe her, I can't." Katie frowned. "Nancy, you have to promise me you won't tell anyone about this, *ya*? You must promise me this will stay between us."

Her sister looked serious. "I won't tell anyone, but I think you need to be careful." She touched Katie's arm. "I know you don't want to believe *Mammi*, but I think she's right. You have to try to stop thinking about Jake or you're going to get into more trouble."

Katie pursed her lips. "I know you're right. Jake and I simply can't be together, and I need to accept that."

Nancy frowned. "I'm sorry, but it's the truth. I'm worried about you, Katie. If things get any worse, *Dat* might send you away." She touched Katie's hand. "I couldn't bear to lose you, *schweschder. Ich liebe dich.*"

Katie hugged her sister. "*Ich liebe dich* too."

Nancy yawned. "We need to get some sleep. It's getting late." Reaching over she flipped off the lantern and snuggled under the covers. "*Gut nacht.*"

"*Danki* for talking this through with me," Katie said. "What you said made perfect sense." She rolled onto her side facing the wall. Her sister's breathing changed, and soon she was snoring in the soft way Katie had become accustomed to hearing every night since they were very young.

Closing her eyes, Katie turned her thoughts to God and silently recited her evening prayers. Soon, however, she found herself pleading with God for help with her predicament.

Why does this have to be so difficult, God? Please show me how You want me to live my life. I need Your guidance.

As tears trickled down Katie's cheeks, she fell asleep.

16

The following evening, Jake steered down Beechdale Road and contemplated his day. Working in the same building with Katie and not being allowed to speak to her had been pure torture. Although he enjoyed his work on the display cabinets, he more than once considered asking Eli if he could go back to working at the store and have one of the other carpenters replace him at the bakery. Yet he knew he'd let Eli down if he did that, and he also wanted to stay in the bakery even if he couldn't see Katie. Just knowing she was there was sort of a comfort to him, as crazy as it seemed.

Jake merged onto his street and then slowed. His thoughts drifted to his conversation with his parents, and he turned around to head back to his grandfather's house.

The truck moved onto the street his grandparents lived on, and he couldn't help but smile. Visiting his grandparents had always been a welcome treat. He spotted the farm and drove into the rock driveway. He studied the house, the same white two-story residence where his mother had grown up as an only child.

Jake looked toward the large barn and the small shed that had been converted into a shop beside it. He'd spent many days playing in the barn and working with his grandfather in his shop. Those were some of his best childhood memories.

As he eased the truck up toward the house, the front door opened to reveal his grandfather smiling and waving. Jake hopped out of the truck and started up the path toward the front porch.

"Jacob!" Elmer came down the stairs and greeted him with a handshake. "What a pleasant surprise. Did you come to join us for supper?"

"Actually, Grandpa," Jake began, "I came to talk with you."

"Oh," Elmer said. "Let's have a seat on the porch, and if you have time after we're finished talking, maybe you can join us for supper. Sound good?"

"Absolutely." Jake followed his grandfather up the steps and took a seat in a rocker next to him. "How was your day?"

"*Gut*," Elmer said, tugging his long, graying beard. "How was yours?"

"Fine." Jake leaned back in the rocker. "The display cabinets are starting to shape up. I think Elizabeth is happy with them."

"*Gut*," Elmer said. "We miss you at the store, but I'm glad you're helping Eli." He folded his hands on his lap. "What did you want to discuss with me, Jacob?"

Jake ran his fingers over the arms of the chair. "This is the rocker I helped you sand when I was about ten, right?"

"It is." Elmer grinned. "You remember that?"

"I remember it like it was yesterday." Jake glanced back toward the shop. "I was thinking on the way over how much I loved spending time here with you and Grandma. My days spent here were some of the best of my childhood."

"*Danki*," his grandfather said with a wide smile. "It makes me quite happy to hear you say that. I'm certain I enjoyed it as much as you. The day you told me you wanted to be a carpenter like me was one of the best days of my life."

"Do you ever regret being Amish?" Jake asked.

"Do I regret being Amish?" Elmer looked confused. "Why would you ask that, Jacob?"

"I've been thinking lately about the differences between the Amish and Mennonite faiths and wondering what inspired you and Grandma to stay in the Amish faith and my mother to leave."

Elmer was silent for a moment while he tugged his beard. "Your grandma and I never wanted any other life for ourselves, but your mother did. In the end, it all worked out, and we're still a family."

"What do you think caused Mom to leave the Amish church?" Jake asked.

"You already know she met your father and fell in love," Elmer said.

"But there had to be more than that, right?" Jake pressed on. "It had to be more than her love for him."

"She felt God put the decision in her heart, and I believe that," Elmer said. "I didn't at first, but I was hurt, as was your grandmother. Once I overcame the hurt, I realized Anna Mary never truly connected with the Amish community like her friends did. Looking back, it made sense she decided to become Mennonite and marry your father."

Jake ran his hands over the arms of the chair while considering his grandfather's words. "Was it a tough transition when Mom became Mennonite?"

Elmer shrugged. "I'm not really certain about that. I wasn't around her when she converted. I'm certain she missed us as much as we missed her. But she had your father and his family. They welcomed her with open arms, which I assume helped her through the pain."

"Do you think Mennonites are more accepting of people who convert than those who convert to the Amish faith?" Jake asked.

Elmer looked surprised. "That's a really tough question, Jake. I'm not sure I can answer it."

"But you just said Mom was accepted with open arms into Dad's family," Jake said. "Would a person who is converting into the Amish faith also be welcomed?"

"I would suppose so. I can't think of anyone who joined our community from another faith."

"Not one?" Jake asked.

Elmer looked suspicious. "Why are you asking all of these questions, Jacob? You already know your mother left the faith. Why is it troubling you after all these years?"

"I guess I have questions about what happened when she left," Jake said. "I'm thinking about the what-ifs, you know? For example, what if my father had converted and become Amish? Would you and Grandma have accepted him?"

Elmer rubbed his beard again, considering the question. "I suppose your grandma and I would've accepted John. It's not our place to judge others. If his intentions had been true in the eyes of God, then he would've been part of the community. However, it's rare for people to convert to our faith. They have to sacrifice quite a bit."

"Do you think I would make a good Amish man?" Jake asked.

"You?" Elmer gestured toward Jake. "I think you'd be a fine Amish man."

"Really and truly, Grandpa?" Jake asked. "Or are you just joking?"

"No, I'm not joking." Elmer looked serious. "You realize what converting would mean though, *ya*? If you were Amish, you'd have to give up your truck, your electricity, your phone in your house, and all of your modern conveniences." He pointed toward his jeans. "And your clothes. You'd have to get a haircut and trade in your jeans for some real trousers and suspenders. No more fancy ball caps; only straw and black felt hats."

"I know, Grandpa," Jake said, smiling. "But being Amish is about more than driving a horse and buggy and dressing a certain way. Do you think I would be a good member of the community if I were Amish instead of Mennonite?"

"You're right, Jacob, it is about more than clothes and buggies." Elmer smiled. "*Ya*, you'd make a fine Amish man. Your grandma and I would have loved it if you were raised Amish. You know I'd love having you with me at worship on Sundays."

Jake's heart warmed at his grandfather's words.

"Jacob!" his grandmother, Malinda, called from the doorway. "What brings you out here?"

"Hi, Grandma," Jake said. "I wanted to talk with Grandpa for a bit."

"Come inside now," Malinda said. "You must eat supper with us." She frowned. "I won't take no for an answer, young man."

"Yes, Grandma." Jake stood and gestured for his grandfather to enter the house first.

Malinda hurried ahead of them. When Jake entered the kitchen, she was setting a place for him. "You sit here," she said, placing the plate, utensils, and glass next to his grandfather.

"*Danki*," Jake said. "I really appreciate the invitation."

"Don't be silly," she said. "Just sit." She brought a pitcher of ice water to the table. "Here's some water."

Jake glanced around the table, taking in the roast, potatoes, carrots, and homemade bread in the center of the table. He breathed in the delicious smells and smiled. "Everything looks *appeditlich*."

"*Danki*," his grandmother said with a grin. "*Kannscht du Pennsilfaanisch Dietsch schwetze?*"

"*Ya*," Jake said with a laugh. "I've been brushing up on *mei Dietsch*."

His grandma looked pleased as she glanced at his grandfather. "That's *gut, ya*?"

"Absolutely." Grandpa winked at Jake before bowing his head in prayer.

Jake followed suit, silently thanking God for the meal and for his family and also asking for guidance with the confusion about Katie burdening his heart. Once the prayer was over, they began to eat, passing the platters and filling their plates with the meal that was causing Jake's stomach to growl.

"Elmer tells me you've been working at the bakery," Malinda began. "Tell me about your project."

Between bites of the food and sips of water, Jake described the display cabinets he and Eli had been designing and installing in the bakery. His grandmother listened with interest while he talked.

"They sound lovely, Jacob," Malinda said. "I'll have to come by to see them sometime."

"Maybe I'll take you over there one day soon," Elmer said. "You haven't been to the bakery in quite a while."

"I'd love to pick up some of Elizabeth's chocolate cake," his grandmother said. "I could never match her recipe. I'm convinced she has a secret ingredient she's not sharing with anyone in the district."

Jake chuckled as he sipped more water. "You just might be right about that."

"What brings you here tonight, Jacob? You said you needed to talk to your grandfather." She looked excited. "Can you share your secret with me? Do you have a wedding date set? Is that what this is about?"

"No, Grandma," Jake began, "I'm sorry I'm not announcing a wedding. I know you'd like to see me married, but I don't think that will happen soon for me."

"Oh." She looked confused as she sliced another piece of roast for herself. "What is it then?"

"Jacob was asking me about when Anna Mary left the Amish faith." His grandfather looked serious. "He has some questions he felt he needed answered."

"Oh." Malinda looked surprised. "What did you want to know?"

"I know it was a hard time for you and Grandpa when my mom left," Jake said. "I've heard the family was healed when my brother and I were born. Is it true it took the birth of your grandchildren to heal your hearts?"

"*Ya*," Malinda said. "It was a very painful and complicated time for us." She glanced at Elmer, and he nodded in agreement. "We felt like we lost our daughter when Anna Mary left, but we always loved her. When you and your brother were born, it was as if our family was renewed. The pain of her leaving wasn't erased, but it was easier to accept she was gone from our community."

"Do you think it's like that when any member leaves the community?" Jake asked. "Is it always that painful for the parents?"

Malinda nodded. "*Ya*, I think so. It's never easy when a member leaves, no matter what the circumstances are." She looked curious. "Why are you asking about this now?"

"Jake was wondering what life would've been like if he'd been raised Amish," Elmer said. "He asked if we would've accepted John if he converted instead of Anna Mary."

"Why not?" She shrugged, buttering a homemade roll. "If he truly wanted to be Amish, we would've welcomed him into our family just like any other family member."

"Jacob asked if I thought he'd make a good Amish man," Elmer said, smiling. "I told him absolutely."

His grandmother's grin was wide. "*Ya*, you would, Jacob. I would've loved to have seen you be baptized into the faith, but we love you no matter what."

"*Danki*," Jake said, and his grandparents laughed.

While his grandparents continued to talk, he contemplated his grandmother's words. After hearing how much pain his mother caused when she left, he knew he could never ask Katie to leave her family and become Mennonite. He couldn't bear the thought of causing her or her family any more pain.

17

Rebecca sat across from Lindsay at a small restaurant on a Thursday afternoon a month later. She sipped her water and smiled. "The doctor said everything looks *gut*. I should stay on complete bed rest, but my blood pressure is excellent, and the *boppli*'s development is perfect."

"That's *wunderbaar gut!*" Lindsay clapped her hands together. "And the ultrasound was *gut* too?"

"*Ya.*" Rebecca sipped her water again to wet her parched throat. "Daniel was excited, and he squeezed my hand so hard, I yelped."

Lindsay smiled. "I wish he could've come to lunch with us, but I guess they're very busy at the store finishing up Christmas orders."

"*Ya*, I know, but it was nice of him to tell us to go ahead and enjoy lunch. I wanted to do something special for you today. You've been working so hard for me." Rebecca leaned forward and took her niece's hands in hers. "I'm so thankful for you, Lindsay. You've been very generous and thoughtful throughout this pregnancy. I know you'd rather be working with your *freinden* and cousins at the bakery, but you've been stuck with me and the *kinner* all day every day. I'm glad Nancy could come over today to relieve you so we could have a special lunch together."

Lindsay waved off Rebecca's words. "You're just *gegisch. Ich liebe dich* and the *kinner* more than anything. At *heemet* with you and them is where I'd rather be. Besides, I'm not with you all day every day. I get to see *mei freinden* at church and at youth gatherings." She looked curious. "Now your due date has stayed the same, *ya?*"

Rebecca nodded. "Early January is what the doctor says."

"Yay." Lindsay clapped her hands again. "I can't wait! I'll have another little cousin."

The waitress arrived with their grilled chicken sandwiches and potato chips, and Rebecca and Lindsay prayed before beginning to eat.

"Have you heard from Jessica?" Rebecca asked, grabbing a chip from her plate.

Lindsay shook her head. "No, it's been quite a while since I've heard from her. I may call her this evening."

"*Ya,*" Rebecca said. "Please do. I'd like to know if she's still planning to come for the holidays. I hope she does. I miss her."

"I do too." Lindsay sipped her soda. "Last I heard, she was coming for Christmas, but she can't get away before then. She's taking a very difficult load of classes this semester and can't afford the time away from her schoolwork the weekend of Thanksgiving."

Rebecca shook her head, thinking of her older niece. "Jessica works awfully hard. Sometimes I worry about her."

"I do too." Lindsay frowned. "I hope she doesn't work so much that she gets sick like she did after her internship. She was putting in about fifty hours per week, and she sounded awful when she finished up. Nothing is worth getting yourself that sick."

"I agree," Rebecca said. "The holidays are coming fast, *ya?*"

"*Ya,* they are." Lindsay placed her sandwich on her plate. "I can't believe Lizzie Anne's wedding is only a few weeks away. The material she bought for her dress and the attendants' dresses is going to be beautiful. It's royal blue."

"That's lovely." Rebecca smiled. "I'm sure she's very excited."

Lindsay nodded while chewing more of her sandwich. "I just wish Katie had been involved in more of the planning. It isn't the same without her around. I hope her *dat* will forgive her before the wedding. Her father said it was indefinite, but surely he will forgive her and lift it at some point."

"Have you heard how she's doing?" Rebecca asked.

"I haven't seen her since church two weeks ago," Lindsay said, lifting a potato chip from her plate. "Lizzie Anne saw her the other day when she went to visit Samuel, and she said Katie is very unhappy." She shook her head. "I feel so bad for her. She tries to make it up to her parents by helping more around the house when she's not at work." She looked incredulous. "I still can't believe she and Jake have feelings for each other. I always hoped Jake and *mei schweschder* would work things out even though they are so very different."

Rebecca considered the comment. "I agree Jake and Jessica are different. They may like each other and be attracted to each other, but I think they want a different kind of life. Jessica wants something fast-paced, and Jake is satisfied working in a furniture store and having a simple life. I don't think they would mesh very well."

Lindsay nodded. "You're right. I thought they gave each other balance, but they could never be together since they want such different things in life." She ate a few more chips. "But Katie and Jake could never be together either. He's not Amish. I feel so bad for her because she's stuck at *heemet* with a broken heart while I'm getting to know Matthew better, and Lizzie Anne is planning her wedding. Poor Katie must be so lonely. I wish I could make things better for her, but I know it's not my place to get involved. I would only make it worse with her *dat* if I said something to him."

Rebecca took another bite of her sandwich, chewed, and

swallowed it. "You're right. It's not our place to get involved, but Katie must be lonely. I wonder if you could go visit her. Do you think her *dat* would allow that?"

A serious expression marred Lindsay's features as she shook her head. "Samuel said Katie is completely cut off from all of her friends, except for seeing us at church. Her *dat* is very strict."

Rebecca ate more of her sandwich and thought of her sweet niece. She'd always known Robert and Sadie were tough on their children. She could recall many times when Robert reprimanded his children for insignificant infractions in front of the whole Kauffman family, embarrassing the children and the rest of the family at once. On one occasion, he'd hollered and then spanked Samuel for turning his head just before one of the younger children fell off the swing set. In reality, it was an honest mistake, but in Robert's eye it was an inexcusable lapse of attention.

After witnessing many incidents like those, Rebecca had always secretly vowed to be more loving and forgiving to her own children if she and Daniel were blessed to become parents. Now she and Daniel were parents, and she hoped she lived up to that promise to herself.

"I'm sorry to hear Katie is having a hard time," Rebecca said. "I hope she is back at your youth gatherings to meet more *buwe* soon." She smiled. "You mentioned you're getting to know Matthew better. How's that going?"

Lindsay's pretty mouth formed an embarrassed smile. "It's going well."

"Oh?" Rebecca leaned in closer. "Can you share more with me?"

"He's very thoughtful and kind." Lindsay stared down at her half-eaten sandwich and moved the remaining pile of chips around on her plate. "He enjoys romantic walks when we're at the youth gatherings. We talk about everything. I feel like I can share things with him without worrying he'll think I'm *gegisch* or immature. He always seems to understand. And when we're together, time flies by. We can start talking about something, and an hour goes by in a flash."

"I remember those days with Daniel," Rebecca said, smiling. "He and I used to talk for hours when we were getting to know each other. Those were some of our best times together. Be sure to enjoy getting to know him."

"Oh, I am." Lindsay picked up a potato chip. "Did you feel like you could see your future when you were dating *Onkel* Daniel? What I mean is—did you feel like you were always meant to be together? Did you know you would someday get married and have a family?"

Rebecca wiped her mouth while considering the questions. "I think I always knew in my heart Daniel was my future."

Lindsay smiled. "I feel that way with Matthew. I think he's my future."

"That's *gut*," Rebecca said, lifting her sandwich. "I'm so glad you met him. I believe he's a very nice young man and will treat you well."

They discussed Lizzie Anne's wedding while they finished their sandwiches.

When Rebecca ate her last chip, she glanced at the clock on the wall. "We'd better get going. I don't want Nancy to worry. I'll go ask if I can use the phone to call the driver."

"No, no." Lindsay stood. "You rest. I'll call."

As Lindsay walked toward the front of the restaurant, Rebecca smiled. She was so very thankful for her wonderful niece.

⊘∾∾∾∾⊘

Lindsay sat on the porch later that evening and smiled at Matthew. "I'm so *froh* you stopped by. I've been thinking of you today."

"Have you?" He grinned and his eyes sparkled. "I'm glad I had to return a few tools to Daniel."

"Did you really have to return them to him today?" she asked.

"No." He moved closer to her on the swing. "I just really had to see you."

"Oh?" Her heart skipped a beat. "Why did you have to see me?"

"Because it's been a few days," he said. "How is your family?"

"Wunderbaar gut," Lindsay said with excitement. "Rebecca, Daniel, and I went to her doctor today, and she received a *gut* report. The *boppli* is growing well, and Rebecca's blood pressure is fantastic. She has to remain on bed rest, but everything is going as it should."

"I'm glad to hear it," he said. "I'm just *froh* to see you, Lindsay."

He looked at her with an intense expression that made her heart thud in her chest. She studied his handsome face and wondered what he would look like with a beard. The thought excited and scared her all at once. Yet, it was difficult not to wonder if Matthew would ask her to marry him since Lizzie Anne and Samuel would marry in only a few weeks. Would Lindsay and Matthew possibly be the next married couple in their youth group?

"Tell me about your day," Lindsay said. She listened with interest while he talked about his current projects at the furniture store. She loved hearing him discuss his work, and she wondered if someday he would create furniture for their home. She smiled at the thought.

The back door opened with a squeak, and Lindsay jumped at the sight of her uncle. "*Onkel* Daniel," she said. "I didn't hear you in the kitchen."

"Matthew," Daniel said, holding out his hand. "*Wie geht's?* I didn't realize you were here."

"I came to return those tools you loaned me last week." Matthew stood and shook Daniel's hand.

"Oh," Daniel said. "You didn't need to do that, but *danki*." He motioned for Matthew to follow him toward the barn. "Since you brought the tools, I guess we might as well put them away."

Matthew glanced back at Lindsay with an apologetic smile before following Daniel to the buggy for the tools.

She watched as Matthew and Daniel disappeared into the barn and bit her lower lip, hoping they would return quickly so that her uncle would go back into the house and she and Matthew could talk more.

She clung to the thought as she stared at the barn door.

Eventually, she frowned.

What's taking so long?

⌒≈⌒

Matthew followed Daniel into the barn and placed the tools on the workbench. "*Danki* for loaning these to me."

"*Gern gschehne,*" Daniel said. "How's your project coming along?"

"Really well." Matthew cleared his throat and folded his arms over his chest in order to stop his hands from shaking. Taking a deep breath, he mustered up the confidence to ask Daniel the question he'd wanted to ask for weeks. "Daniel, I wanted to talk to you about something."

"Oh?" Daniel asked as he hung the tools on the pegboard. "What did you need to discuss?"

"It's about Lindsay," Matthew began, hoping he'd choose the right words. "You know I care for her, *ya*?"

After hanging up the last tool, Daniel faced him. "Of course

I do. I see how you two are together. In fact, you and Lindsay remind me of Rebecca and me when we were your age."

"We do?" Matthew asked with surprise.

"You do." Daniel hopped up on a stool nearby. "What did you want to discuss about Lindsay?"

"I've been doing a lot of thinking," Matthew said. "And I'm at a point in my life when I'm ready to be out on my own. I love *mei schweschder* and her family, but I'm a man now and ready to have my own *heemet*. I can't live with Betsy forever."

Daniel nodded. "I understand."

"*Mei schweschder* and her husband offered me a piece of their land, and I plan to start building a *haus* soon." Matthew paused, gathering his thoughts. "Daniel, I want to ask Lindsay to marry me, but I need your blessing before I ask her."

"Matthew." Daniel jumped up from the stool and shook his hand. "*Ach*, of course you have my blessing, and I know you have Rebecca's too. We think the world of you, son."

Matthew blew out a sigh. "*Danki. Danki* so much, Daniel."

Daniel slapped Matthew's arm. "This is *wunderbaar* news. I know Lindsay will be thrilled."

"Please keep it to yourself, *ya?*" Matthew asked. "I'm not going to ask her until Christmastime. I want to finish the project for her first."

"I won't tell a soul, Matthew." Daniel smiled again. "What a *wunderbaar* Christmas gift for Lindsay. And my brothers and I will help you with your new *haus*. You'll have a crew of carpenters at your disposal."

Matthew smiled while he thought of his future with Lindsay.

⚬⚬⚬

After what seemed like fifteen minutes, the men reappeared. Lindsay stood by the porch railing while they continued their conversation. She wondered what two men who worked together every day could possibly have to talk about for so long. She considered walking down to the barn and breaking up the conversation, but she knew it would be rude. Yet, it was still tempting.

Matthew and Daniel sauntered back toward the porch, and Lindsay tried her best to catch Matthew's eye. He met her gaze before he climbed the stairs, and he looked apologetic.

"It was *gut* talking to you," Daniel said while holding his hand out again. "I'll see you at the shop."

Matthew shook his hand. "*Danki* again for the use of your tools, Daniel. I truly appreciate it. I'll see you tomorrow."

Daniel turned his gaze up to the sky. "You better head *heemet* soon. It'll be getting dark shortly."

"I plan to leave very soon," Matthew said. "I was going to say *gut nacht* to Lindsay now."

Lindsay shot Matthew a sideways glance. *And I hope we can talk a little before you leave.*

Daniel turned to Lindsay. "Don't be out here too late."

"I won't," she said. "I want to call Jessica, but I'll be in after I talk to her."

"Keep it short," Daniel said. "It's almost bedtime." He smiled at them both. *"Gut nacht."*

"Gut nacht," Matthew repeated as Daniel disappeared through the door. Once Daniel was out of sight, Matthew took Lindsay's hand and gently pulled her down the porch steps.

"Where are you taking me?" she asked, as the warmth of his skin radiated up her arm.

Letting go of her hand, Matthew gestured toward the buggy. "I thought we could stand by the buggy so we're out of sight of the kitchen windows." They reached the buggy and he faced her. "I brought you something," he said.

"You did?" Lindsay asked, smiling.

"Open your hand." He pulled something from his pocket.

Lindsay held out her hand and he placed something into it. She looked down and found a duck carved out of wood. "Matthew," she said. "It's gorgeous."

"I hope you don't think it's *gegisch*." He looked embarrassed. "I was working on a project in my shop at the house, and I had an extra little piece of wood. I was thinking about the time we walked around the pond at Lizzie Anne's house and we saw those ducks. You said the ducks reminded you of the pond behind your parents' house back in Virginia. I thought maybe this would help you remember your former *heemet*."

"I love it, Matthew." She couldn't hide her smile. "It's beautiful." She pulled the heart from her apron pocket. "I'll keep it close like the heart you made for me." She held up the heart, and he looked surprised.

"You carry the heart with you?" he asked.

"Always." She stared into his eyes and warmth filled her as he smiled back at her. "*Danki*. I love the duck."

"*Gern gschehne*." He glanced back toward the house. "I better go. I don't want your *onkel* to be upset by my overstaying my welcome. I need him to like me so I can see you often."

"I know he likes you. You're like a son to him." She held the wooden heart and duck up. "I'll treasure these always. *Danki* so much." She gestured toward the buggy. "Drive safely *heemet*."

"I promise I will. *Gut nacht*, my Lindsay." He climbed into the buggy. "Sleep well tonight."

"*Gut nacht*, my Matthew," she said. "You sleep well too."

She waved as the horse started down the driveway toward the road. She felt as if she were walking on clouds as she made her way to the phone shanty. She couldn't believe Matthew had made her another special gift. He was so thoughtful and sweet.

She checked the messages and, after finding none, dialed her sister's cell phone.

"Lindsay?" Jessica asked as she answered. "Is that you?"

"Yes, stranger," Lindsay said. "It's me. Long time, no talk."

"Wow," Jessica said. "You sound awfully happy. How are things?"

"Wonderful. Amazing. Perfect." Lindsay sighed while winding the phone cord around her fingers. "I just had the most amazing day."

"Tell me all about it," Jessica said. "I'm all ears."

Lindsay filled her in on Rebecca's doctor's visit and their nice lunch.

"I'm so glad to hear Aunt Rebecca is doing well," Jessica said. "I've been praying for her and the baby. I'm thankful you can help her, so she can concentrate on resting and saving all of her strength for the baby."

"I know. I am thankful I can be here too." Lindsay settled back in the chair. "Matthew came to see me tonight." She couldn't stop her grin. "We had a really nice visit."

"Oh?" Jessica sounded curious. "How nice was it?"

"He made me the cutest gift," Lindsay said. She then explained how he'd previously made her a heart and how now he'd given her a duck to remind her of home in Virginia. "Isn't that the sweetest thing you've ever heard, Jess?"

"That's so romantic," Jessica said. "He obviously loves you. I'm so happy for you. What else is going on there in Bird-in-Hand?"

"Naomi had her baby a few days ago," Lindsay said. "They're both doing great."

"Really?" Jessica asked. "What did she have?"

"She had a girl, and she and Caleb named her Priscilla," Lindsay said.

"That's a pretty name," Jessica said. "I bet Susie and little Millie love her."

"They do," Lindsay said. "Everyone is very happy, and Lizzie Anne is enjoying babysitting for them." She paused, thinking of the rest of the news. "Lizzie Anne and Samuel's wedding is coming up fast. It's only a few weeks away." She crossed her legs at her ankles while she talked. "She bought the material for the dresses, and she and her mom will be working on making them."

"That's great. I wish I could come, but classes are just too much this semester."

"Are you pulling straight A's again?"

"I'm trying really hard," Jessica said. "I think I may have all A's but one B. I'm really disappointed, but Trig is just not agreeing with me."

"I'm surprised. You're so good at math. But still, a B is fantastic."

"Thanks," Jessica said. "I guess it'll have to do. Oh, I talked to Aunt Trisha a few days ago. She's doing great. She's made a full recovery with her leg, but she's not taking any chances climbing onto railings or even step ladders anymore."

"That's good." Lindsay asked Jessica about her friends and listened while Jessica shared how everyone was doing.

"Oh," Jessica said. "I meant to ask you if you've seen Jake lately."

Lindsay paused, wondering if she should tell Jessica about Jake and Katie. Her inner voice told her to just keep the information to herself. "No, I haven't." It wasn't a lie. She hadn't seen Jake in at least two months. "Why do you ask?"

"Just wondering how he is. I talked to him over a month ago."

"You did?" Lindsay asked with surprise. "You hadn't told me that."

"Yeah, I know. I finally got up enough nerve to call him."

"And?" Lindsay asked. "What did you say and what did he say?"

"We didn't talk very long," she said. "I'd been looking through a box, and I found a photo of us from the time he came to visit me and we went to the beach. When I brought it up, he seemed annoyed at me for mentioning the trip. He said he didn't know what to say, and I reminded him that we always wind up stuck in the same holding pattern."

"You know that's the truth," Lindsay said.

"I know." Jessica sighed. "I really want to settle things with him, you know? I think he's still angry with me. I can never say the right thing to him."

Lindsay was silent for a beat. She knew Jake and Katie had feelings for each other but couldn't see each other due to their religious differences. Now Jessica was admitting things were unsettled with Jake. What a tangled web!

"Linds?" Jessica asked. "Are you there?"

"Yeah," Lindsay said. "I'm here. I just don't know what to say."

"What can you say?" Jessica asked.

"I guess it's like Dad used to say, the more things change, the more they stay the same, right?" Lindsay said.

"Right."

"Are you coming for Christmas?" Lindsay asked.

"Oh yes," Jessica said. "I'm not exactly sure what day I'm coming, but I'll be there."

"That's great," Lindsay said. "I'll let *Aenti* Rebecca know."

"Thanks." Jessica yawned. "I guess I'd better let you go. I have a big test tomorrow in my accounting class."

"Don't be up too late," Lindsay said. "You need your sleep."

Jessica laughed. "There you go again acting like the big sister. Give my love to Aunt Rebecca, Uncle Daniel, and the kids."

"I will. Tell Kim I said hello," Lindsay said, referring to Jessica's roommate.

"I will," Jessica said. "Love you."

"Love you too," Lindsay repeated before hanging up. She sat on the stool and studied the receiver for a few moments while contemplating the situation with Jessica, Jake, and Katie. She couldn't help but wonder what would happen when the three of them were reunited at Christmastime.

"Christmas will be interesting for certain," Lindsay muttered, walking back toward the house.

18

Three weeks later, Katie sniffed and wiped her eyes as the bride and groom recited their vows in front of nearly two hundred members of the community who were gathered in Lizzie Anne's home. Weddings always made Katie cry, which made her feel silly. After all, it was a very happy occasion, and it wasn't as if she were the one getting married.

Katie had once attended an English wedding ceremony with her grandmother when one of their customers invited them. She found the English weddings were very different from the Amish ceremonies. English weddings were usually held on Saturdays throughout the year. Amish weddings were scheduled for Tuesdays and Thursdays in the fall and didn't include flowers, tuxedoes, or gowns.

Just like a typical church service, Katie sat next to Lindsay with the other young, unmarried women on backless benches. The service had begun with Lizzie Anne and Samuel meeting with the minister while the congregation sang hymns from the *Ausbund.*

When the hymns were complete, Lizzie Anne and Samuel returned to the congregation and sat with their attendants: her sisters Naomi and Levina, his brother Raymond, and her brother Elam. Katie couldn't help but think Lizzie Anne looked stunning in her blue dress, especially with her attendants by her side in their matching dresses. Naomi, who had given birth to her second daughter, Priscilla, only three weeks ago, looked beautiful too. The women sat facing Samuel, Raymond, and Elam, who were clad in their traditional Sunday black-and-white clothing.

After another hymn, the minister delivered a thirty-minute sermon based on Old Testament stories of marriages. Katie tried her best to concentrate on the sermon but her mind was racing with thoughts of the scene playing out in front of her. It all seemed surreal—as if life were moving ahead of Katie at hyper-speed. How could her brother be old enough to be getting married? And when had he fallen in love with one of her best friends? Katie had to be dreaming.

Lindsay elbowed Katie in the rib cage. "Katie?" she whispered. "Are you okay? You look a little green."

"I'm feeling green," Katie whispered. "This all seems so unreal."

Lindsay looked confused, but Katie didn't reply as they joined the rest of the congregation in kneeling for silent prayer. Once the prayer was complete, everyone rose for the minister's reading of Matthew 19:1–12.

Bishop Abner Chupp then stood and began to preach the main sermon, continuing with the Book of Genesis, recounting the story of Abraham and the other patriarchs included in the book.

Lindsay leaned over to Katie. "What do you mean by *unreal?*"

Katie shook her head. "I just can't believe *mei bruder* is marrying one of *mei* best *freinden*," she whispered. "It seems like only yesterday Samuel was taking my favorite doll and running around the pasture laughing at me while I whined for him to bring it back."

Lindsay cupped a hand over her mouth as she stifled a laugh, and Katie bit back a sigh. She knew she should be happy for Lizzie Anne and Samuel, and she was, deep down. Yet it all seemed to be happening so fast.

Katie looked toward the soon-to-be newlyweds. Lizzie Anne beamed at her groom, whose eyes shone with love for her. Katie hoped she found that love someday, and she prayed somehow she could still enjoy that love with Jake.

Her eyes moved to the sea of young, unmarried men at the other side of the room, and she was astonished to find Jake in the back sitting next to Matthew. Her heart slammed against her rib cage when she saw that he was studying her. She wondered if he was hoping they could someday find happiness despite the rules and traditions that separated them.

Katie kept her eyes locked on Jake's. She wondered if they could possibly sneak in a moment to talk. She missed him so much her heart ached. Oh, how she wished things could be different, and they could be together!

Tearing her eyes away from Jake, she turned back to the bride and groom, who seemed to be listening intently to the bishop's lecture on the apostle Paul's instructions for marriage, which were included in 1 Corinthians and Ephesians.

The bishop continued his sermon, instructing Lizzie Anne and Samuel on how to run a godly household, and then he moved on to a forty-five minute sermon on the story of Sarah and Tobias from the intertestamental book of Tobit.

When the sermon was over, the bishop looked between Lizzie Anne and Samuel. "Now here are two in one faith," he said. "Elizabeth Anne King and Samuel Robert Kauffman." The bishop asked the congregation if they knew any scriptural reason for the couple to not be married. Hearing no response, he continued. "If it is your desire to be married, you may in the name of the Lord come forth."

Samuel took Lizzie Anne's hand in his, and they stood before the bishop to take their vows.

While the couple responded to the bishop's questions, Katie glanced over at Jake. She gnawed her lower lip when she found

him still watching her. He smiled, and she couldn't help but
return the sweet gesture. Oh, how she wished she could read
his thoughts! Was he thinking of her and what their relationship could've been if they were both Amish?

Katie held his gaze with her heart pounding in her chest
while the bishop read "A Prayer for Those About to Be Married"
from an Amish prayer book called the *Christenpflict*.

Once the bishop returned to the sermon, Katie broke the
trance and directed her attention back to the service. She wanted
to talk to Jake, because she needed to know how he felt about
her. Did he still care even though they hadn't spoken for more
than a month? Although she wasn't allowed to speak to Jake,
she'd never let her feelings for him evaporate. He still haunted
her thoughts during the day and her dreams at night. She knew
she was in love with him, and the feelings were as strong today as
they were the day he saved her from the men who attacked her.

When the sermon ended, the congregation knelt while the
bishop again read from the *Christenpflict*. After the bishop recited the Lord's Prayer, the congregation stood, and the three-
hour service ended with the singing of another hymn.

Once the ceremony was over, the men began rearranging
furniture while Katie, Lindsay, and the rest of the women set
out to serve the wedding dinner, which included chicken with
stuffing, mashed potatoes with gravy, pepper cabbage, and
cooked cream of celery. The bountiful desserts that would follow the meal were cookies, pie, fruit, and Jell-O salad.

Katie glanced back toward the newly married couple, who
were surrounded by well-wishers.

"It was a beautiful wedding, *ya?*" Lindsay asked while they
walked to the kitchen.

"*Ya,*" Katie said. "It truly was."

"Lizzie Anne looks so *froh*." Lindsay sighed. "I can't imagine
what it feels like to be the bride. I used to wonder if I'd ever

fall in love and get married. But now it feels like it could really happen, you know?"

"Oh, my," Katie said. "It's serious with Matthew and you, *ya?*"

"*Ya*," Lindsay said. "I'm really happy. I never thought I could find this kind of happiness. It's really nice."

Katie smiled, despite the jealousy nipping at her. She knew jealousy was a sin, but it was difficult for her to watch her two best friends fall in love while she sat alone wishing she could be with Jake. "I think it's *wunderbaar gut*, and I wish you all the best." She glanced toward the women preparing trays of food for the waiting wedding guests. "I'm going to see what I can carry out."

"I'll come too," Lindsay said, falling into step beside her.

Katie chose a bowl of mashed potatoes while Lindsay took a bowl of gravy and a ladle.

"I guess we'll serve the bride and groom," Lindsay said as they started out to the family room. "They always get served first."

"That's right."

Katie and Lindsay moved toward the corner where the bride and groom sat with their attendants.

"Katie!" Lizzie Anne squealed, pulling Katie into her arms for a tight hug. "Lindsay!" She hugged Lindsay next. "I'm so glad you're both here."

"Congratulations." Katie gestured toward Lizzie Anne's dress. "You look *schee*. I'm so *froh* for you." Tears filled her eyes. She truly was happy for her friend and her brother.

While Lindsay and Lizzie Anne prattled on about the service, Katie turned toward Samuel. "Congratulations. I'm really sorry I was so negative when you got engaged. You and Lizzie Anne belong together, and I'm sorry I couldn't see that before. I never meant to be so mean."

"*Danki*, Katie," Samuel said with a smile. "That means a lot."

"I guess I can finally call you a man now since you have a *fraa*." Katie grinned.

Samuel laughed. "I guess so. Don't worry, *schweschder*. Your time will come soon enough." He hugged her, and Katie wished she could believe his words.

Lizzie Anne and Samuel were engulfed in a group of friends, while Lindsay stepped over to talk to Matthew. Not wanting to intrude on either conversation, Katie moved back toward the kitchen to retrieve more food. She spotted her parents across the room engrossed in a conversation with Lizzie Anne's parents.

"Katie," her aunt Beth Anne called from the kitchen. "Would you run out to see if there are any guests to greet? I'm supposed to be out there, but I'm tied up with the meal preparation and need to finish what I'm doing here."

"*Ya*," Katie said. "Of course." Turning back toward the doorway, she walked directly into Jake. "Jake," she said with surprise. "I didn't see you there."

"I know." He frowned. "I had to talk to you. It's been too long. How are you, Katie?"

"I'm fine," she said. "I have to go outside and greet guests for *mei aenti* Beth Anne. Enjoy your meal. Excuse me."

She rushed to the door, retrieved her wrap from a hook, and hurried out to see if any guests had arrived for the reception. As much as she longed to talk to Jake, she didn't want to encourage him to break her father's rules and create more problems for her. She hoped he wouldn't follow her outside. She knew if he followed her, it would mean more trouble since her father was just inside the house.

Katie glanced around the sea of buggies and didn't spot any guests arriving. She turned toward the house and gasped as she spotted Jake smiling at her. "Jake," she said, walking over to him. "What are you doing out here?" She craned her neck to see past him, hoping no one had spotted them together.

"I had to see you," Jake said, his eyes pleading with her. "How are you doing, Katie? How are you really?"

"Jake, you can't be here." She motioned toward the house. "I can't disobey *mei dat* again." She looked around, hoping no one had followed Jake. "Did anyone see you come out here?"

"No," he said. "I snuck out the back door when no one was around." He shivered, and she glanced at his button-down black shirt and trousers.

She hugged her wrap closer to her body. "Why didn't you get your coat?"

He shrugged. "I was in a hurry and didn't want to attract too much attention." He gestured toward her. "It's been too long since we've talked."

"I know, but we can't be seen together, Jake." Frowning, she shook her head. "You have to go. Please, Jake."

He looked pained, causing her heart to shatter.

"I know I shouldn't have followed you," he said. "I'm sorry. I don't want to cause more problems for you, but I just wanted to make sure you were okay."

"I'm fine," she whispered. "Please just go."

As he disappeared up the stairs to the porch, Katie sent a silent prayer up to God asking Him to please guide her and Jake so that they could somehow find a way to be together.

⟊

Jake's body shook like a leaf in a windstorm as he rushed up the back porch and through the door. Glancing left and then right, he spotted groups of wedding guests talking, but no one looked toward him.

He weaved through one knot of guests to reach the bathroom, and he breathed a sigh of relief when he found the door open and the room unoccupied. He stepped into the small room and shut and locked the door behind him.

Leaning against the wall, Jake hugged his arms to his chest and shivered. Although the cold had seeped into his body, warmth had filled him as he thought of Katie. He'd only hoped to say hello to her after watching her during the three-hour wedding ceremony. He'd dared to approach her after noticing her parents were busy visiting with other wedding guests. Jake had wanted to get a chance to talk to her, but she'd dismissed him. He knew trying to talk to her was a risk, but he couldn't bear the thought of being in the same building as her without speaking to her.

The bitter cold had stung his exposed skin as soon as he stepped out the door, and the discomfort increased as their time outside wore on. However, standing with her, even in the cold of December, was exhilarating.

He knew she was the only girl for him. And he loved her. From the depth of his soul he felt the words — *I love Katie Kauffman*. He had to find a way to be with her, but he didn't know how.

After taking a deep breath and rubbing his arms a few times, Jake stepped back into the crowd of wedding guests, slipping over to stand by Matthew and Lindsay near the warm woodstove by the kitchen. They were discussing the upcoming plans for visiting friends during the Christmas season, and Jake did his best to join in the conversation, smiling and nodding while they spoke.

Glancing across the room, he spotted Katie standing with her sister Nancy. Her eyes met his and she quickly looked away.

Jake held his breath and sent up a prayer to God asking Him for guidance. He needed to find a way to be with Katie Kauffman. Jake wanted to be able to tell the rest of the world that he loved her.

❦

Later that evening, Jake tossed his keys onto the small table by his door and kicked off his shoes. Heading through the kitchen, he spotted a red light blinking on his answering machine, so he hit the button.

"Jake," a familiar feminine voice said. "It's Jessica. I wanted to just say hi. I hope you're doing well." She paused as if to gather her thoughts. "I'll be in town for the holidays, and I'd love to see you. I'm arriving next week. Hopefully we'll run into each other, or maybe we can sneak away for a bite to eat. I'd love to get caught up. Anyway, I hope you're having a nice week. I hope to talk to you soon. Bye."

Jake knew he should call Jessica back and tell her he hoped to see her during the holidays, but he was too emotionally spent. His thoughts were only focused on Katie. He needed to find a way to be with her. He couldn't bear being forbidden from talking to her.

He climbed the steep stairs to his bedroom while contemplating his predicament. Having Katie avoid him tonight was too much for his already broken heart. He knew he'd been wrong to follow her outside, but the need to talk to her had been overwhelming. He didn't want to cause more problems for her by being too forward, but he also couldn't walk away from her and forget her after all they'd been through together.

While he changed for bed, Jake again thought of Katie. He'd felt a resurgence of hope after praying for guidance with their relationship. He hoped the solution would come to him soon.

19

Jessica burst through the back door of Rebecca's house. "Merry Christmas!" Dropping her bags on the kitchen floor, she opened her arms as her little cousins ran over to her. "Hi," she said, hugging them close. "Emma! Junior! You've gotten so big."

"Jess," Junior said. *"Willkumm heemet."*

"Oh, thank you," Jessica said. "It's good to be back."

Lindsay burst into the room. "Jess!" She hugged her. "How are you?"

"I'm great." She studied her sister, who seemed to glow. "You look different, Sis. You're happier."

"I guess I am." Lindsay began picking up bags from the floor. "I'll help you take your things upstairs."

"Oh, thanks." Jessica grabbed her wheeled suitcase and matching tote bag and followed Lindsay toward the stairs. "I brought a lot of gifts for the kids. We're going to the Kauffman gathering, right?"

"Ya," Lindsay said. "It's at Katie's house this year." She started up the stairs.

"Cool." Jessica hiked her bag further up on her shoulder while they climbed the steep flight. "How's Aunt Rebecca?"

"Doing really well." Lindsay smiled. "She had an appointment last week, and everything looks great. The doctor said she could even deliver early."

"Oh, wow." Jessica shook her head. "What a miracle that Aunt Rebecca thought she'd never have children, and now she'll have three."

"God is good." Lindsay stood outside her doorway. "You can have my room. I'll sleep in the other room with Emma. We still have the extra bed in there. There's a new crib already set up in Rebecca's room for the baby. We can't wait to find out what the baby will be. If it's a girl, she'll eventually share a room with Emma, and, of course, a boy would share with Junior when he's older."

"Are you certain about giving up your room for me again this time?" Jessica asked. "I don't mind sleeping in the room with Emma."

"It's not a problem at all." Lindsay placed the bags on the bed. "I'm just glad you're here."

Jessica dropped her bags on the floor next to the bed. "You missed me, huh?"

"Yes, I did." Lindsay leaned on the doorframe. "How's school?"

"Good." Jessica lowered herself onto the bed next to her suitcase. "It seems like the projects and tests don't stop, but I'm muddling through it. I can't wait until this year is over."

"Do you ever have time for fun?" Lindsay asked, looking concerned. "You know you can really wear yourself out if you don't have any downtime for yourself."

Jessica shrugged. "Kim and I sometimes go out to eat or see a movie. It's not very often, but it's something."

"That's good, I guess," Lindsay said. "Just remember what Dad used to say when we were working ourselves to death in school. You need to work hard but also find time for fun."

Jessica frowned. "I think about that statement a lot, but I figure college isn't going to last forever. I'll eventually get to have some fun, right?" She gestured toward Lindsay. "I want to hear about you. I'm glad Aunt Rebecca is doing much better, but how are you doing? How are things with your friends?"

"*Gut.*" Lindsay smiled. "Matthew and I are doing really well."

"I'm so happy for you," Jessica said. "I hoped you'd find someone nice. You know I worry about you all the time. I feel like it's my job to make sure you're okay since Mom and Dad are gone. Sometimes it's really difficult to be so far away from you, but I know that sounds silly. After all, you're eighteen and a woman now. And you have Aunt Rebecca here to watch out for you."

Lindsay shook her head. "You're so silly, Jessica. You don't need to worry about me. You just take care of yourself." She tilted her head in question. "Are you staying through the holidays?"

"Yes," Jessica said, absently running her fingers over the quilt on Lindsay's bed. Her thoughts turned from the Kauffman family and school to Jake. "Have you seen Jake lately?"

Her sister paused and then shook her head. "Not since Lizzie Anne and Samuel's wedding. I haven't been to the furniture store in a long time. Why do you ask?"

"Oh, no reason." Jessica hoped she looked casual. "I called him last week, and he hasn't called me back. It just seemed strange I hadn't heard from him. We used to try to keep in touch. At least, we did last year before we had our little falling out. I guess I just miss his friendship."

"Do you still care for him?" Lindsay looked a little hesitant. "I thought you said you were trying to get over him. Have you changed your mind?"

Jessica sighed. "The truth is I know there's no chance for us, but I want to end it better than we did last spring."

"I don't think that's necessary," Lindsay said. "You two pretty much went your separate ways."

"I know, but I would feel better if we ended it on a better note," Jessica said. "He was a good friend to me, and I miss that friendship."

"Just a moment." Lindsay stuck her head out into the hallway as if listening to something. "It's awfully quiet down there. I should make sure the kids are okay. I always worry they'll wander out the back door when I'm not looking." She pointed toward the bags. "You can get unpacked and then go visit *Aenti* Rebecca. Take your time." She stepped out into the hallway. "I'm going to start cooking soon. When you're done, maybe you can play with the kids while I cook. I know they'll enjoy visiting with you again."

After Lindsay left, Jessica pulled out a few of her skirts and blouses, which she'd packed for Christmas parties, and hung them on the unoccupied hooks on the wall next to Lindsay's frocks and aprons. She then pushed her bags to the corner of the room and out of the way.

Jessica stepped into the hallway and made her way down to Rebecca's room. Finding the door ajar, she knocked on it and stepped into the doorway.

"Jessica!" Rebecca said with her arms opened. "How are you, dear?"

"Hi, Aunt Rebecca." Jessica leaned down and hugged her. She then examined her aunt's smile and pink complexion. "You look great." She sat on a chair across from the bed. "Lindsay said your last visit to the doctor went well. How are you feeling?"

Rebecca ran her hands over her protruding baby bump. "I'm feeling much stronger. I guess that's God's way of helping me get ready for the big day." She sat up straighter in the bed and placed a Christian novel next to her on the bed. "Tell me all about school. I want to hear everything."

Jessica shared stories about her classmates, research projects, and professors. Her aunt listened with interest, smiling and nodding often.

"You're a very busy young lady," Rebecca said, rubbing her

belly. "I'm so glad school is going well for you. Lindsay said your internship was grueling last summer. Are you planning to go back to work there again over the summer this coming year?"

Jessica shrugged. "I don't know. It was exhausting, but I'll see how I feel next year. I might want to stay in the local area and work there. New York City was amazing, but I don't know if I want to do it again." She gestured toward her aunt's abdomen. "Do you have a hunch if it's a girl or a boy?"

"No, I don't. All three of my pregnancies were very different." Her aunt smiled. "I'm just so *froh* it's all working out. I was worried for a while we might not get to enjoy this *boppli*. It seemed like the complications might cause me to lose the *boppli*. However, it's a miracle we've made it this far. Only a few weeks left."

"I hope I get to see the baby before I leave." Jessica crossed her legs at the ankles. "If not, then I'll have to make a trip back for certain."

"Will you stay until New Year's?"

"Yes. I'm thinking about going back to Virginia on January second," Jessica said.

"That will give us a little bit of time to visit. Everyone will be happy to see you while you're here."

"I'll enjoy seeing the family too," Jessica said. "I heard Katie's family is hosting the gathering. It will be nice to see everyone again. How was Lizzie Anne and Samuel's wedding? Were you able to attend?"

Rebecca frowned. "No, I couldn't go, but Lindsay filled me in on everything. I'm hoping Lizzie Anne and Samuel will visit me soon. I heard they're busy moving into the apartment in his parents' house, but they said they'd come by to see me after they get settled. It's a shame I had to miss it, but everyone understands."

"Of course they do." Jessica gestured toward the empty glass on the nightstand. "Would you like another drink and maybe a snack?"

"That would be nice. Thank you." Rebecca rubbed her belly some more. "It's good to have you here, Jessica."

"Thank you. It's nice to be here again." Jessica took the glass from the nightstand and then kissed her aunt's cheek. "I'll be back soon with your drink and snack."

ᢙᡇᡐ

Jessica dried the last dish after supper. She placed it in the cabinet and then used a sponge to wipe down the counter. Once the counter was clean, she wiped down the kitchen table and swept the floor. She put the dustpan and broom back in place and heard a burst of giggles sound from the bathroom.

With a grin, Jessica made her way to the bathroom. Emma sat splashing in the tub while Lindsay knelt beside the tub and shielded herself from the spray of water with a towel.

"She likes her bath, huh?" Jessica said, laughing with her little cousin.

Lindsay grinned. "You could say that. Want to bathe her?"

"Sure!" Jessica squatted over the tub and grabbed the face cloth. "Are you getting clean, Emmie?"

Her little cousin giggled and splashed, spraying water over Jessica's jeans and long-sleeved shirt.

"She got you." Lindsay stood and wiped a towel over her black bib apron and dark blue dress. "She's something else, *ya?*"

"Yes, she is." Jessica finished washing her while the little girl smiled up at her. "You're so cute, Emma. I'm so glad I'm here with you."

Lindsay snickered while holding a towel out toward her. "I'm certain you'd rather be somewhere else than getting soaked."

"That's not true." Jessica lifted Emma, and Lindsay engulfed her in the towel. "I love being here. I may not live here, but I love

212

visiting." She kissed Emma's cheek, and the little girl squealed. "She is a cutie pie." Leaning down, Jessica let the water out of the tub. "What else can I do?"

"I think I'm fine." Lindsay sat on the commode while drying Emma. "Do you need help in the kitchen? I can put Emma in her high chair if you do."

"It's all done." Jessica touched her phone shielded in the pocket of her jeans. She'd been hoping to sneak away to make a call. "I think I'm going to walk outside for a minute."

"Walk outside?" Lindsay's eyes widened. "It's freezing out there. Why would you want to go outside?" She looked suspicious. "Don't tell me you took up smoking. Did all of the stress do it to you?"

"Are you serious? You think I'm a smoker? Never in a million years." Jessica waved off the comment. "I just want to make a phone call."

Lindsay's eyebrows flew to her hairline. "Make a phone call? You don't have to go outside to do that."

"I'll be right back." Jessica headed through the kitchen to the back door.

She pulled on her heavy coat and then stepped out into the cold December night. She clutched the coat to her body and she sat on the porch swing. The frigid air seeped through her wet jeans causing her to shiver. She pulled her phone from her pocket and pushed a few buttons. Soon the line on the other end began to ring.

After four rings and a click, a recording picked up. "This is Jake. Leave me a message."

Jessica glowered. *Is he ever home?*

After the beep sounded, she sucked in a deep breath. "Hey, Jake," she said, nervously pushing her long, dark hair behind her shoulder. "It's Jessica. I wanted to let you know I'm in town. I plan to be here until January second. I was hoping I could see you." She paused, wondering if she sounded desperate. "Call me. My number is still the same. Bye."

Jessica disconnected the call and then stared at her phone. She wondered why Jake wasn't calling her back. Was he out of town? She pushed that thought away. Why would he be out of town? Lindsay said Jake still worked for the furniture store, and Jessica remembered his work ethic. Not only did Jake love his job, but he was the kind of person who would stay late and come in on Saturday to finish a project by the deadline. Perhaps he was working late on a project.

She tried to convince herself Jake was only working, but she remained unconvinced. He'd never returned her call from last week. He couldn't possibly be working so much that he had no time at all to call her. Maybe his answering machine didn't work. What if he never got the message?

While staring across the dark pasture, another thought occurred to her. What if Jake simply didn't want to talk to her?

Her stomach ached at the thought. Even though she knew she didn't want to date Jake, she couldn't stand the idea of him pushing her out of his life. Her gaze moved to her SUV, and she briefly considered driving over to Jake's house to find out if he was truly avoiding her. However, that plan made her seem desperate and needy, and Jessica couldn't stand girls like that. She'd seen plenty of girls at college who threw themselves at boys, doing anything in their power to get the boys' attention. Jessica had vowed never to be like that. She had more self-esteem and self-worth than they displayed in public.

Jessica stood and stepped back into the kitchen. She hung up her coat and then glanced down at her phone. She knew one thing for certain—she was going to find out why Jake was avoiding her before she returned to her home in Virginia.

20

Katie glanced across the family room toward Jake and considered marching over to talk to him and wish him a Merry Christmas. She couldn't stand how awful she'd felt ever since she'd sent him away at Lizzie Anne and Samuel's wedding. It seemed unfair that she wasn't permitted to speak to all of the guests at the Christmas gathering she and her family were hosting. Yet, she knew the outcome if she did speak to him. Even though her father had permitted her to leave the house as an early Christmas gift to her, he'd warned her to steer clear of Jake.

She turned to her left and spotted her father talking with his brothers, Daniel and Timothy. Grabbing two cups of hot cider, she started toward Jake, who stood with Matthew and Lindsay. A tiny twinge of envy nipped at her while she watched Lindsay smile up at Matthew. Katie wished she could find that happiness too.

"Hi," Katie said, approaching the group. *"Frehlicher Grischtdaag!"* She handed Jake the mug of cider.

Jake's expression was full of surprise. *"Frehlicher Grischtdaag."*

Lindsay and Matthew echoed the greeting.

"The party is *wunderbaar gut,"* Lindsay said, touching Katie's arm. "The *haus* looks so *schee.* I love how you decorated with the greenery and poinsettias."

"*Danki,*" Katie said. "I better go check and see if *mei mamm* needs help in the kitchen. I just wanted to say hello."

Jake nodded before she weaved through the crowd toward the kitchen.

⁂

Jessica glanced across the room and spotted Jake standing with Matthew and Lindsay. Now was her time to finally get him to talk to her.

Jessica looked back at Lizzie Anne and Samuel, who had been talking to her with a few other Kauffman cousins. "Would you excuse me for a moment?" She held up her empty cider mug. "I'm going to go get a refill."

Jessica had noticed when Jake arrived, and she was almost certain he'd been avoiding her in person, just like he'd avoided the phone calls. Every time she tried to approach him, it seemed he deliberately moved to speak to someone else. She was going to face him and find out what his problem was. She walked over to him, finding him engrossed in a conversation with Matthew.

"Jessica!" Lindsay said with a smile. "Are you enjoying the party?"

"I am," Jessica said, nodding a greeting to Matthew. She turned to Jake. "Jake," she said. "I've been looking for you."

"Jessica," Jake said. "Good to see you. Merry Christmas."

Jessica touched his arm. "Can we talk in private? I promise it will only take a moment." She gestured toward the back door. "Let's just go for a quick walk. I won't keep you away from the party long."

Jake nodded. "That's fine."

Jessica fetched her coat from the hook by the door and followed Jake down the back porch steps. The cold air hit her legs like a solid wall, and she wondered why she'd decided to wear a skirt and hose today. After all, it was December in Pennsylvania.

"Let's go over by the barn," Jake said, walking fast and hugging his coat to his body.

Jessica tried in vain to keep up with him as they walked around to the back of the barn. When they rounded it, Jake faced her. She wondered why he was frowning. He seemed to be upset about something, and she hoped she wasn't upsetting him.

"Jake," she said. "I've been trying to talk to you all evening."

"I'm sorry," he said. "I've been really distracted."

"Distracted?" She folded her arms over her coat. "Is that why you haven't called me back? I've left two messages on your voice mail. Are you avoiding me?"

He paused. "No, I'm not avoiding you. I should've called you back, but I've had a lot on my mind. Also, I don't mean to hurt your feelings, but I'm not certain we have anything else to talk about. We said it all last spring."

"I don't think we've said it all," she said, hugging her arms closer to her body as the cold seeped through her like ice. Was it the frigid air or his words that stung so badly?

"What else is there to say?" he asked. "I honestly can't think of anything more to say to you. What do you want to talk about?"

"I thought after everything that happened between us we were still friends. Isn't that what you said when we talked back in the spring? Aren't we friends, Jake?" Her voice quavered with hurt. Oh, how she wished she could turn off her emotions. Why did this hurt so badly? She sounded like one of those girls she'd seen embarrass themselves at college. She'd never wanted to be like them, but here she stood begging Jake to talk to her. Where had she gone wrong?

"Yes, Jessica." Jake's expression softened. "I told you I'll always be your friend, and I meant it."

"So then why haven't you called me back?" She wished she didn't sound so desperate.

"I've been busy." He looked behind her. "I've had a lot going on and a lot on my mind. It's too much to explain right now, but I promise I'll tell you when I have the time."

"You've been busy?" she asked with disbelief radiating in her tone.

"I'm really sorry I haven't had time to call you," he said. "I'll try to be a better friend."

"Fine," she said. "I wanted to tell you I'm sorry things ended the way they did in the spring. You were a tremendous help to me after I lost my parents and was thrown into this strange environment." She gestured around the farm. "I needed a friend, and you were there for me, always listening and putting up with my moods. I grew up a lot last summer during the internship. I've realized what's most important in life and those things are family and close friends. You were both to me, and I'm thankful for you. I know you and I could never be more than friends, but I'm thankful for our friendship. I truly am, Jake."

"Thank you," he said, and he looked sincere. "I am too, Jess."

"That's what I wanted to say, Jake. Thanks for finally listening." She turned to go and then stopped. "Do you still care about me?"

"Yes," he said. "I do care about you, Jessica. I always will. You're my first love."

A choked sob sounded behind her.

Turning, Jessica found Katie Kauffman looking at her and Jake with tears shining in her eyes.

⌒◯⌒

Katie couldn't believe her ears or stop the tears from flooding her eyes as she looked between Jake and Jessica. *Jake still loves Jessica! This can't be true. I had hoped he loved me!*

"Katie?" Jessica asked, looking confused.

"Katie!" Jake rushed toward her. "Wait. Let me explain."

"You're seeing Katie?" Jessica asked Jake with a shocked expression.

Katie turned and started toward her house. She felt as if her world were crumbling around her.

"Wait!" Jake yelled.

A strong arm pulled her back before she reached the other side of the barn. "Let me go!" Katie smacked Jake's hand away. "You still love her, Jake." She spat the words at him. "I can't tell you how stupid I feel."

"No, no." He reached for her cheek, and she backed away from his touch. "I don't love her anymore."

"That's not what you said!" Katie swiped away her hot tears. "You said you care for her, and you'll always care for her because she's your first love. I was so naive. I thought you might actually love me." She pointed toward her chest. "I thought you only cared for *me*!" She couldn't stop the sobs from racking her body. "How could I be so stupid to think you cared about me?"

"Because it's true. I do love you, Katie." He pulled her into a hug. "I only love you."

"That's enough!" A voice boomed behind them.

Katie sucked in a breath as she turned and found her father glaring at them. *"Dat?"*

"Jake Miller," her father bellowed. "Get off my property now and stay off!" He turned his smoldering gaze on Katie. "You! Get to your room, Katie Joy, and don't come out."

Katie ran toward the house. Her tears continued to flow as she rushed in through the back door, nearly knocking Lindsay over on her way up the stairs. When she reached her room, Katie slammed her door and fell onto her bed, letting her tears flow into her pillow.

After a few moments, her door squeaked open and closed once more.

"Katie?" Lindsay asked. "Katie? What happened?"

"I'm so naive," Katie said, rolling onto her side. "I can't believe I thought he cared for me. And *mei daed* heard everything! I'll be shunned now for certain."

"Katie," Lindsay said, sinking down onto the bed beside her and pushing the ribbons from Katie's prayer covering away from her face. "I don't know what you're talking about. Please tell me so I can help you."

"Jake Miller." Katie grimaced as if the name were laced with poison. "I thought he cared about me, but he doesn't. He still loves your sister." She shook her head. "I was so naive. I saw him go outside, and I followed him behind the barn. When I got out there, he was talking to Jessica, telling her he'll always care for her because she's his first love. I thought he wanted to be with me."

Katie swallowed a sob as she stared at the white wall across from her bed. "I told him I never should've been so stupid, and he said he does love me. *Mei daed* walked over just as Jake hugged me, and he told Jake to get off his property and sent me to my room." She shook her head. "I can't even imagine what *mei daed* is going to say to me, but I know I'm in big trouble. And I risked it all for someone who doesn't even love me!"

"I'm sorry your *dat* interrupted, but I don't think Jake loves Jessica." Lindsay shook her head. "Jessica told me Jake doesn't return her phone calls. She's tried to call him more than once before she came here."

Katie frowned at Lindsay. "I know what I heard." She turned toward the pillow. "I'm going to be shunned. You shouldn't even be in here."

"I don't think you'll be shunned." Lindsay touched Katie's arm. "Your *dat* will be upset, but it will be okay."

Katie sniffed, wishing she could take away everything she'd done in the last twenty minutes. "I'm certain I'll be shunned. He's already warned me. What was I thinking? I should've stayed inside and helped serve the food for the guests. I had no business going outside at all."

"Don't be so hard on yourself." Lindsay rubbed Katie's shoulder.

"That's easy for you to say." Katie glared at Lindsay. "You have no idea how I feel. Your boyfriend is Amish. You don't have to risk getting into trouble by being with him." She paused and cleared her throat. "Jake isn't Amish. I have no chance of a relationship with him even if your sister wasn't here to ruin everything." She shook her head. "Jessica needs to go back to her fancy job in New York City and just leave us alone! It's all her fault that Jake and I quarreled."

Lindsay's expression darkened slightly. "I don't think it's Jessica's fault. She has a right to come and see me and the rest of the family for Christmas."

"Her being here is ruining everything," Katie said as new tears pooled in her eyes. "She should just leave."

Lindsay stood. "Maybe I should too."

"*Ya.*" Katie wiped away more tears. "Maybe you should."

Lindsay grimaced. "I only came up here because I saw how upset you were. I wanted to try to help you. I didn't mean to make it worse." She started toward the door but stopped before opening it. "And as I said before, I don't think Jake loves Jessica. If he did, he would've been more interested in talking to her when she got here. As far as I know, he hadn't made any attempt to talk to her before today."

"Please go," Katie whispered through a sob. "Close the door behind you."

"Fine." Lindsay pulled the door open, and it squeaked in response. "I hope your *daed* listens to you when you talk to him. You don't deserve to be punished."

Katie buried her face into her pillow as the door closed behind Lindsay. Grief and frustration rained down on her as she thought about the conversation she'd witnessed between Jake and Jessica.

It was all so confusing, and it hurt her all the way to her soul. To make matters worse, her father was going to punish her again for her seeing Jake and the punishment would certainly be worse than before.

Closing her eyes, Katie succumbed to her tears and silently prayed her father would witness her heartache and have mercy on her.

21

"Did you hear me, Jacob Miller?" Robert Kauffman asked. "I told you to get off my property and I mean *now.*"

"Mr. Kauffman," Jake began. The cold seeped into his skin, causing his toes to go numb while they stood by the barn. "I wanted to try to explain to you that I—"

"There's nothing to explain," Robert said, his eyes full of animosity. "You had no right to come to *mei heemet* and try to date *mei dochder.* How dare you fill her head with notions of your love for her! You know she's been forbidden to see you. Yet you have the audacity to meet her in private so you can touch her again!" His voice rose and shook with fury. "You need to stay away from my family and my property. Leave now!"

"But Mr.—" Jake attempted to explain his actions.

"Leave now!" Robert repeated while stomping back toward the house.

"But I don't have any transportation," Jake called after him. "I drove with my grandparents in their buggy."

Robert spun, facing Jake. "I don't care if you have to walk *heemet,* Jacob. Just get out of here before I escort you off my property." He then marched toward the porch, slamming the door on his way into the house.

"I'll drive you," a small voice said behind him. "I have my Jeep."

"You heard everything," Jake said, frowning at Jessica. "You stayed and eavesdropped."

"I didn't mean to." Jessica shook her head. "I know I should've left, but I didn't want to walk through the conversation either." She gestured toward his face. "You look as if you might freeze to death. Your lips are turning blue. Let's get in my truck and I can drive you home." Jessica started toward her SUV, her shoes crunching on the frozen ground.

He stood still, debating if he should go into the house and try to talk to Katie. But he knew her father meant business, and the last thing he wanted to do was make the situation worse than it already was.

"Come on," she called, walking backward while facing him. "I think my legs are frozen."

He followed her, but he couldn't stop the longing to go make things right. "I hate leaving her when I know she's so upset."

"You heard her father," Jessica said. "I don't think he'd take it well if you tried to go into the house. You know how Robert Kauffman is."

"Yes," Jake said with a scowl. "I certainly do."

Jessica pushed a button on her key ring and the door locks popped open. "Get in. I'll get the heat going."

Jake climbed into the passenger seat and buckled his belt while she climbed in beside him. She cranked the engine over and then blasted the heat.

"This SUV may be old, but the heater works like a charm." She rubbed her hands together and shivered. "It's so cold. I'd forgotten how cold it gets here in the winter."

Jake stared at the dashboard and thought of Katie while Jessica rambled on about the weather and how she wished she'd worn jeans instead of a skirt. He glanced up at the second-story windows and wondered how Katie was while the Jeep rumbled past the house. He wished he could console her and explain to her he loved her and only her. He couldn't take the hurt anymore. He needed to be with her. He had to do something now to make it work between them. But what should he do?

"So ... you and Katie Kauffman, huh?" Jessica asked. "I never would've guessed that."

Jake glanced at Jessica. "It wasn't planned. It just sort of happened."

"I'm really surprised." Jessica shook her head while steering onto the main road.

Instead of responding, he stared out the window and studied the farms they passed. He wondered if he could ever afford to buy a piece of property. And if he could, would he be able to convince Katie he wanted her to be his wife and help him run a little farm?

"Do you love her?" Jessica asked.

"Yes," he said without hesitation.

"Jake, she's Amish and you're not," Jessica said. "You know you can't be with her. You're playing with fire, and of course you're going to get burned."

He frowned at her, but she kept her eyes on the road. "I know that good and well, Jessica. I'm not stupid. I'm trying to find a way to make it work."

"You are?" Jessica looked confused as she faced him. "How can you possibly make it work with her?"

"I'll figure it out," Jake said, wishing he could go back and relive the evening.

Slowing at a stoplight, Jessica sighed. "I'm sorry," she said with a frown. "I never meant to interfere in your life. I made a mess of things with you and Katie."

Her apology caught him off guard and rendered him speechless for a moment. "I forgive you," he said. "You had no idea, and I was wrong to not call you back. You at least deserved a phone call. I was a lousy friend to you."

"No, you weren't, Jake. I know I hurt you too." She accelerated through the intersection. "I hope you and Katie can work things out somehow. I know my parents found a way, and your parents did also."

"Thanks," Jake said. "I appreciate that."

They were both quiet as Jessica steered the Jeep into the driveway of his two-family house. Jake thought of Katie again and wondered how he could speak with her alone.

"Here we are," Jessica said. "I'm sorry things didn't go as you'd hoped today."

"Thank you," he said. "I appreciate the ride home."

"It's the least I could do." She faced him. "I truly hope things work out for you and Katie. You deserve to be happy."

"Thank you," he said.

Jessica tilted her head in question. "Did you want me to give Katie a message for you? I'm sure I could sneak up to her room for you."

He shook his head. "No, but thanks for offering. I'll contact her when I'm ready. I don't want anything misconstrued in the delivery of the message." He wrenched the door open. "Have a good night."

"You too," she said. "Hopefully I'll see you before I go back to Virginia."

"I'm certain you will," he said, climbing from the SUV. "Good-bye."

Jake waved as Jessica pulled out of the driveway.

Turning, he faced his truck and the solution hit him like a bolt of lightning—Jake needed to make a sacrifice in order to be with the woman he loved. Jake needed to abandon his possessions and become Amish. It was the only way they could ever be together, and he couldn't live without her.

He didn't need his truck or his electricity. Yes, he would miss them, but he needed Katie more than he needed the modern conveniences. Becoming Amish was the only way for him to be with Katie, and he was willing to give up his English lifestyle all for her.

Closing his eyes, Jake sent a prayer up to God, asking if this was the solution God wanted for him. A calmness settled on his heart, and he knew this was the right path. It was as if God put it in his heart, just as his mother had felt when she left the church.

Pulling his keys from his pocket, he rushed over to his truck. He needed to go see Bishop Abner Chupp now and ask for permission to be baptized so he could finally begin his new life with Katie Kauffman.

⌒⌒⌒

Jessica stepped into Katie's house and glanced around at the group of party guests, absently wondering whether anyone had noticed when she and Jake had left or that Katie had been sent to her room. She nodded and smiled at members of the Kauffman family and their friends and helped herself to another cup of cider. The spicy drink warmed her body while she sipped it and crossed the room.

"Jess," Lindsay said, approaching her. "Where have you been?"

Jessica smiled at her and took another sip. "That, little sister, is a very long story."

Lindsay glanced around before taking Jessica's arm and tugging her to a quiet hallway off the kitchen.

"Slow down. You're going to make me spill my drink," Jessica muttered, balancing her mug in her hand.

They stopped outside the bathroom, and Lindsay looked past Jessica before meeting her gaze. "I haven't seen you in a while. Where were you?"

"I had to drive Jake home," Jessica said. "There was an incident outside, and he was told to leave."

"Katie," Lindsay said, frowning. "She's upstairs sobbing in her room." Her expression was accusatory. "You apparently stirred up things you shouldn't have."

Jessica held her hand up in protest of the accusation. "I didn't mean to. I apologized to Jake while we drove to his house. I just wanted to tell him I was sorry about how things ended and I want to be his friend. I thanked him for all he did to help me through my adjustment when we moved here. I realized how much his friendship meant to me, and I wanted to tell him. I didn't mean to come between him and Katie." Her expression softened. "Is Katie okay? I feel really bad."

"You need to tell her that the next time you see her," Lindsay said. "She's blaming you for taking Jake away from her."

"I didn't take him away," Jessica said. "Jake and I both know things could never work out between us. We're just friends."

Lindsay shook her head. "She's really worried her father is going to shun her."

Jessica grimaced. "Do you think he will?"

Lindsay shrugged. "I don't know. *Onkel* Robert is really strict, and he punished her quite severely when he caught them together once before."

"I'm so sorry to hear that," Jessica said, shaking her head. "That's a harsh punishment for talking to a boy. I hope he's not hard on her this time. She didn't do anything wrong. They were only talking."

"But he told her not to see him. She disobeyed him. To make matters worse, Jake hugged her, and her father witnessed it." Lindsay folded her arms over her blue frock. "I feel really bad for her. She loves Jake. Her heart is broken."

Jessica sipped her drink and thought of everything Jake had said in the car. She hoped they could work things out.

Lindsay turned her eyes to the hallway. "I guess we better get back. Matthew wants to leave soon."

"Do you need a ride?" Jessica said.

"No, thank you." Lindsay smiled. "He wants to take me *heemet*. He said he has something for me."

"Oh." Jessica bumped Lindsay's arm with her elbow. "Sounds serious."

"I don't know." Lindsay's ivory cheeks blushed a light pink. "I guess I'll find out."

"And then you'll tell me," Jessica said. "I'm your sister, so I'm first to know what his gift is."

"I'll see you later," Lindsay said before heading back toward the party.

Jessica finished her cider as her sister walked away. She smiled while thinking of how happy Lindsay looked. The Amish lifestyle fit her little sister well, and she prayed Lindsay would have a life of happiness. She also prayed Katie and Jake could find the same happiness.

⌒➴♡

"Like I said earlier, I have to stop by *mei haus* for a moment," Matthew said while they walked next door. He guided Lindsay toward the barn next to his sister's house. "It shouldn't take too long." He glanced at her. "I promise I'll hitch up my horse and take you *heemet* afterward. Does that sound okay?"

"*Ya*," Lindsay said, her stomach tingling with butterflies. *What does he need to get? Is it the gift he mentioned earlier? What could it possibly be?* Her thoughts swirled with possibilities—A small wooden trinket box? A set of tea towels? What would Matthew give her?

When they reached the barn, Matthew opened the door.

"Do you want me to come with you?" she asked.

He grinned. "Of course I do. The item I need to get is for you."

"Oh." She gnawed her lower lip with anticipation and followed him through the barn to his workshop in the back.

Matthew stepped through the doorway of the workshop and flipped on a few battery-powered lanterns that supplemented the low light seeping in through the high windows.

Lindsay entered the small shop. The sweet smell of stain mixed with the scent of wood dust reminded her of being in the furniture store. She glanced around at the array of tools cluttering the workbench and smiled. She enjoyed seeing Matthew in his favorite environment.

He pointed toward a cedar hope chest. "What do you think of it?" he asked with a sheepish expression.

Lindsay studied the beautiful chest that glistened with new stain. The brass lock and key were also shiny and new. "It's a gorgeous piece of furniture. Are you going to sell it in the store?"

He shook his head. "No, Lindsay. This is for you and only you."

She gasped. "Matthew, I can't possibly accept anything so extravagant. You must sell this. I'm certain you worked hard on it."

Matthew looked disappointed. "Lindsay, I worked hard on this for you. It belonged to *mei mamm*, and I refinished it for you."

Her mouth gaped as she took in his words and their sentiment. "This belonged to your mother?" she asked, her voice small and unsure. "And you want me to have it?"

"*Ya.*" He moved close to her and smiled. "*Frehlicher Grischtdaag, mei liewe.*"

"Matthew," she said, her mind swirling with the meaning of the gift. "This is such an elaborate gift. I never expected you to do something so tremendous for me. I only got you a couple of tools *Onkel* Daniel told me you'd needed."

"*Danki,*" he said. "I'm certain I'll need the tools while I start to build my new *haus* this year."

"Your new *haus*?" Her eyes widened. "You're moving?"

"I won't be far." He gestured in the direction of the pasture beyond the barn. "I already told you *mei schweschder* is going to give me some land. I'm ready to start building."

"Oh." She studied his eyes, wondering what this all meant. "I'm *froh* for you."

"I am too." He took her hands in his. "But I need to know how many bedrooms you want."

"How many bedrooms I want?" Her heart thudded against her rib cage and her mind raced with questions.

"Ya," he said. "How many bedrooms should our *haus* have?"

She swallowed a gasp. *Is he asking what I think he's asking?*

His smile was wide. "You haven't answered me. I need to know so I can start on the plans right away."

"I don't know." Her response was a trembling whisper. "How many do you want?"

"I would like *mei fraa* to decide that," he said, squeezing her hands. "That's if you'll be *mei fraa*."

She couldn't take this game anymore. Matthew had to say what he meant before she screamed in frustration. "What are you asking me, Matthew Glick?"

"Lindsay Bedford," he began, "will you marry me next fall?"

"Yes," she said as her eyes filled with tears and her heart pounded in her chest.

"Danki," he said. *"Frehlicher Grischtdaag, mei liewe,"* he repeated.

"Frehlicher Grischtdaag," she said. "This is the best Christmas ever!"

Lindsay couldn't wipe the smile off her face as Matthew guided his horse into her uncle's driveway. Lindsay was engaged! Never in her wildest dreams did she imagine Matthew would ask her this soon.

She climbed from the buggy just as her uncle appeared from the barn.

"Hello," Daniel said. "I was wondering when you would be *heemet*."

"We made a stop at Matthew's house," Lindsay said before turning to Matthew. "I'm going to go tell *mei aenti* and Jessica."

Matthew smiled. "You go ahead. I'll have Daniel help me with the hope chest."

Lindsay hurried up the porch steps and through the kitchen. When she found the family room empty, she continued up the stairs. She found her sister and cousins visiting with her aunt Rebecca.

"Lindsay!" Rebecca said, sitting up in bed. "You look like you just ran a mile."

"I feel like I did," Lindsay said. Her heart pounded in her chest both from running and from the news she had to share. She sank onto the bed next to Rebecca. Emma held up her arms, and Lindsay pulled her little cousin onto her lap and kissed her cheek. "Hi, Emmy!"

"What took you so long to get home?" Jessica asked with a suspicious expression. She sat in the chair across from the bed with Junior in her lap.

"I told you I had to stop at Matthew's *haus*," Lindsay said. "He had something to give me."

"Did he leave already?" Rebecca asked, adjusting her pillow behind her back. "I was hoping to see him and wish him and his *schweschder*'s family a *Frehlicher Grischtdaag*."

"He'll be up soon with my gift." Lindsay sucked in a deep breath. "He got me something special. It's heavy too. His *bruder*-in-law had to help him load it, and *Onkel* Daniel has to help him carry it into the house and up to my room."

"What is it?" Jessica asked, annoyance sounding in her voice. "The anticipation is killing me."

Lindsay smiled. "It's a hope chest. It used to be his *mamm*'s. He refinished it for me."

"Oh, my," Jessica said. "That sounds pretty special. Like it has a hidden meaning."

"That's very extravagant," Rebecca said. "Most Amish *buwe* don't give a gift that expensive to their girlfriends at Christmas, Lindsay."

"I know," Lindsay said. "I told him I couldn't accept it, but he insisted. I also said I only got him a couple of tools, and he said he'll need them to build his new *haus*."

"New house?" Jessica said.

"He asked me how many bedrooms I want in the *haus*," Lindsay said, her voice quaking with excitement. She placed Emma on the bed next to her aunt.

"Oh, Lindsay," her aunt said. "He asked you to marry him?"

Lindsay nodded. Rebecca pulled her into a hug while Jessica squealed.

"When are you getting married, Linds?" Jessica asked.

"Next fall." Lindsay wiped her eyes where tears had gathered. "I'm so excited."

"I can't believe it," Jessica said. "My little sister is getting married!" She placed Junior onto the floor. "Wow! This is unexpected news."

"I know," Lindsay said, hugging her sister. "I never expected him to ask me this soon."

"I'm not surprised," Rebecca said, wiping her eyes. "I knew he cared for you. I'm glad you're going to wait a year, though. There's no rush. Maybe the *haus* will be almost complete before the wedding. I guess it depends on how quickly he gets started."

Lindsay smiled at her aunt. "I'm so very *froh*. This is the most *wunderbaar gut* Christmas."

Jessica opened her arms. "Give me a hug, Linds. This is big news."

Lindsay laughed as she hugged her. "Yes, it is big news. I wish Mom was here."

"Me too," Jessica said softly. "But I'm glad I'm here to celebrate with you."

Boots scraped the stairs, and Lindsay took Jessica's hand. "Come with me and see my hope chest. It's so beautiful!" She pulled her sister down the hall to where Matthew and Daniel were entering her room with the hope chest in their hands. "I'm glad you're here too."

While looking at the hope chest, Lindsay said a silent prayer for Katie, asking God to bring her the same happiness He'd bestowed upon Lindsay.

22

Katie glanced out her bedroom window and watched the last horse and buggy make its way toward the road. She knew once the guests were gone she'd have to face her parents. Dread filled her at the thought of enduring another painful conversation with her father about Jake. She had to swallow her heartbreak and face her punishment with all of the strength she could muster in her body.

Her stomach rumbled as she sat on her bed. Until that moment, she hadn't realized her last meal had been breakfast early this morning. It was now after six, and her stomach felt hollow.

Heavy footsteps in the hallway caused her body to quake. She moved to the chair by her bed and took a deep breath. A loud knock sounded on her door.

"Come in." Her voice was tiny, making her sound like a scared little girl. She sat up straight, hoping to look mature and ready to handle her punishment.

The door banged open in a fast whoosh, and her father entered the room. His large body seemed to dwarf the doorway like a giant. "Katie," he began, "you've had ample time to consider your behavior today."

She nodded while he stood near the doorway.

"I'm still trying to understand why you would disobey me. I

took pity on you and let you off your punishment earlier than I had originally intended. Yet you continue to break the rules. Have you learned nothing?" His eyes bore into hers, causing her posture to wilt. "Why would you think sneaking out to the barn to meet Jake Miller would be acceptable?"

"I didn't sneak out," she said. "I just wanted to talk to him."

"But you knew you weren't allowed to talk to him." His voice rose. "What do I have to do to get you to stop being disobedient?"

"I don't know," she said.

"You don't know?" He pointed his finger toward her. "I can tell you this, Katie Joy. If you speak to Jacob Miller again, I will tell the bishop about your behavior, and you will have to confess your transgressions in front of the community or be sent to live with cousins in western Pennsylvania."

Katie cleared her throat and ignored the tears pooling in the corners of her eyes. She was strong, and she wouldn't appear weak and cry in front of him. She had to stand up for herself. "I love Jake, and nothing can change that."

"What?" Her father's voice reverberated against the walls. "You're continuing to defy me?"

"I can't stop loving him," Katie said. "If that's considered defiance, then, yes, I'm defying you."

"And your community. You shouldn't even consider a *bu* outside of our community, Katie Joy." His expression was filled with frustration. "You took a vow, and then you proceeded to break it not even six months after your baptism. I don't understand you at all."

His words stung. Didn't her father remember what falling in love for the first time felt like? Didn't her father have any feelings at all? What made him so cold and unfeeling?

"We can't help who we love," she whispered. "Don't you remember when you fell in love with *Mamm*? I'm certain it wasn't planned."

"How dare you compare my love for your *mamm* with your inappropriate feelings for that Mennonite *bu*!" He jabbed his finger at her in anger. "You knew not to get involved with a Mennonite *bu*. You made a conscious decision to behave improperly and embarrass our family. I'm very disappointed in you, Katie Joy."

His words caused anger to flood through her. How could he accuse her of all of those horrible things? Although it would appear even more disobedient, she was determined to stand up for herself and the truth.

"Embarrass our family?" she asked, gesturing widely with her arms. "How did I embarrass our family, *Daed*? No one saw me with Jake. Members of our family speak to *Englishers* and Mennonites all the time."

Her father glared at her. "Don't twist this around, Katie. I heard the conversation. You were speaking of love and relationship. You want to be his girlfriend. This was about more than just a friendly conversation. He's touched you before. And he hugged you again!"

"It's true," she said, tears spilling from her eyes. "He hugged me. I do want to be his girlfriend and I love him. I'm confused, *Daed*. I don't know how to turn these feelings off."

"You can control your feelings, Katie Joy," he said. "You're old enough to know and understand the rules by which we live."

"What's my punishment?" She wanted to finish this conversation and move on. The pain in her heart was enough to endure without her father's cold and accusing words.

His eyes narrowed. "Don't be so prideful, Katie Joy. This is a serious situation."

"I know." She kept her voice even, despite her frustration. "Please tell me what you'd like my punishment to be, *Daed*."

"I want you out of this *haus*. You're not a good influence or role model for your younger *schweschdern*." He shook a finger at her again. "I'll call my cousin in the morning and buy a bus ticket for you to go out there and stay with him and his family for a while. Maybe they can instill some respect in you."

"That's it?" Her voice squeaked with her emotional pain. "You're sending me away? I'm your flesh and blood, but you disown me so easily?"

"I've tried with you, Katie," he shouted. "I've tried and tried with you, but you never learn. You're not the *dochder* I raised. You're not a part of this family anymore. You're dead to me."

"Dead to you?" she whispered, a sob choking her voice.

"Start packing your things. Samuel will take you to your grandparents' *haus*. I'll call and leave a message, telling them why I'm sending you there. You'll leave for western Pennsylvania in the morning. I want you downstairs in ten minutes." He marched through the door and slammed it closed.

With her tears splattering her hot cheeks, Katie filled a small suitcase with clothing and a few toiletries.

Katie glanced around her room and wondered if she would ever be welcome in her father's home again. How she would miss her late-night chats with Nancy and her cooking projects with Janie. Life would not be the same without her family.

❦

Jake considered what he would say to the bishop while he drove toward the Chupp farm. His instinct told him to speak from his heart, which was what he planned to do. He prayed the Lord would give him the right words to convince the bishop becoming Amish was the right path for him.

After parking near the front door of the bishop's two-story white house, Jake sucked in a deep breath. His hands trembled as he yanked his keys from the ignition. He knew this conversation would be life changing, and a mixture of excitement and anxiety surged through him while he strode up the path to the porch.

Jake climbed the stairs and knocked on the door. He folded his arms over his chest in order to prevent himself from wringing his hands. After a few minutes, he knocked again.

Receiving no answer, Jake jogged down the steps and headed to the back of the house, where he spotted Abner Chupp walking from the barn to the back door. Jake moved toward him and waved when the bishop met his gaze.

The old man stopped and squinted toward Jake. "Jacob Miller?"

"Hi, Bishop," Jake said with a little wave. "How are you?"

"I'm well," Abner said, looking curious. "Is there something that you need, Jacob?"

"I was hoping to speak with you. Is now a good time?" Jake cleared his throat while gathering his thoughts. "It's a personal matter."

"Oh." Abner glanced toward a picnic table sitting next to a swing set. "Would you like to have a seat?"

"*Danki.*" Jake followed him to the picnic table where they sat across from each other on the cold wooden planks. "I appreciate your time. I know I should've called first."

"It's no problem," Abner said, folding his hands in front of him on the table. "What can I do for you, Jacob?"

Jake paused for a moment and then decided to plow forward with the full truth. "I've been doing a lot of thinking and praying, and I want to know what I would need to do to become Amish."

"*Ach.*" The bishop's eyes flew open as if he were startled by an unexpected noise. "You want to be Amish?" He asked the question slowly as if trying to comprehend the words.

"Yes," Jake said. "I know this year's baptism class is over, and I will have to go to another district, but I felt I should speak with you first since you're my grandparents' bishop. You also know my parents."

The bishop studied Jake while fingering his long, gray beard. "This is something you've been considering for a while?"

"Yes and no," Jake said, shaking his head and wondering how to explain his confusing feelings. "I've spent the past two months in prayer about my life, and today I realized I belong here in this community." He tapped the picnic table for emphasis. "I feel God has told me to become a part of the Amish church."

"But your *mamm* left before you were born." The bishop's expression was pointed. "It's rare an *Englisher* joins our community. What are your true intentions?"

"I know it's rare, but it happens," Jake said. "What about Lindsay Bedford? She joined this year."

The bishop looked unconvinced. "She's living among the Amish currently. Of course she wanted to join the community."

"My life is very similar to Lindsay's," Jake said. "I work with the Amish and my relatives are Amish. My closest friends are Amish." He paused and considered what else was in his heart. "My grandfather taught me how to work with wood in his shop on his farm. I knew when I was a little boy I wanted to be a carpenter. I also loved being at his house. I remember going to worship with him a few times when I spent the weekend at his house. I learned *Dietsch* from my grandparents, and I understood most of the sermon at Samuel Kauffman's wedding." He cupped his hand to his chest. "My heart belongs in this community, and I'm ready to start living like a true member of the community."

The bishop's expression softened. "Are you certain your reasons are pure?"

Jake paused and thought of Katie and knew he needed to be honest with the bishop. "The truth is, I'm in love with Katie Kauffman. I need to find a way to bridge the gap between our religions. We can't be together unless she becomes Mennonite or I become Amish. I can't expect her to become Mennonite because she loves her family and this community too much. It makes more sense for me to become Amish, and I want to do that for her. I love her that much."

Abner studied Jake. "You're saying you want to convert in order to date Katie Kauffman?" He looked suspicious. "It's not my place to judge, but I'm not certain that's a pure reason to become Amish, son."

"My reasons are pure because it was God who brought me to this decision after weeks and weeks of praying. This wasn't a hasty decision," Jake said. "I've searched my heart and soul, and I know I need to convert in order to be with her. It's the only way for us to be together. I feel God brought us together, and His path has led me here." He tapped the table again. "I can't live without Katie. I can't take the pain of being forbidden from seeing her, and I'll sacrifice anything to be with her. She's suffered a lot because of me, and I can't stand to see her suffer anymore."

The bishop rubbed his beard and was silent for a moment. "You truly believe God put this decision in your heart?"

"Absolutely," Jake said, emphasizing the word. "I could never have decided this without His guidance."

Abner paused. "I believe you. And I also know the truth about that day you were hugging Katie by the side of the road."

"What do you mean?" Jake asked, his words cautious.

"Katie had been attacked by three young men," Abner said. "You saved her. I was wrong to accuse her of behaving inappropriately in public with you."

Jake gasped. "How did you find out the truth?"

"Someone who witnessed it from afar told *mei fraa*." Abner frowned and shook his head. "I'm so sorry for not believing Katie. I need to apologize to her and tell Robert the truth."

"That would be helpful, Bishop," Jake said. "Thank you."

"Now, back to your request to be baptized," Abner continued. "What would your family say about your converting?"

"I've spoken with my parents and my grandparents about why my mother left. I understand why my mother left the faith, but I also believe my parents and grandparents would support my converting." Jake held his breath, praying Abner believed him.

"*Gut.*" Abner smiled. "You and I will have to speak to Bishop Gideon Swartzendruber and see if he will allow you into his class in order to be baptized next year."

Jake smiled. "That would be wonderful. *Danki*, Bishop. I truly appreciate your support in this."

"*Gern gschehne.*" The bishop stood. "Do you want to go speak to Bishop Gideon Swartzendruber today?"

"Would that be convenient for you?" Jake asked with surprise.

"It's fine." Abner shrugged while heading toward the house. "I'll go tell *mei fraa* we're running out for a bit. We can run over there in your truck, and then we can go see Robert Kauffman and set him straight."

"Oh, thank you so much." Standing, Jake faced the old man and shook his head while hope swelled in his heart. He then considered his truck and frowned. "Will my truck give Bishop Swartzendruber the wrong impression?"

Abner held open the storm door and chuckled. "You're English. He'd be surprised if you didn't have a vehicle. Besides, it would take nearly an hour by buggy. I'll be right back."

Jake's heart pounded in his chest while Abner disappeared into his house. *This is really happening! I'm going to become Amish, and Katie and I will finally be together!*

⟨∾⟩

Thirty minutes later, Jake sat across from the two bishops in Gideon Swartzendruber's kitchen. As if mirror images, they both studied him while fingering their long, gray beards.

"You want to be Amish, *ya?*" Gideon asked. "And your *mamm* left the faith before you were born. She was shunned, *ya?*"

"She was." Jake folded his hands on the table and sat erect, hoping to look serious and respectful. "However, once my twin brother, Jeremy, and I were born, she and my grandparents rebuilt their relationship. My grandparents have been a great source of strength to me, especially after my twin brother was killed in a car accident. I've always been very close to my grandparents, and I have a great love and respect for the Amish faith. I feel as if I was always meant to be Amish. Now it seems God is leading me to the faith more than ever."

The two bishops spoke to each other in Pennsylvania Dutch, and Jake picked up a few words here and there. It sounded as if they were discussing his sincerity. He listened while they spoke and waited for them to face him.

"I know that this seems sudden, but I have truly thought this through." Jake gestured toward the front of the house. "I plan to advertise my truck beginning next week after I change the oil and check a few things on it. Once my truck is sold, I'll walk to work since I live close by."

The bishops nodded in unison, and Jake couldn't help but think they almost looked like fraternal twins.

"You realize you can't simply decide to be Amish and then quickly convert. You must be a part of the community for approximately six months," Gideon said. "You'll need to live as we do without any of your modern conveniences. After that, you must complete baptism classes. That will include six months of instruction since you're converting."

"I understand, and I'm prepared to do everything that's required. My uncle owns my house," Jake explained. "I'll tell him I plan to move out soon. I'll move in with my grandparents until I can afford a farm of my own. I'll begin worshipping with them and acquiring Amish clothes. I'm ready to make a full commitment to this community and to my new life right away, and I'll be ready for my instruction."

"Is there anything else that is influencing this decision?" Gideon asked.

"Yes," Jake said. "I'm in love with an Amish girl, and my converting to the Amish faith is the only way we can be together. She's suffered a lot since we met because we're forbidden from seeing each other. She's newly baptized, and I can't imagine asking her to be shunned for me. I'm willing to sacrifice my modern conveniences to be with her. I truly love her, and as I explained to Abner, I believe God brought our paths together. I want to be with her for the rest of my life. I want to purchase some land, build a farm, and have a family with her. I know in my heart we're meant to be together."

The bishops exchanged serious expressions, and then Abner turned back to Jake. "Would you please wait outside on the porch for a moment? We would like to speak in private."

"Of course. Take your time." Jake stood and moved through the family room and stepped out on the porch.

Lowering himself onto the porch swing, he closed his eyes and prayed, asking God to guide the bishops in their decision about his future. After his prayer was complete, he gently moved the swing back and forth while thinking of Katie. He couldn't help but wonder what she would say if she knew he was sitting on Gideon Swartzendruber's front porch awaiting an answer to his request to be baptized.

Jake hugged his coat closer to his body and shivered while staring out at the traffic moving past the farm. He glanced up at the sky as dusk began to set in on Lancaster County. The day had taken such an unexpected twist. Jake felt his life taking a more meaningful and fulfilling path.

"Jacob," Abner called from the doorway. "Would you please come back in and join us?"

"Of course." Jake rose and followed the elderly man back to the kitchen. His body quaked anew with anticipation as he sat in the chair across from them.

"We've made our decision," Abner began.

"We would like to welcome you to the Amish community," Gideon began, his lips curving into a smile. "You're invited to join the baptism class in my district next spring."

"Oh, thank you!" Jake clapped his hands together. "I mean, *danki*! This is so wonderful." Jumping up, he shook their hands with such vigor they each moved forward in their chairs. "I'm so thankful. I appreciate your time."

The men chuckled.

"You are a very eager young man, Jacob," Gideon said. "Your enthusiasm tells me this is genuine."

"I agree," Abner said as he stood. "Jacob, let's head to Robert Kauffman's house. I'm eager to set him straight on a few things."

After thanking Gideon again, Jake and Abner headed out to his truck. Jake's stomach flip-flopped with a mixture of worry and excitement as they drove to Robert Kauffman's farm.

23

Katie gnawed her bottom lip and hugged her small suitcase to her chest while riding in the buggy next to Samuel. She'd cried so much her eyes felt dry and void of tears. She'd lost everything in a matter of a few hours—her family, her home, and Jake—everything and everyone that meant the most to her. Now she was alone.

"I'm sorry," Samuel finally said, breaking the long silence that had hung over them like a black cloud during the trip. "I really think *Dat* is overreacting, but you know how he gets when he's angry."

"*Danki*," Katie whispered, her voice weak and exhausted. "But it's all my fault."

"No," Samuel said, frowning. "It's not your fault you fell in love with Jake. It just happened. God put it in your heart. *Mammi* always says everything happens in God's perfect time."

Katie studied her brother, stunned by his empathy for her situation. "But if this happened in God's perfect time, it means I'm supposed to lose my family. I never wanted that. I only wanted to date Jake."

Samuel shook his head. "I don't understand why you have to go through all of this, Katie. I hate seeing you suffer. I just wish you could be *froh* like Lizzie Anne and I am."

"I do too." Katie gripped her suitcase as the buggy bounced

past the bakery. She'd never imagined the bakery would be taken away from her. Gone were her dreams of becoming the best baker and taking over the business from her grandmother. Her heart thudded in her chest as Samuel guided the horse toward her grandparents' driveway. How would her grandparents react when they heard her father had kicked her out of the house? Would they support her father or listen to Katie when she attempted to explain what had happened?

Samuel brought the buggy to a stop by the back door before facing her. "Do you want me to go in with you?"

Katie shook her head as a lump swelled in her throat. "No, I need to face this alone." She touched his arm. "*Danki* for understanding, Samuel. I'm going to miss you."

Leaning over, Samuel hugged her. "Lizzie Anne and I will come visit you. I promise."

"I hope you will," Katie said, sniffing. "I better go. Delaying this won't lessen the heartache or the punishment." Hefting her bag onto her shoulder, she climbed out and waved as the buggy disappeared down the driveway.

Katie pulled herself up the back stairs while the weight of the world hunched her shoulders and weighed down her feet. As she reached the top step, the back door flew open and her grandmother studied her. "Hi, *Mammi*," she said, wishing she sounded more confident.

"We've been expecting you," her grandmother said, frowning.

"You received *mei dat*'s message?" Katie asked, stepping into the kitchen.

"Your *daadi* spoke to him," Elizabeth said. "He heard the phone ringing in the barn while he was feeding the animals."

Katie's stomach growled, and she hugged her arms around her waist.

Elizabeth looked surprised. "Have you eaten?"

Katie shook her head.

"Sit," Elizabeth said, taking Katie's cloak and bag. "I have some fresh *brot* and peanut butter."

"That sounds *appeditlich*." Katie sat at the table, and her stomach gurgled again. "I feel as if I haven't eaten in a week."

Elizabeth brought the bread and peanut butter, along with a plate of cookies, to the table. She then grabbed a glass of water and set it in front of Katie before sitting across from her.

After a prayer, Katie began to eat. Although the bread and peanut butter were delicious, the food didn't ease the hollow feeling in her stomach.

Elizabeth studied Katie for a moment, and Katie wondered what she should say. She knew she couldn't defend her actions, but the silence was unbearable.

"Do you want to talk about it?" Elizabeth asked.

"I don't know what else to say." Katie shook her head. "I've lost everything I cared about today—my family, *mei heemet*, my job at the bakery, my community, and Jake Miller. I'm left with nothing at all. I'm all alone." Her voice choked on the last words, and she took a deep breath, willing herself not to cry again.

Elizabeth placed her hand over Katie's. "You haven't lost me or your *daadi*."

Fresh tears filled Katie's eyes. "*Danki*," she whispered. "I don't know what to do now, *Mammi*. This isn't how I expected things to turn out for me. I'm not welcome at *mei heemet*, and I can't be with Jake. I never wanted to be shunned. I never wanted to leave the church and become Mennonite like Jake. My heart belongs to this community and the Amish church. But now I've lost everything and have to go live with people I've never even met. It's all so unfair." She stared down at a cookie and crumbled the edge. "Why do we fall in love with someone we know we can't be with? Why does God put love in our hearts for unattainable people?"

"God gave us free will," Elizabeth said. "It's up to us to make the right choices. Sometimes we consider something that may not be a *gut* choice, but it's up to us to make the right decision. Do you understand what I mean?"

Katie nodded. "I know it's up to me to make the right choice, but sometimes I wonder why God would put a wrong choice in front of me when it feels so right." She shook her head. "That doesn't make sense. My emotions are all jumbled up. I can't deny I love Jake, even though I know I can't be with him."

Her grandmother reached over and touched her hand again. "I know what you mean, Katie. But you must remember the verse from Matthew, ' ... let your light shine before others, that they may see your good deeds and glorify your Father in heaven.' We're to shine like Jesus as much as we can. Even if in your heart you want to do something that feels right, you shouldn't do it when you know it's wrong."

"But how can love be wrong?" Katie asked. "If Jake loves me, and I love him, why is it wrong?"

"You know the answer to that, Katie. We've talked about this before, and I warned you that this could turn out badly."

Katie blew out a frustrated sigh. "I know." She studied her grandmother's kind face. "Have you ever had your heart broken? I mean, before you met *Daadi*."

Her grandmother paused and then looked serious. "I did, but you can't tell anyone if I share the story with you."

Katie held her hand up. "I won't tell a soul, *Mammi*." She bit off a piece of bread, thankful for the food.

"There was a *bu* I liked in my district," her grandmother said with a faraway look in her eye. "His name was Chester. He was a few years older than I was, and he was *freinden* with my cousins. I liked him and I thought he liked me. We talked at singings, so I was so heartbroken when he started dating *mei* best *freind*." Her expression brightened. "Soon after that I met your *daadi*, and we began to date. It wasn't meant to be with

Chester, but it did hurt. I cried myself to sleep a few nights."
She squeezed Katie's hand. "I know it seems like the world is
ending and you'll never find happiness, but trust in God to lead
you to your future husband."

Katie shook her head. "I can't even think about finding a
husband. Right now I need to know how to get my family back."

"You'll get your family and your *heemet* back, Katie," Elizabeth said with a serious expression. "Just follow your *daed*'s
orders and let him calm down. He'll realize how much he over-
reacted. I imagine he won't even let you get on that bus tomorrow. And you'll also meet the right *bu* for you, Katie. I promise
you that. I have faith."

"Sometimes I'm convinced I'll be alone for the rest of my
life," Katie said. "I've never met an Amish *bu* I wanted to have
as a boyfriend, and it's been difficult watching Lizzie Anne and
Samuel and then Lindsay and Matthew." She felt guilty saying
the words, but the truth rang forth from her lips. "I want to find
the happiness and love Lizzie Anne and Lindsay have found.
And I want to have that happiness with Jake. I feel as if God
brought us together."

"You will find that happiness, but it may not be with Jake."
Elizabeth smiled. "God has *wunderbaar gut* plans for you. He
will guide you, Katie Joy." She stood. "I think you need some
chocolate cake and ice cream instead of those *kichlin*." She
crossed the room to the refrigerator and rummaged through the
freezer. "Everything will be fine. You'll get your family back,
and you will find happiness. I promise you it will happen in
God's perfect time. *Ich liebe dich, mei liewe.*"

"*Danki*," Katie said, her voice hoarse with emotion. "*Ich liebe
dich* too."

"Katie," her grandfather said, stepping into the kitchen. "I
don't want to interfere in your conversation with your *Mammi*,
but I want to remind you about something. It's a scripture verse

from John 16 that gives me comfort when I desperately need it. Jesus said, 'In this world you will have trouble. But take heart! I have overcome the world.'"

"*Danki, Daadi,*" Katie said with a sniff.

"Let's all have some ice cream and chocolate cake," Elizabeth said. "Sit at the table, Eli."

As her grandmother gathered up the desserts, Katie prayed her grandparents' words would ring true and everything would be all right.

⁂

Jake's heart was lodged in his throat and his hands trembled as he stood in front of Abner Chupp on Robert Kauffman's porch. He knocked on the back door and then prayed Robert would listen to him and the bishop and give them a chance to explain all of his misconceptions about him and Katie.

The door opened and Robert glared down at Jake. "Jacob Miller," he growled. "How dare you come back here again! I warned you to stay off my property."

"Robert," Abner said, stepping in front of Jake. "Is that how you treat guests who come to pay you a visit?"

"Bishop. Excuse my rudeness." With an embarrassed expression, Robert opened the door and gestured for him to come in. "Please come in."

Jake followed Abner into the kitchen where Sadie sat at the table, wiping tears from her face. He wondered why she'd been crying.

"Bishop," Sadie said, standing. "What brings you here?"

"Jacob and I have some news," Abner said. "Tell them, son."

"I'm going to be baptized into the Amish church," Jake said, squaring his shoulders. "I want to be with Katie, and I know converting to the Amish faith is the only way she and I can be together. I don't expect her to leave the church, and I don't want her to be shunned. She's suffered enough because of me, and I want to make things right. I'm going to be baptized next spring with Bishop Swartzendruber's district."

Robert scowled and shook his head. "You're too late."

"What do you mean?" Jake asked, confused.

"Katie's gone," Robert said. "I sent her away. Punishing her didn't work, and her behavior is unbearable. I'm sending her to live with my cousin in western Pennsylvania."

"You can't do that!" Jake yelled. "She's an adult, and she's entitled to make her own decisions."

Abner placed his hand on Jake's shoulder. "Calm down," he said. "Robert, you need to rethink your decisions. Katie needn't be sent away."

"What are you saying?" Robert shook his head. "You told me you saw my Katie hugging this Mennonite *bu* on a street corner." He gestured toward Jake. "You warned me she could be shunned if I didn't get her under control. I tried over and over again to get her to behave like a proper baptized *maedel*, and she continued to defy me. I had no choice but to send her away."

"I was wrong." Abner frowned.

"What?" Sadie's eyes flew open with shock. "What do you mean you were wrong?"

"Katie did nothing wrong the day I saw her on the street corner," Abner said. "One of my neighbors witnessed the whole scene and explained it all to *mei fraa*. Katie was attacked by three men, and Jacob saved her."

Sadie gasped. "She was telling the truth," she whispered, tears trickling down her chubby cheeks.

"What do you mean he saved her?" Robert asked, looking unconvinced.

"He drove up and stopped the men," Abner said. "He held up a piece of wood and threatened them and then the men left."

"I only hugged Katie to calm her down. She was terrified,"

Jake said, hoping to keep his voice even despite his frustration. "I was trying to help her, Mr. Kauffman, because I care about her." He looked between her parents. "Katie needed to be consoled, not blamed for what those men did to her. And if I hadn't come along, the situation could've been much worse."

Sadie wiped her tears and shot Robert an accusing look. "How could you not believe your own *dochder?*" she said.

"Don't speak to me in that tone, *fraa*," Robert bellowed. "I will not be spoken to that way by my own *fraa* in my own *haus!*"

"Where's Katie now?" Jake asked. "Where did you send her?"

"She's gone," Robert said. "And you have no right to interfere. You will stay out of this family's business."

"You're wrong, Robert," Abner said. "Katie doesn't deserve to be treated this way."

Robert shook his head. "I've heard enough. You have no business telling me how to raise *mei kinner*." He stomped from the kitchen toward the back of the house.

Jake stared after him. His stomach twisted as he wondered what to do. How would he ever find Katie? He turned to Abner. "I'm too late. She's gone."

Frowning, Sadie touched Jake's arm. "She's heading to Robert's cousin's house in western Pennsylvania tomorrow," she whispered. "She's gone to Elizabeth Kauffman's *haus* for the night. Please go get her and bring her *heemet*."

"I'll stay here and try to talk some sense into Robert," Abner said. "Go to your *maedel*."

"*Danki*," Jake said before rushing out the back door. He jogged over to his truck and stopped. Driving his pickup over to Elizabeth's was counterproductive to proving to Katie he wanted to be Amish. He turned toward Matthew's sister's house and spotted a light glowing in the kitchen.

Jake walked over to the kitchen door and knocked.

Betsy opened the door. "Jake," she said with surprise. "Is everything okay?"

"Yes. At least, I think it will be," he said, wringing his hands. "I'm sorry to bother you, but is Matthew available?"

"*Ya*," Betsy said. "Come in."

Jake stepped into the kitchen while Betsy disappeared into the family room and called her brother. Jake paced back and forth in front of the kitchen until Matthew appeared in the doorway.

"Jake?" Matthew asked, looking concerned. "What's going on?"

"I need your help," Jake said. "May I borrow your horse and buggy?"

"Of course, but what's wrong with your truck?" Matthew asked.

"Nothing," Jake said, starting toward the door. "I'll explain while we hitch the horse up."

"This sounds like an interesting story," Matthew quipped, following Jake to the door.

24

Less than ten minutes later, Jake climbed into the buggy and nodded toward Matthew. "*Danki, freind.* I'll bring your horse and buggy back as soon as I can."

"*Gern gschehne,*" Matthew said, grinning. "We'll have to work on your Amish before you get baptized."

Jake raised his eyebrows. "I think I do pretty well."

"I'm just joking." Matthew gestured toward the road. "Go get Katie. We'll celebrate your decision to join the community later. I know there will be a lot of *froh* people when they hear the news. We already consider you one of us."

"*Danki* for your friendship, Matthew," Jake said. "I mean that."

"Go on," Matthew said, gesturing again. "Get out of here. Katie's waiting for you."

"I hope so," Jake said with a nervous frown.

"You know she is," Matthew said. "See you later."

Jake waved as he left. He gripped the reins with both of his hands and sent up a silent prayer as he guided the horse toward Elizabeth Kauffman's house. He hoped Katie would be as happy to see him as he was to see her and tell her his news.

❧

Katie wondered where Jake was and if he was thinking of her while she stood at the sink and washed the dishes after finishing dessert with her grandparents. She insisted on doing the dishes while her grandparents retired to the family room. Cleaning up the kitchen was the best way Katie knew to stay busy and try to not dwell too much on her problems.

Despite her grandparents' insistence that everything would work out for her, she couldn't escape her heartbreak over losing her family or her worries about her future. She dreaded her trip to western Pennsylvania and her new life with a family she'd never met before.

The sound of hooves drew her gaze to the small window above the sink. Peering out, she spotted a buggy moving up the driveway toward the back door.

Katie moved to the doorway leading to the family room, where her grandparents sat reading. "*Mammi*, were you expecting more company this evening?"

Her grandmother looked up from her Amish novel and shook her head. "No. Why do you ask?"

"There's a buggy pulling up to the house," Katie said as a knock sounded on the back door.

"I wonder who that could be?" her grandfather asked, glancing up from *The Budget* newspaper.

"Go on," Elizabeth said. "You may answer it."

"I will." Katie headed to the door and wrenched it open. She gasped when she found Jake standing on the porch smiling at her. "Jake?" she asked. "What are you doing here?" She looked over her shoulder and then stepped out on the porch, closing the door behind her. "You shouldn't be here." She shivered.

"You need a coat." Jake removed his jacket and draped it over her shoulders. "It's freezing out here."

"You need to go," she said. "I'm in so much trouble now, and your being here will only make it worse."

"I know all about it," he said, frowning. "Your father sent you away, but Abner Chupp is at your house right now trying to talk some sense into him."

"What?" Katie asked with surprise. "Why is the bishop at *mei haus* talking to *mei dat*?"

"I went to see the bishop when I left the party today," Jake said. "He and I talked about a lot of things, and he knows the truth about the day you were attacked."

Katie stared at him, wide eyed. "What are you saying?"

"One of Abner's neighbors witnessed the whole scene and told Mrs. Chupp what happened," Jake explained. "Abner told your *dat* he was wrong to punish you because you did nothing wrong that day. You hugged me because I saved you from those horrible men."

Katie's heart swelled with hope that father would forgive her. "What did *mei dat* say?"

Jake shook his head, and Katie's hope deflated.

"Abner is working on him," Jake said. "But your *mamm* is very upset. I think she believed you all along, but your *dat* over-powered her."

Katie glowered. "He always does."

"But there's hope," Jake said, touching her arm. "The bishop and your *mamm* believe you, and they both think your *dat* over-reacted today. Your *mamm* told me to bring you home."

Katie clapped her hands together. "I can go home!"

"Yes, but we need to talk first." Jake took a deep breath.

Katie's heart fluttered with anticipation of what he might say.

"I'll be brief," Jake began. "First, I want to apologize. I never meant to hurt you today. Jessica wanted to talk to me outside because I'd been so busy worrying about my relationship with you that I hadn't returned her phone calls."

"I don't see what that has to do with me," Katie said, hoping to keep her voice even despite the emotions raging within her.

"When I told Jessica I cared for her, I only meant I would be her friend no matter what." Jake's expression pleaded with her. "I loved Jessica a long time ago, but I don't love her anymore. I only love you, Katie. You're the love of my life."

Katie bit the inside of her lip to keep it from trembling. "It's too late, Jake. We can't be together. Our lives are too different." She started to back up toward the door. "I really want to get ready to go home. I should go tell my grandparents the good news."

"I don't want you to be shunned either." He followed her and took her hands in his. "Please listen to me."

"We shouldn't do this," Katie whispered, her voice thick with emotion.

"Yes, we should." Jake took a deep breath. "My mother was Amish, as you know. She felt in her heart that she had to leave the church when she met my father."

"I know all this," she said, frustration building in her voice. "Why are you telling me this again?"

"Please." His expression begged her to listen. "Let me finish. You are the one I want to be with. And God has put it in my heart that in order to do that, I need to change. I need to become Amish."

"What?" Her voice cracked. "You're just playing a cruel trick on me. This can't be true."

"It is true, Katie," Jake said. "I'm going to join the Amish church. I've prayed about it for quite awhile, and I know the choice is the right one for me. That's why I went to see Abner Chupp tonight. After I saw you in the barn, I knew I needed to do something so we could be together. I can't live without you, and I can't stand to watch you suffer anymore."

Katie shook her head. *This is too good to be true.* "I don't understand."

"After I had Bishop Chupp's blessing to join the church, he and I went to visit Bishop Swartzendruber," he continued, holding her hands. "I'm going to join Bishop Swartzendruber's baptism class next spring and be baptized in the fall with his district. Once I join the church, I want to marry you, Katie. I want to start a life with you. We can buy some land and have a little farm and someday have a family."

She felt tears pool in her eyes while his words sank into her heart. *Can this be real? Is Jake truly going to be Amish?*

"I never meant to hurt you, Katie," he said, pulling her closer to him. "I only want to be with you."

Katie couldn't contain her tears. His words filled her with a mixture of happiness and fear. She was happy to hear he loved her and wanted to convert, but she was afraid that it was all too good to be true.

He studied her eyes. "Are you crying because you're happy or because you're sad?"

"I don't know," she said. "All I know is that I'm confused."

"Please tell me why you're confused," he said.

"Earlier this evening, I was certain you and I would never be together," she began. "When *mei daed* sent me away, I prayed and asked God to heal my broken heart and guide me toward the path I'm supposed to follow. All evening long, I've struggled because I couldn't stop believing the path would lead to you. And now here I am standing with you, and you're telling me you want to be Amish. I think God is telling me the path has led to you all along."

Before she could speak another word, Jake leaned down and placed his finger on her lips. "I love you, Katie Kauffman," he said. "I want to be with you. My path has always led to you."

"*Ich liebe dich* too." Her smiled suddenly faded as she thought of her parents. "What do we do about *mei daed*? We can't meet in secret until you're baptized."

"No, we can't." He nodded toward the back door. "Let's get your things and then I'll take you home. We'll go talk to your *dat* right now."

"No." Her stomach twisted as she shook her head. "He'll never accept us before you're baptized. It's not a *gut* idea."

"I have to do this," Jake said. "I have to make things right with your parents or we can never be together."

She hesitated, and he tugged her toward the kitchen door. Together, they walked into the family room. Katie's grandparents both looked stunned.

"Jake," Eli said, standing. "What brings you out here?"

Elizabeth also stood and looked curious.

Jake stood erect with a confident expression on his handsome face. "I came to tell Katie I love her, and I'm going to be baptized into the Amish faith in Gideon Swartzendruber's district next spring."

"You're going to become Amish?" Eli asked.

"When did you decide this, Jacob?" Elizabeth asked. "This is a very serious decision."

"I know." Jake smiled at Katie, and her heart swelled with love for him. "I want to be with Katie, and I can't stand watching her suffer because of me. This is the only way we can be together. I don't want her to be shunned, and I don't want her to leave the family and community she loves. Instead, I'll sacrifice my modern way of life and become Amish. I want to do this for her. I can't bear living without her."

"*Danki,*" Katie whispered, her eyes filling with fresh tears.

"That's *wunderbaar!*" Elizabeth said, clapping her hands together.

Katie smiled as her grandmother hugged her. "The Lord found a way to bring us together, *Mammi,*" Katie whispered. "It was meant to be all along."

Elizabeth smiled and touched Katie's cheek. "I'm so *froh* for you."

Eli and Jake shook hands.

"*Mei mamm* told Jake to bring me *heemet,*" Katie said.

"She did?" Elizabeth looked surprised again. "What happened to change her mind?"

Jake explained his visit with the bishop and how the bishop knew the truth about the day of the attack. He told

Katie's grandparents the bishop went with him to visit Katie's parents.

"What a miracle," Eli said. "My son may soon see the light and realize he's mistreated Katie all along."

"I hope so." Katie motioned toward the kitchen. "I'm going to get my things and try to make things right with *mei dat*. I can't stand the distance between us anymore."

Elizabeth touched Katie's arm. "Go." She smiled at Jake. "Take *gut* care of my Katie Joy."

"I will," Jake said with a tender smile. "I promise."

⊙≈⊙

Katie's stomach fluttered with excitement and worry as she and Jake climbed out of the buggy in her father's driveway. "I don't know if I can do this," she said. "*Mei dat* was so angry with me earlier. I can't handle more yelling and accusations."

Jake's expression encouraged her. "Have faith, Katie," he said. "You said you believed God led you to me. Don't you think He'll also lead your parents to support our relationship?"

Her hesitation vanished while she gazed into his determined eyes. "*Ya,* I think you're right."

"*Gut,*" he said. "Let's go tell your parents about our future."

Although Katie knew in her heart she and Jake belonged together, her father's warning echoed in her ears as they headed toward the back porch.

When they reached the back door, Jake stopped and faced her. "Remember, Katie, have faith. We're in this together."

Katie attempted to force a smile, but her lips formed a grimace.

Jake pushed open the door and motioned for her to follow him. They found her mother and her sister Nancy sitting at the kitchen table.

Her mother's eyes widened and she jumped up. "Katie!

You're *heemet*." She pulled Katie into her arms and hugged her, and Katie thought she might pass out from the shock.

"*Danki, Mamm*," Katie said. "It's *gut* to be home."

"It's *gut* to see you," Nancy said, hugging Katie.

"*Danki*, Nancy," Katie said. "Where's *Dat*?"

Sadie motioned toward the door. "He went out to the barn after the bishop was taken home. I think he's contemplating everything the bishop said to him. They had a very intense conversation."

"Do you want me to go get him?" Nancy offered.

"No," Katie said. "I will."

Jake looked surprised. "Are you certain?"

Katie nodded. "I am certain. I need to face him and tell him my plans for my future with you."

Jake smiled. "I like the sound of that."

Katie started out the door and met her father coming up the porch steps. "I was just coming to see you. Jake and I want to talk to you."

"Go back in the *haus*," he said. "I'm coming in."

With her hands trembling, Katie stepped back into the kitchen, and her father followed. Nancy shot Katie an encouraging smile before slipping into the family room and out of sight. For a brief moment, Katie wished she could follow Nancy, but she knew she had to stay in the kitchen and face her father once and for all.

"Why are you back here, Katie?" Robert asked, pulling off his heavy coat. "You know you're no longer welcome in this *haus*."

"I told Jake to go get Katie and bring her *heemet*," Sadie said, her voice loud and confident. "We need to listen to her, Robert."

Katie met her mother's gaze, and her mother winked unexpectedly. Katie smiled in response and was thankful for her mother's encouragement.

Her father looked stunned while facing Sadie. "You're going to tell me what to do, Sadie?"

"*Ya,*" Sadie said. "I am. For nearly twenty-five years I've stood by you, Robert, and I've never doubted your decisions. Today, however, is the first time I can't stand here and listen without disagreeing. Katie has been through enough during these past few months. Let's give her a chance and hear what she and her *freind* have to say. It might be something you'd like to hear."

Katie held her breath while her father studied her mother. She prayed he would agree to her request, but in her heart, she doubted he would overcome his own stubborn nature for once in his life.

Her father trained his unwavering frown on Katie. "You have two minutes."

"I want to come *heemet,*" Katie said, her voice thick with emotion. "I belong here, and you need to admit I've done nothing wrong. And I want your blessing for Jake and me to be together."

"Katie and I are in love," Jake added. "I told you I'm joining the church with two bishops' blessings, so now you must accept that Katie and I will be together."

"Falling in love is not a reason to join the church," her father said, looking unconvinced. "You join because God has called you to it."

"I'm a solid Christian," Jake said with a serious expression. "I've taken a lot of time to consider this. I've spoken to my parents, my grandparents, my friends, and two bishops. I know the conversion will be difficult, but it's important Katie and I share the same faith. I want to be with her, and I'm willing to sacrifice for her. She's suffered enough for me." He smiled at Katie, and her heart turned over in her chest. "I hope by the time I'm baptized I'll have my own house, and I can ask Katie to officially be my girlfriend once I am finished with the class. I look forward to living the life I feel God is leading me to live with the woman I'm meant to be with. I want to marry her next fall."

A surge of confidence filled Katie, and she looked at her parents. "I want you to accept that Jake and I will be together," she said, her voice steady and strong. "We want your blessing. He's a *gut* man, and you know his family. He's already thought this through, and he's gotten two bishops to support him. You should too." She looked at her father. "I never did anything wrong, and you need to let me come back *heemet* and be a part of this family."

"The bishop told you the truth about what happened the day he saw us on the corner," Jake said.

Sadie nodded and touched Katie's hand. "I'm so sorry I didn't believe you, Katie. You needed my love, not my rejection that day."

"I forgive you," Katie said, hugging her mother again. She then looked at her father and thought she saw tears glistening in his eyes despite his frown.

Sadie touched Jake's arm. "*Danki* for saving my Katie that day. Abner told us what his neighbor saw, and I shudder to think what could've happened if you hadn't come along. You're a blessing to my Katie, Jake."

"*Danki, Mamm,*" Katie said. "I'm so *froh* you feel that way."

"I'm sorry I was wrong that day," Robert said. "I should've listened to you instead of worrying about what the bishop said."

Katie launched herself into her father's arms as more tears sprinkled her cheeks. "*Danki, Dat,*" she said.

He nodded without responding.

"Mr. and Mrs. Kauffman," Jake began, "will you give us your blessing? Katie and I want you to support our relationship."

"I give you my blessing," Sadie said. "You're a *gut bu*. You will be *gut* to my Katie."

When her mother leaned over and shook Jake's hand, Katie couldn't help but smile as she turned her gaze to her father. She hoped he, too, would have a change of heart.

"This is unusual," Robert said, his expression hardening once again. "You're converting, and it's rare folks who aren't Amish convert."

"My grandparents are Amish, and my mother was raised in the community. It's not foreign to me," Jake said. "I've worked in the furniture store for years and I've always spent a lot of time with my grandparents. I'm a part of this community whether I am Amish or not." He looked at Katie. "Now I know my heart is here, and I can't wait to join it."

Her father's expression softened. "You'll be welcome here at the *haus*, but I would like you and Katie to not start dating until after you're a member of the church. You know that's the rule we live by."

Katie swallowed a squeal of joy.

"*Danki!*" Jake said, shaking Robert's hand. "*Danki*. I will respect all of your rules. I promise you that."

"*Danki* for listening to us," Katie said, touching her father's hand. "*Ich liebe dich* so much. I never wanted to hurt you. We won't let you down." She paused. "Does this mean I can come home?"

Still frowning, her father's nod was stiff. "*Ya*, you can come back. This is your *heemet*. Now I'm going to the *schtupp* to read the paper." He then disappeared into the family room.

Katie touched her mother's hand. "*Danki* for standing up to him," she whispered in her ear. "I can't *danki* enough."

"I just wanted to see you *froh*, Katie," her mother said, cupping her hands to Katie's cheeks. "I couldn't stand watching you suffer anymore. And, again, I'm so sorry I didn't listen to you. I was not a *gut mamm*."

"I forgive you," Katie repeated. "It was all a horrible misunderstanding."

"*Danki*, Sadie," Jake said. "I'll make Katie very *froh*. I promise you."

Her mother's expression sobered. "You two can't visit all evening. It's getting late. Jake, the youth singings are on Sundays as you know. You can attend them now if you're joining the community."

"That's right!" Katie smiled at Jake. "Now you can come and join them. That would be so much fun."

"*Wunderbaar gut,*" Jake said with a smile. "I need to get used to using *Dietsch.*"

"*Ya,*" Katie said as they headed through the door. "You do." She glanced at her mother. "I'm going to walk Jake out. I'll be right back."

"Don't be out long," her mother warned before they slipped out the door.

"I need to return Matthew's horse and buggy before he thinks I stole them," Jake said.

She walked beside him. "Why did you bring Matthew's buggy over to get me when your truck was sitting right here all the time?"

"I wanted you to know I was serious about becoming Amish when I came to tell you the news." He smiled down at her. "I've never been this *froh* in my life, Katie. I'm so thankful for you."

"And this is only the beginning," she said, smiling up at him.

They crossed over to Matthew's sister's property and found Matthew, Lizzie Anne, and Samuel standing on the back porch waiting for them.

"Why are you all here?" Katie asked.

"Matthew came over and told us Jake had gone to get you," Lizzie Anne said. "We've been waiting for you to get back."

"What happened when you talked to *Dat?*" Samuel asked. "We've been waiting to hear the news."

"You're smiling, so it must be *gut,*" Lizzie Anne chimed in, looking curious.

"I'm welcome to come *heemet,* and *Mamm* and *Dat* apologized for not believing I was attacked. The best news is we got their blessing," Katie said. "I can date Jake once he joins the church next fall."

"*Dat* gave his blessing?" Samuel asked with surprise.

"You're joining the church?" Lizzie Anne asked. "I missed that part of the story."

"This is *wunderbaar*!" Matthew said. "It went much better than I ever imagined."

"I agree with that. *Danki* for your help, Matthew," Jake said. He then shared his story of visiting the bishops while Katie beamed beside him.

"I'm so excited for you!" Lizzie Anne hugged Katie. "This is so *wunderbaar gut*! You're going to be so *froh* together."

"I know," Katie said. "God has blessed us."

25

Lindsay! *Dummle!*" Rebecca called from upstairs. "Lindsay, come quickly! It's time!"

Lindsay glanced across the kitchen to where Jessica sat helping Emma with her breakfast. "It's time!"

"Time for the baby to come?" Jessica said, looking surprised. "What do you need me to do?"

"Please stay with the *kinner* for now." Lindsay dashed upstairs and flew down the hallway to Rebecca's room. "Is it time for the *boppli* to come?" she asked, bounding through the doorway.

Rebecca stood next to the bed with her eyes wide with excitement. "My water broke. I need to get to the hospital. Tell Daniel. I'll get dressed and get my bag." She pointed toward a small bag on the floor.

"Do you need help getting dressed?" Lindsay offered, wringing her hands. She needed to calm down. She'd been through this with Rebecca twice before. Yet, it was still just as exciting as when Daniel Junior was born.

"No, I can manage it." Rebecca's lips formed a nervous smile. "I can't believe it. Today is Christmas Eve, and it's the day the Lord has chosen for our new *boppli* to arrive."

"It's a miracle!" Lindsay said. "I'll go get *Onkel* Daniel." She ran down the stairs and to the kitchen, where Jessica sat between their cousins.

"What happened?" Jessica asked. "Is she okay?"

"Her water broke." Lindsay continued across the room and pulled on her cloak. "I need to go get *Onkel* Daniel."

"I'll take them to the hospital," Jessica said. "You can stay with the children."

"That sounds *gut*," Lindsay said, but she wished she could be there too. "I'll be right back." She trotted out into the bitter cold and entered the barn where her uncle was feeding the animals. "*Onkel* Daniel!" she called, walking to the back of the barn. "*Aenti* Rebecca's water broke. It's time! You need to get to the hospital."

"It's time?" Daniel appeared from a horse stall. "Already? But it's not January yet."

Lindsay smiled. "Sometimes they come early. Remember Emma was a week early."

"*Ya*," he said, rubbing his beard. "She was. We'd better go. I'll call a driver."

"Jessica can drive you," Lindsay said, falling in step with him as they headed for the house.

"Oh, right." He turned toward the phone shanty. "I'm going to call *mei mamm* and *dat*. *Ach*, and I better call the doctor too! I'll be right in."

Lindsay rushed into the kitchen and hung her cloak on a peg by the door. "I'm going to go check on *Aenti* Rebecca. *Onkel* Daniel is calling his parents." She hurried back up the stairs and found Rebecca fully clothed while sitting on a chair struggling to pull on her shoes.

"I don't think my shoes fit anymore," Rebecca said, frowning. "I may have to wear a pair of Daniel's."

"I don't think they'd be comfortable." Lindsay took one of the shoes. "Let me try." She loosened the laces on the black sneaker and tried to slip it onto her aunt's pudgy foot. She pushed and twisted, but the shoe wouldn't go on.

"My feet are really swollen. Actually my whole body is swollen." Rebecca rubbed her abdomen and grimaced. "Oh, the contractions are starting. I'm so uncomfortable. I hope this *boppli* is born today."

"I do too." Lindsay dropped the shoe onto the floor. "These don't fit. Let me find your slippers."

"That's a *wunderbaar gut* idea," Rebecca said as she continued to rub her abdomen. "I keep you around because you're a smart *maedel*."

Lindsay laughed. "Is that why? I thought it was because I'm an extraordinary babysitter."

"That too," Rebecca said before sucking in a breath.

Lindsay searched around the floor, finding the pink fuzzy slippers under Rebecca's bed. "Here you go. These are the slippers I gave you last Christmas. They will be just perfect." She slipped them on Rebecca's feet. "You're ready to go." Lindsay picked up the bag. "Let's get you downstairs. *Onkel* Daniel should be ready to go soon. He was just calling his parents." She hefted the tote bag onto her shoulder and then held out her hand to her aunt. "Let me help you up."

"*Danki.*" Holding onto Lindsay's hand, Rebecca grunted while coming to her feet. "I'm not looking forward to those stairs."

"We'll take them slowly," Lindsay said.

Holding her aunt's hand, she guided her down the hallway to the staircase. She then slowly walked down with her aunt gripping her shoulder and the banister. When they entered the kitchen, they found Daniel standing by the table.

The children greeted Rebecca with smiles and claps.

"Where's Jessica?" Lindsay asked while Rebecca kissed the children.

"She's warming up her vehicle." Daniel looked concerned while studying Rebecca. "How are you, *mei liewe*?"

"Uncomfortable." Rebecca stood up straight. "It's started."

He took her hand. "Let's get you in the car."

"Let me say good-bye to the *kinner*." Rebecca leaned down to them. "I'm going out for a little while, but I will be back soon. You be *gut* for Lindsay, *ya?*"

The children nodded and kissed her cheek.

Rebecca stood. "I'm ready."

Lindsay tried her best to smile at her aunt. *I wish I could go, but I know I'm needed here.* "I'll be thinking of you." She hugged her.

Rebecca kissed her cheek. "*Danki* for caring for *mei kinner.* I'm certain Jessica will be in touch with you soon."

The back door opened, and Jessica stepped in. "The Jeep is warm. I'm ready when you are." She held out her aunt's wrap.

Daniel took the tote bag from Lindsay. "*Danki,*" he said.

"*Gern gschehne,*" Lindsay said. She met Jessica's gaze. "Call me."

Jessica frowned. "I wish you still had your cell phone."

"I'll check the shanty as often as I can," Lindsay said.

"Let's go," Daniel said, helping Rebecca to the door. "We'll pick up Elizabeth and Eli on the way."

Jessica wrapped the cloak around Rebecca's shoulder. "Let's go have this baby."

Lindsay smiled as they disappeared out the door. Glancing toward her little cousins, she sent up a silent prayer that their newborn sibling would arrive safely.

⌘

Six hours later, Rebecca held her newborn baby in her arms. "It's a girl," she whispered while Daniel leaned over her shoulder.

"She's perfect," he said before kissing her cheek. "She's just as *schee* as you are."

Rebecca grinned. "I'm so *froh.*" She glanced up at Daniel. "I know what I want to name her."

"What name is that?" he asked, pulling a chair up next to the bed.

"Grace," she said with tears filling her eyes. "After *mei schweschder.*"

He nodded. "Grace it is."

A knock sounded on the door.

"It's probably my parents and Jessica," Daniel said as he stood. "They've been anxious to come in."

"Invite them in," Rebecca said, sitting up straight and adjusting her new baby in her arms.

Daniel opened the door, and Elizabeth, Eli, and Jessica filed in, scrubbing their hands with the liquid provided by a hand cleaner dispenser on the wall. As if on cue, Elizabeth and Jessica rushed to the bed while cooing.

"She's so beautiful, Aunt Rebecca," Jessica said. "May I hold her?"

"Of course," Rebecca said as she pointed toward the chair. "Sit down and I'll hand her to you."

"Oh, Rebecca." Elizabeth leaned over and hugged her shoulders. "She's perfect, *mei liewe.* I'm so very *froh.* What a beautiful little *grossdochder.*"

"She's my Christmas *boppli,*" Rebecca said, handing the baby to Jessica. "My best little Christmas gift."

"That's so true," Jessica said, smiling. "I'm so glad she decided to come early so I can enjoy her."

"How are you feeling?" Elizabeth asked Rebecca.

"I'm doing fine," Rebecca said. "I'm just a little sore, but the doctor said I can go home tomorrow if everything continues going well for me." She looked up at Daniel. "It's a *gut* thing you got the crib set up early, *ya?*"

Daniel nodded while standing next to his father. "*Ya,* I'll admit it. You were right, Becky."

"Did you call Lindsay?" Rebecca asked Jessica, who cooed and whispered to the baby.

"I did." Jessica looked up at her. "Does my newest cousin have a name?"

"Grace," Rebecca said.

"Grace?" Jessica looked surprised. "After my mother?"

Rebecca nodded, and tears filled Jessica's eyes.

"That's beautiful," Jessica said. "I can't wait to tell Lindsay. She'll be so happy."

"I think she will." Rebecca settled back in the bed. "I'm so glad Grace is healthy and perfect. I was so worried for the last few months."

"We all were." Elizabeth patted her hand. "You gave us quite a scare."

Jessica glanced at Elizabeth. "Do you want to hold her now? I don't want to take over everyone else's time."

"No, no," Elizabeth said. "You enjoy her. I can hold her when you're done. You're going to have to go back to Virginia soon, but I'll have little Gracie for a long time."

"Gracie," Rebecca repeated. "I like the sound of that." She watched her niece holding her newborn and smiled. She was so thankful her sister had made Rebecca their guardian. The last four years with them had been the most rewarding of her life. Although she missed Grace dearly, she was so thankful for the gift Grace had given her—her beautiful nieces who were now mature young ladies.

Elizabeth and Jessica discussed how adorable the baby was, and Daniel and Eli talked while sitting at a small table on the other side of the room.

Soon Rebecca's eyes began to feel heavy and she cupped her hand to her mouth as she yawned. She pushed the button on the remote to recline the bed. "I think I'm going to try to get a little rest now," she said, closing her eyes. "Wake me if you need me."

As she fell asleep, she thanked God for her beautiful Gracie.

26

Lindsay rushed around the house the next afternoon making sure everything was ready for Rebecca and Gracie's homecoming. She'd cleaned the kitchen, swept the floors, and straightened the poinsettias and greenery decorating in the family room. The house was perfect for Christmas!

A knock sounded at the door, and Lindsay hurried through the kitchen where the children sat at the table eating snacks. She hoped it was Rebecca and Daniel arriving home with the new baby.

Pulling the door open, she found Matthew standing with a host of Kauffman friends and relatives on the porch.

"*Frehlicher Grischtdaag!*" they called in unison.

"We all wanted to help welcome Rebecca and the *boppli* home," Matthew explained, walking through the doorway. "*Frehlicher Grischtdaag,*" he said softly in her ear as he moved past her into the kitchen.

"*Frehlicher Grischtdaag,*" Lindsay echoed as the line of visitors made their way from the cold into the warm house. "Please make yourself comfortable. I don't know when they'll be home, but they'll be *froh* to see you all." She greeted them all with smiles and handshakes as they filed into the house.

The women left covered dishes and desserts on the counter

on their way to sit in the family room. Delicious smells wafted through the kitchen.

"All of the *kinner* follow me!" Eli called from the family room. "It's time to hear the Christmas story."

Lindsay stood in the doorway leading to the family room as the children cheered and rushed to him. With Emma on his lap and the rest of his grandchildren on the floor in front of the rocking chair, Eli began to tell the story from the Book of Luke.

Matthew sidled up to Lindsay. "He tells the story every year, *ya*?"

"*Ya*," Lindsay said, smiling. "I love watching the way the *kinner* smile and their eyes light up. It's magical to them every year."

"They do look excited." Matthew gestured toward the children. "*Mei daadi* used to tell us the story each year too. I miss him."

"I'm certain you do." Lindsay glanced across the room and spotted her gifts for Matthew. "I have to give you your presents." She motioned for him to follow her to the corner of the room where a pile of gifts sat. She lifted the two heavy wrapped boxes. "I hope this is what you need. Daniel helped me pick them out," she whispered in order to not interfere with the storytelling nearby.

"*Danki*." He gestured toward the stairs. "Let's go sit there so we can have a little privacy."

"*Gut* idea," she said, following him to the staircase. They climbed up to the landing and sat beside each other.

He examined the drill and accessories, and a smile turned up his lips. "They're perfect, Lindsay," he said. "They're just what I need to start on our *haus*."

Her stomach flipped at the mention of the future house. *Next Christmas we'll be married.* "Frehlicher Grischtdaag, *mei liewe*," she said.

He echoed the words. "Now I have a question for you," he

said. "Have you decided how many bedrooms you want in your *haus*?"

"*Ya*," she said. "How about five?"

"Five?" he asked, grinning. "You're expecting a big family, ya?"

"I can hope so, right?" She laughed. "Matthew, I don't care how many bedrooms we have as long as we're together."

"I agree, but without bedrooms, all we'll only have are a kitchen, *schtupp*, and a bathroom." He nodded toward the tools. "But if you want five, then five it is."

"That will be an awfully large house for a couple just starting out," Lindsay said. "I'll be satisfied with three bedrooms."

"Let's start with five and see how the plans come out." Matthew's expression became intense. "*Ich liebe dich*, Lindsay."

"*Ich liebe dich* too," Lindsay said.

While he continued to discuss the house, Lindsay sighed to herself. *Yes, this is absolutely the best Christmas ever.*

⚮

Katie glanced around the group of family members and friends clogging up Rebecca's kitchen. When the word got around yesterday that Rebecca had had her baby and everyone was going to surprise her with Christmas dinner, Katie hoped someone would invite Jake. She'd spent the past couple of days making a gift for him, and she wanted to give it to him on Christmas.

Moving through the family room, she spotted her grandfather telling the Christmas story to the little ones, and she smiled. She remembered gathering around him every year to hear the story when she was a girl. Even though she knew the words nearly by heart, it was fun and exciting to hear it again, especially since only her grandfather could tell it so well.

She gripped the little gift in her hand and headed toward the front door, trying to ignore the disappointment filling her. She stood by the door and glanced out at the road, spotting small snowflakes dancing their way down from heaven.

"It's snowing," she whispered to herself.

"I know," a voice behind her said. "I noticed it when I climbed the back porch."

Turning, Katie found Jake smiling at her.

"Jake," she said, "you're here!"

"*Ya*, I'm here," he said. "*Frehlicher Grischtdaag.*"

She touched his arm, noticing that his body was cold. "Did you just get here?" she asked. "You feel like you've been walking outside."

"I did just arrive." He sat on a bench by the front door and motioned for him to join her. "*Mei daadi* got a slow start this morning, and I was waiting for him to pick me up." He pulled a small item from his pocket. "I have something for you. It's not much, but I made it myself."

"Oh," she said, placing his gift on her lap. "I have something for you too."

"I'll go first," Jake said, handing her a small package wrapped in red paper. "I hope you like it." His smile was shy, and she couldn't help but think he looked adorable.

"I'm certain I will." She unwrapped the package to reveal a small, wooden box with *Katie* carved in the top. It had brass hinges.

"It's a prayer box," he said. "You write down your special prayers on small pieces of paper, fold them up, and put them in the box for safekeeping."

"Oh, Jake," she said, running her fingers over the wood. "It's the most *schee* box I've ever seen. *Danki*. I love it so very much."

"*Gern gschehne,*" he said. "I'd hoped you'd like it."

A commotion sounded from the direction of the kitchen, but Katie ignored it, concentrating only on Jake.

"My gift isn't much." She held up the little package. "But I hope you like it."

"I'll like anything you give me." He ripped open the green paper and found a knitted, dark blue blanket. "I love it, Katie."

"I'm so glad," she said. "It's a blanket for when you get your first buggy. You put it on the seat to keep it warm. When I have more time, I'll make you a larger blanket too."

"It's perfect," he said. "Celebrating our Lord's birth with you today makes this day perfect. *Danki.* This is the best gift I could ever receive this year, other than being here with you."

"*Danki,*" she said. "I'm glad you liked it."

"Hey," a voice called.

Katie looked up as Jessica walked over.

"I'm sorry," Jessica said, looking embarrassed. "I didn't mean to interrupt you two." She started to walk away.

"No," Jake said, standing. "It's okay. Merry Christmas." He shook Jessica's hand.

"Hello, Jessica," Katie said. "Merry Christmas."

"Merry Christmas." Jessica jammed her thumb toward the family room. "I just got back from the hospital. I brought Rebecca, Daniel, and the baby home."

"They're back," Katie said with excitement. "I can't wait to see my new cousin."

"She's gorgeous," Jessica said, smiling. "She's the most beautiful baby I've ever seen." Her smile faded, and her expression became serious. "I wanted to speak with you both, especially Katie."

Katie's stomach tightened. "Oh?"

"I owe you both an apology." Jessica looked between Jake and Katie. "I didn't mean to come between you. I also never wanted to make you feel uncomfortable or cause you to think Jake wanted to be with me. I know he belongs with you, Katie." She touched Katie's arm. "I wish you and Jake happiness."

With surprise, Katie smiled and hugged Jessica. "I forgive you, Jessica. Thank you so much for your honesty."

"You're welcome," Jessica said. She gestured toward the family room. "I'll let you two celebrate together. I'm going to go get some of that yummy food that's in the kitchen. I'm going to miss this Amish food when I head home and go back to being a poor college student."

Jake smiled as Jessica walked away. "I'm glad she apologized. She told me she felt really bad about interfering, and I suggested she express her feelings to you."

Katie smiled up at him. "No one can interfere between us now."

"That's right," he said. "Let's go meet your new cousin."

"I can't wait," she said.

As Katie and Jake started walking toward the kitchen, Katie spotted Lindsay and Matthew coming down the stairs. Katie suddenly remembered how nasty she'd been to Lindsay the night of the Christmas party. *Now it's my turn to apologize.* She turned to Jake. "I need to talk to Lindsay for a minute."

Jake raised his eyebrows. "Oh. Let me know when you're done. I'll go talk to Timothy and Luke."

"Danki." Katie caught up with Lindsay and touched her arm. "Lindsay."

"Katie!" Lindsay said. *"Frehlicher Grischtdaag."* She hugged her. "It's so *gut* to see you."

"You too." Katie pointed toward the front door. "May I talk to you for a moment?"

"Of course." Lindsay glanced at Matthew. "I'll be right back."

"Danki, Matthew, for allowing me to borrow her for a moment," Katie said before following Lindsay to the front door.

Lindsay grinned at Katie. "I heard the news about Jake. I'm so glad you worked things out. That's *wunderbaar* he's going to join the church, and you two can be together. I know how much you care about him."

"Danki." Katie smiled. "I never expected things to work out as well as they did."

"I know. I was surprised when Matthew told me Jake wanted to be Amish, but it all makes sense." Lindsay smiled. "Did you hear my news?"

"No," Katie said. "What is it?"

"Matthew asked me to marry him next season." Lindsay beamed.

"What?" Lizzie Anne sidled up to them. "Lindsay, did you say Matthew proposed?"

"*Ya,*" Lindsay said.

"*Ach!*" Lizzie Anne said, squeezing Lindsay's arm. "That's so exciting."

"Oh, Lindsay!" Katie said. "That's *wunderbaar gut.* I'm so *froh* for you."

"*Danki,*" Lindsay said. "Now what did you want to talk about, Katie?"

Katie took a deep breath. "I want to apologize."

"For what?" Lindsay asked, looking confused.

"For being so awful to you the day of the party at *mei haus.* I shouldn't have said those mean things to you." Shaking her head, Katie thought back to the last couple of months. "I've been really moody during the past few months, and I'm sorry you both took the brunt of it." She glanced at Lizzie Anne. "I'm sorry for being nasty to you too, Lizzie Anne. I was a horrible *freind* to you both."

Lindsay waved off the comment. "Please don't apologize. There's no need. You're *mei freind.* We're always going to have bad days and say things we don't mean in the heat of the moment. But no matter what, we forgive and love each other."

"*Ya,*" Lizzie Anne chimed in. "We're always best *freinden,* even on the rough days."

Katie held their hands. "I'm so thankful for you both."

"I'm thankful for you both too," Lindsay said.

"*Frehlicher Grischtdaag, mei freinden,*" Lizzie Anne said.

Rebecca held Gracie close as she stepped through the back door of her house. Her eyes widened with surprise when she found all of the members of the Kauffman family waiting for her. Kathryn and David stood over in the corner with Beth Anne and Paul. Timothy and Luke stood by the doorway, and Sarah Rose and Miriam spoke to Caleb and Naomi. Children zoomed in and out of the kitchen, snatching goodies off the counter.

The crowd spotted Rebecca. *"Frehlicher Grischtdaag!"* they called before rushing toward her to coo at the baby.

"Ach," Rebecca said. "This is so *wunderbaar gut! Danki* all of you for coming to see us." She glanced down at her sleeping newborn. "This is your family, Gracie. They all love you."

Elizabeth emerged from the crowd. *"Willkumm heemet,* Rebecca and Gracie." She held out her arms. "I just washed my hands. May I take her from you?"

"Ya," Rebecca said, handing over the baby. *"Danki."* She looked at the sea of food that covered the counters and table. "Everything smells so *appeditlich.* I appreciate this warm welcome."

Elizabeth took Rebecca's cloak off her shoulders. *"Gern gschehne.* Would you like to rest in the *schtupp* or in here?"

"I'm very sore," Rebecca said. "I think I'd like to go to the *schtupp.*"

Daniel appeared behind her. "I'll walk with you."

Taking her hand, he led her through the crowd to her favorite chair in the family room. Rebecca greeted family members on her way, thanking them for coming and for bringing the delicious food.

"I'll bring you a plate," Daniel said. "You relax."

"Danki." Rebecca smiled up at him and then glanced over at Eli, who was in the middle of telling the Christmas story. She

spotted Emma curled up in his lap. Junior sat with his cousins and his eyes were trained on Eli. Happiness filled her. Someday soon, Gracie would be in the middle of the group, enjoying the sacred story with her siblings and cousins.

"*Aenti*," Lindsay said, rushing over to her, "I'm so glad you're home! How are you?"

"I'm fine." Rebecca held her arms out and hugged her. "How are you, Lindsay?"

"I'm *wunderbaar gut. Frehlicher Grischtdaag*," Lindsay said. "Where's the *boppli*?"

"Elizabeth has her." Rebecca gestured toward the kitchen, where Elizabeth was holding Gracie while talking to Sarah Rose and Naomi.

"Oh." Lindsay sat in a chair next to Rebecca. "Are you feeling well?"

"*Ya*," Rebecca said. "I'm just sore."

Daniel returned with a heaping plate of food and a cup of hot cider. He placed the cider on the table beside Rebecca and handed her the plate. "I'm going to go get myself something to eat. I'll be right back."

"Okay," Rebecca said, before sipping some cider.

Elizabeth stepped into the family room and held Gracie out to Lindsay. "Here's your new cousin," she said, passing the bundle to her. "Isn't she *schee*?"

"Oh," Lindsay said, her eyes filling with tears. "She's the perfect Christmas gift."

Rebecca smiled. "*Ya*, she is."

Jessica rushed over. "Isn't she exquisite, Lindsay?"

"She is," Lindsay said, smiling up at her sister. "She's adorable."

"And she's named after Mom," Jessica added, squatting next to Lindsay to be close to the baby. "Isn't that awesome?"

Rebecca smiled. *Yes, it's awesome.*

"Mom would be so honored," Lindsay said.

Across the room, Eli finished up the Christmas story, and the children began talking and playing. A small roar of noise rose with their little voices.

"Mamm!" Junior called, rushing over to Rebecca.

"Mamm!" Emma echoed as she leaped from Eli's lap and hurried over with her arms extended.

"Hello!" Rebecca placed the plate on the table and opened her arms. Both children buried themselves in her hug. *"Frehlicher Grischtdaag."* She leaned down and kissed their cheeks.

"Emma. Junior." Lindsay motioned for them to come over to her. "Come and meet your new *schweschder."*

With their eyes round with curiosity, Emma and Junior made their way over to the baby. They stared at her.

"Boppli!" Emma exclaimed with a giggle. *"Boppli!"*

"She's tiny," Junior said. "What's her name?"

"Her name is Grace," Jessica said, sitting on the floor next to them. "We call her Gracie. Do you like that name?"

With a serious expression, Junior nodded. *"Ya*, it's a *gut* name."

Jessica and Lindsay continued to talk to Emma and Junior about their new baby sister, explaining how much babies like to sleep. Gracie yawned, and the children laughed.

Daniel appeared next to Rebecca and touched her shoulder. "I think they like their *schweschder, ya?"*

"Ya," Rebecca said. "They do." She took his hand. "We have the perfect family, Daniel. God has blessed us."

"Ya, He has." Leaning down, he kissed her cheek. "I was blessed the day I met you, Becky."

"I was blessed the day I met you as well, *mei liewe."* Rebecca turned back to her children and smiled. "And I was blessed the day Jessica and Lindsay came to live with us."

DISCUSSION QUESTIONS

1. When Katie and Jake become close friends, Katie feels as if she's finally found her soul mate. Due to the rules by which she lives, her father forbids her from seeing Jake. The bishop and Katie's parents misconstrue her innocent encounters with Jake. Take a walk in Katie's shoes. If you were in her situation, how would you have handled the conflict she faced at home? Share this with the group.

2. The birth of Rebecca's third child intensifies her love for her family and the joy she's felt while serving as guardian for her nieces. Have you ever had a life-changing experience that strengthened your love for your family or a certain family member? Share this with the group.

3. Elizabeth Kauffman quotes Matthew 5:16 (print out the verse). What does this verse mean to you?

4. Jake realizes during the story that he longs to convert to the Amish way of life rather than continue to live as a Mennonite. Have you ever longed to make a huge change in your life? If so, did you follow through with that change? How did your family and friends react? What Bible verses helped you with your choice? Share this with the group.

5. Before Katie becomes close friends with Jake, she feels like the fifth wheel when she spends time with her friends. Think of a time when you felt lost and alone. Where did you find your strength? What Bible verses would help with this?

6. By the end of the book, Lindsay's and Jessica's relationship has grown from one filled with disagreements to one of mutual respect and love. Have you ever had a tumultuous relationship with a sibling or family member that flourished into one of mutual respect? Share this with the group.

7. The verse Joel 2:23 (print out the verse) is mentioned in the book. What does this verse mean to you? Share this with the group.

8. Jessica grows as a character throughout the book. What do you think caused her to mature throughout the story?

9. Which character can you identify with the most? Which character seemed to carry the most emotional stake in the story? Was it Lindsay, Rebecca, Katie, or possibly Jessica?

10. What did you know about the Amish before reading this book? What did you learn?

ACKNOWLEDGMENTS

As always, I'm thankful for my loving family members, including my mother, Lola Goebelbecker; my husband, Joe; my sons, Zac and Matt.

I'm more grateful than words can express to my patient friends who critique for me—Stacey Barbalace, Sue McKlveen, Janet Pecorella, and Lauran Rodriguez.

Special thanks to my special Amish friends who patiently answer my endless stream of questions. You're a blessing in my life.

Thank you to my wonderful church family at Morning Star Lutheran in Matthews, North Carolina, for your encouragement, prayers, love, and friendship. You all mean so much to me and my family.

To my agent, Mary Sue Seymour—I am grateful for your friendship, support, and guidance in my writing career. Thank you for all you do!

Thank you to my amazing editors—Sue Brower, Becky Philpott, and Tonya Osterhouse. I appreciate your guidance and friendship. I also would like to thank Alicia Mey and Jennifer VerHage for tirelessly working to promote my books. I'm grateful to each and every person at Zondervan who helped make this book a reality. I'm so blessed to be a part of the Zondervan family.

ACKNOWLEDGMENTS

To my readers—thank you for choosing my books. The Kauffman Amish Bakery series has been a blessing in my life for many reasons, including the special friendships I've formed with my readers.

Thank you most of all to God for giving me the inspiration and the words to glorify You. I'm so grateful and humbled You've chosen this path for me.

Special thanks to Cathy and Dennis Zimmermann for their hospitality and research assistance in Lancaster County, Pennsylvania.

Cathy & Dennis Zimmermann, Innkeepers
The Creekside Inn
44 Leacock Road—PO Box 435
Paradise, PA 17562
Toll Free: (866) 604–2574
Local Phone: (717) 687–0333

The author and publisher gratefully acknowledge the following resource that was used to research information for this book:

C. Richard Beam, *Revised Pennsylvania German Dictionary* (Lancaster: Brooksire Publications, Inc., 1991).

9780310343998-A

Don't miss Amy's
debut for the Amish
Heirloom series

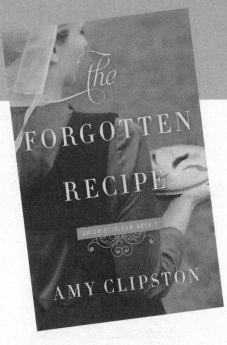

After a tragic accident, Veronica Fisher finds solace
in the old recipes stored in her mother's hope chest—
and in a special visitor who comes to her bake stand
to purchase the old-fashioned raspberry pies.

Available December 2015 in print and e-book

A SEASON of LOVE

Book Five

AMY CLIPSTON

ZONDERVAN®

ZONDERVAN

A Season of Love
Copyright © 2012 by Amy Clipston

This title is also available as a Zondervan ebook.
Visit www.zondervan.com/ebooks.

This title is also available in a Zondervan audio edition.
Visit www.zondervan.fm.

Requests for information should be addressed to:

Zondervan, *Grand Rapids, Michigan 49546*

Library of Congress Cataloging-in-Publication Data

Clipston, Amy.
    A season of love / Amy Clipston.
      p. cm. — (Kauffman Amish bakery series ; bk. 5)
      ISBN 978-0-310-31997-9 1. Amish—Fiction. 2. Amish Country (Pa—Fiction. 3.
    Domestic fiction. I. Title.
    PS3603.L58S43 2012
    813'.6—dc23   2012006944

Cover design: Tim Green, Faceout Studio
Cover illustration: Brandon Hill
Interior design: Mallory Perkins

ISBN: 978-0-310-34415-5 (RPK)

Printed in the United States of America

15 16 17 18 19 20 21 22 /RRD/ 21 20 19 18 17 16 15 14 13 12 11 10 9 8 7 6 5 4 3 2 1